THE LIBRARIAN'S SPELL

SCHOOL OF MAGIC, BOOK 4

PATRICIA RICE

The Librarian's Spell
Patricia Rice

Published by Rice Enterprises, Dana Point, CA, an affiliate of Book View Café Publishing Cooperative P.O. Box 1624, Cedar Crest, NM 87008-1624
Cover design by Kim Killion
ISBN 978-1-61138-946-3 ebook
978-1-61138-947-0 print

ONE

"I don't want your book of secrets, Mr. C." Lydia Wystan brushed aside her employer's long white beard and gently pried the aging volume from his gnarled hands. "I simply want you to sleep so I won't worry you've killed yourself when you make noises like that."

She helped him from the chair by his tower window. He muttered crankily, but since the apoplexy, his words were lost. The Librarian had so very many words in his head. . .

Lydia shook off her sorrow—and fear. She didn't have the ability to fix Mr. Cadwallader any more than she could fix the crumbling castle— or her life, what little there was of it.

He was still muttering and gesturing for his book when she tucked him between the covers. He had a manservant, but Lloyd was entitled to the occasional night off. It was just her luck that it was one of the nights Mr. C felt well enough to get up on his own. She wrapped his arms around the book.

She wished she could see inside her employer's journal, but Malcolm journals were private as long as the owner was alive. Having to wait until he died to learn if he knew the next librarian. . . Worried her beyond measure.

Mr. C had been reticent even when he could speak. She was barely his secretary, after all, a stranger who had arrived on his doorstep one summer day and never left. He had no reason to trust her or anyone.

Once assured her scholarly employer was settled, Lydia wondered what had drawn Mr. C from his bed. They didn't usually have night skies this clear in mid-summer. Had he been studying the stars? The crisp fresh scent of the open air drew her to the mullioned casement window.

The tower was ancient and almost certainly had possessed only arrow slits at one time. But over the centuries, modern conveniences had been added throughout Calder Castle. Windows were among them.

The skies were beautiful at this hour before dawn, with just a rosy tint in the distance. But a wind had picked up. She reached out to swing in the panes and glanced downward.

She drew in her breath in shock.

A dead body lay spread-eagled on the lawn. A very large one.

Oh, no, she couldn't go through this again. Her knees melted, and she almost sank into Mr. C's chair. This must have been what had him agitated. If she closed her eyes, could she make it go away?

The only dead body she'd ever seen had been her father's, after he'd fallen off the roof attempting to repair it himself. Vicars should not repair roofs. The pain of that day affected her every decision—she did nothing without worrying over consequences.

She doubted the man below was a vicar, however. Anglicans were few and far between in rural Scotland.

Shaken by the painful memories, Lydia pulled on one of Mr. C's old cloaks, hoping the image would fade with the dew. The castle seldom had visitors. Neither she nor Mr. C had friends or family here. Their servants were, by necessity, limited. And they were too far from the city and up in the hills for travelers to stumble upon them by accident. The lane to this ancient, isolated fortress was torturous.

She glanced out again. The body lay flat on his back, as if he'd actually fallen from a roof. Why else would anyone sprawl on the rocky damp ground like that? From up here, the man appeared reasonably young, if she were to judge by his thick, wavy, dark hair. No horrid mustache marred what appeared to be broad square cheeks and jaw. Was his nose maybe just a little large. . . ?

Ives men often had Roman noses. And dark wavy hair. A missing Ives had recently requested aid. . .

Swallowing hard, Lydia pulled up the hood on the cloak. She was taller than Mr. C, taller than most men, so the cloak didn't drag as she ran down the narrow tower stairs.

If this was Lady Agnes's missing son. . . Oh, please, don't let him be dead!

The dew-drenched yard soaked her shabby slippers as she hurried through the unmown weeds that served as lawn. The gardeners had been let go after Mr. C's apoplexy. She had no way to pay them.

Keeping the cloak pulled tight against the morning chill, Lydia halted a few feet from the still figure. He seemed much larger from down here —taller than her by half a foot or more, which was to say very tall indeed. And several stone heavier—a giant of a man.

He was breathing. Thank all the heavens, he was alive! There was no blood. There had been a lot of blood when her father had fallen.

She stepped closer. She could almost swear he was *asleep*. On the lawn, in the dew. He didn't smell of gin. He smelled of raw male and a faint hint of bay rum.

She took another moment to wipe out her horrid memories and compose her stammering pulse. She was quite certain she'd never seen this man before. His bones were too square and solid for handsomeness, but he had curved, sensual lips and laugh lines—and a very large nose, all with a weathered, sun-bronzed coloring rarely seen in these cool climes. She wasn't usually given to unmaidenly desires but if anyone could stir them, it would be a man who looked as if he were forged in steel.

She almost hated to wake him and discover he was as small-minded and venal as most men.

His eyes suddenly popped open, and Lydia stepped back in surprise.

"Ah, Mr. Cadwallader," he said in an amiable baritone. "I heeded your call, at last. Did you know your tower is leaning?"

• • •

NEARLY INVISIBLE IN THE DARK SHADOWS BEFORE DAWN, THE GRAY-CLOAKED figure of his host glanced back at the tower. "You're here to study the foundation?" the librarian asked in a low, husky tone.

The man was elderly, after all, and living here alone, he probably seldom spoke. That *living alone* part was the main reason Max was here. He didn't have to worry about gossiping servants.

Maxwell Ives stretched his road-weary limbs and adjusted the pack beneath his head. "No, I simply thought to refresh my memory of the stars of home and must have fallen asleep. I hope my early arrival didn't disturb you."

"We had no word of your coming," the monk-shrouded figure said in a voice almost certainly hinting of disapproval.

The only approval Max had ever known was his mother's, so he was impervious. "Sorry. The train ran late. There were no horses or carriages to be had. So I walked."

"All the way up the mountain?" Astonishment didn't quite replace disapproval. "That had to have taken all night. Surely you could have stopped in the village."

Explaining why he didn't want anyone to know he'd returned shouldn't be done before breakfast. He hoped to leave as soon as he accomplished his errands.

Aware of the damp seeping through his travel-worn clothes, Max scrambled up, hauling his pack over his shoulder. His host was a good height, but Max still looked down on the librarian's hood. He was accustomed to that. "Oh, aye, but I'd forgotten how lovely a Scottish summer is. After the humid furnaces of other continents, the mist nourishes my soul."

"More likely, you're dehydrated," the Librarian said pragmatically. "Come in. There'll be tea ready at least."

Max searched his weary brain for what little he knew of the recluse who lived here. Malcolm librarians weren't known for their social skills. He'd exchanged letters upon occasion and knew Cadwallader was an older man devoted to his studies and the library.

The librarian's last letter had been insistent that Max come home and take care of his mother and bring his journals with him. Max's mother was a Malcolm. The family expected him to contribute to their Malcolm library of weird knowledge.

And therein lay the rub.

The only word Max could write with any certainty was his name. He'd been eight before he'd accomplished that, and even then, he'd reduced it to Max Ives for clarity.

"Tea, real tea?" he asked, with the pleasantry he'd learned to divert the inevitable disapproval. "You cannot imagine the bilge water that passes for tea elsewhere."

"From that, I deduce your travels have not taken you to China or India," the low husky voice said from the confines of the hood, still sounding like a disapproving schoolteacher.

"On the contrary, I've been to both, but the poorer parts near the mines don't indulge in expensive niceties. They'd have drunk brewed coal had it been cheap. I learned to carry my own when I could, but the water was often like boiling mud."

"Unhealthy," the librarian concluded, leading the way through a side entrance and into a parlor so unused that Max could smell the must.

His host lit an oil lamp, and the light confirmed Max's suspicion. Linen adorned most of the furniture. Dust covered all else. He was fairly certain there were immense cobwebs decorating the dark corners.

He'd lived in far worse.

"I would appreciate it if you didn't tell anyone I'm back," he finally admitted. "I'll only be here briefly and don't want to disturb the family."

His host hesitated, then pulled an actual bell pull. Amazing. A medieval castle with amenities. And servants—*damn*.

"I had hoped you gathered from my replies that your mother is beside herself with worry." Cadwallader removed a dustcover from a sofa and gestured before taking a wing chair across from it.

Beside herself with worry? Did men still talk like that here? It seemed odd after the rough, usually crude discourse in the places he'd been inhabiting. Max took the seat offered and put his road-weary boots on a heavy chest that appeared as old and sturdy as the castle.

How did he explain that he preferred that his family think him dead? He hadn't been able to put it into the letters he'd dictated to the family librarian.

"My mother is prescient. She knows I'm alive. She simply wants me to come home and produce grandchildren." He'd produced children, three to be exact, one of the reasons he was here now. His mother would prefer a wife to go with them. He didn't have that.

A thickset woman with a limp, wearing a pristine apron, appeared with a silver tea tray. She scowled at Max's boots on the furniture. He quickly removed them so she could set down the tray. An older woman, she didn't seem perturbed by his presence, he realized with relief.

His mouth watered at the array of breads and pastries set before him. The place might not have a housekeeper, but it had a baker. He could live with that.

His host poured the tea while the cook lumbered away. "Your mother is about to lose her home, and the school that is her heart and soul. I wrote you about that."

"And I sent funds," Max retorted. "There is utterly no reason for her to be short of resources unless she's frittering them away. That's not like her. She simply wants me home. My uncle and cousin are far better executors of my father's estate than I'll ever be."

Ominously silent, Mr. Cadwallader sipped his tea, probably with disapproval.

The librarian's missives had been curt. Long distance arguments did not hold much persuasion. But Max had a favor to ask, so he tried to be patient. He was a patient man. He had to be.

Cadwallader set down his cup. "Your *uncle* is the one preparing to sell your mother's home. He says the estate is bankrupt."

"*What?*" Max almost jumped from his seat, but he wasn't an impulsive youth anymore. He bit angrily into a scone and chewed while he sorted his thoughts. "That's impossible. My father left a substantial estate. The house was part of my mother's dower. He can't sell it. And I've sent a bloody fortune to help with repairs and expenses." He'd simply sent them through a third party so no one knew from whence the funds came, except as income from an *investment* his father had purportedly made before he died.

"Then it seems your uncle isn't the executor you think he is," his host said dryly.

"I don't have time for this," Max muttered. "I'm only here for a few days. I have a job waiting for me in Burma."

"I do hope the situation is more important than your mother, her home, and a school of ladies who need their positions." Mr. Cadwallader rose from his chair.

The librarian rose from her chair like a woman pulling her skirts around her.

He was still wearing his hood inside.

Admittedly, the unheated parlor was freezing. . . Max found himself rising as if his host were a lady. He had no words to explain himself. Apparently, the librarian was brief on words as well.

"Marta will show you to a room. I have work to do." Cadwallader walked away.

It was hard to tell beneath the thick cloak if the librarian walked like a woman too.

TWO

LYDIA PACED HER OFFICE, ROLLING HER FINGERS INTO FISTS. SHE WAS NOT the type of person to fret overmuch. She had a very good brain and the strength of an ox. She had responded to life's punches by picking herself up and marching onward. She could do it again.

But she wanted to bash Maxwell Ives' head against a wall.

What was the matter with the man?

He had a mother and an aunt about to be put out of the homes they'd lived in all their lives! The pair were a little dotty, to be sure, but they were generous, kind-hearted ladies who provided homes for women who had none. They provided education for children who could not fit into normal schools. The School of Malcolms was absolutely essential.

And he would let his uncle sell it off?

Without telling the old ladies that the heir was alive and home.

Really, he should be strangled.

Lloyd arrived bearing that day's box of correspondence. She usually enjoyed reading these missives from all over the world. Due to Mr. C's arthritis, she'd been handling most of the librarian's work even before the apoplexy. Which meant she had seen Mr. Ives' correspondence over the years. He obviously had his own secretary penning his letters, since the handwriting differed from country to country as he traveled. Talking through third parties over very long periods of time and distance made conversation difficult.

Her recent letters may have been a little more insistent that he return than Mr. C had been previously.

Sifting through that day's mail, Lydia calmed her fury. Mr. Ives was a busy man who thought in terms of business and projects and gave little thought to women and children. An unmarried man had little understanding of hearth and home, especially one who traveled as extensively as Mr. Ives.

He was accustomed to dealing with men. He'd thought he'd been corresponding with a man. He would dismiss Lydia's advice as feminine foolishness.

Mr. C was in no condition to talk sense into him. It was up to her to convince Mr. Ives that he must visit his mother.

He'd seen her and *thought she was a man!*

The office possessed no mirror. She couldn't tell how her overall appearance had given Mr. Ives the impression that she was Mr. C. Perhaps she looked like a monk in this overlarge cloak. Could she—did she dare—continue the pretense that she was the librarian long enough to persuade their guest that he had a large responsibility he must assume?

His letter had only said he would bring his journal and seek some advice before he traveled on. If he were here only a day or two. . .

Mr. C had always been elusive, locking himself in his hidden library for days at a time. She could pretend the same. Perhaps she might only don the cloak as Mr. C and join Mr. Ives when he was outside. Surely a gentleman as restless as he would want to walk about the countryside a bit.

How she would convince him to visit his mother was another problem entirely.

In any case, she needed to be dressed instead of slipping around in her nightclothes. Making certain no one was about, she tiptoed up the tower stairs to her small chamber.

For the first time since she'd arrived here, she actually studied her limited wardrobe. A vicar's daughter didn't own much, and mostly, it was practical black or gray wool. She'd had a few gowns made up since she'd moved into the castle, but they were inexpensive and locally made, nothing fashionable. Perhaps that was for the best. An old maid should look like one.

She'd never worn crinolines or bustles, but she did have some lovely lace her mother had given her. Lydia draped it over the plain bodice of her black gown and fastened it with a cameo. She squinted in her tiny mirror as she brushed her brassy orange hair into a chignon and pinned it tight. Curls inevitably escaped but she could start the day looking presentable.

While Mr. Ives was presumably sleeping, she ran upstairs to check on Mr. C. He finally slumbered soundly. Lloyd should be up to take care of him before long. She longed to make off with the book her employer slept with, but she had been taught upon pain of losing her position to respect his privacy and that of the other Malcolms who might turn their journals in while still alive.

Pushing open the hidden door in Mr. C's parlor, she took the spiraling secret stairs through the library. The enormous tower of books called to her, whispered in her ear, begged to be read. They were the reason she lingered in this desolate outpost. She'd heeded their call.

Unfortunately, they'd never spoken louder than a vague whistling breeze.

On the ground floor of the tower was the librarian's private study. Dark paneled walls, a fading woven carpet, and a soot-blackened fireplace spoke of recent male occupancy. The oak desk had probably been made from wood cut from the estate in medieval times. But she wasn't a small woman, and the chair suited her comfortably as she settled into the familiar seat. Their guest wouldn't find her here.

The Malcolm librarian's purpose was to answer questions from the extended family about their often odd and not necessarily controllable gifts. Lydia had spent these past six years memorizing tomes applicable to the people who wrote to Mr. C. As far as she could ascertain, there was no journal advising how to bring home a straying son. All she could do was gather Lady Agnes' letters and pleas and place them in a folder for Mr. Ives to see.

When she heard Lloyd in the outer office, she slipped through the hidden door as herself. She could never fool the manservant into believing she was Mr. C.

Explaining about their visitor, she handed him the folder of letters and asked him to take it to Mr. Ives. If those letters didn't sway their guest, she might just have to resort to writing Lady Agnes directly. Mr. C would not be happy if she violated his privacy—Mr. Ives, even less so.

Duty done, Lydia returned to her search of the library for any clue as to how the next librarian might be chosen—and who would inherit the castle. The physician had said Mr. C's days were numbered. She was doing her best to suppress panic and sorrow, but with no book catalog and no librarian gift for hearing the pages speak, her task seemed futile.

MAX HAD LEARNED TO SLEEP LIGHTLY. HE WAS ON HIS FEET BEFORE THE servant knocked. Still in his dirty clothes, he opened the door, and a servant handed him a folder—a male servant, thank all that was holy.

"Thank you, my good man. Might I trouble you for a pitcher of hot water? Or could you direct me to the kitchen so I might fetch it myself?" Max set aside the folder and watched the other man's reaction to his request. It was always good in a strange place to learn the inhabitants first.

His visitor stood a good foot smaller than Max. Slender, thinning gray hair, soft hands. . . probably an assistant or valet or both. He didn't wear livery, and his coat was shiny with age. Mr. Cadwallader might own a castle, but he wasn't wealthy.

"There's a bath at the end of the hall," the servant informed him stiffly. "I'll turn on the hot water and give it time to heat."

"A hot bath! You have no idea how long it's been since I've had the luxury. Ship travel leaves much to be desired. If you would be so good as to set the water heating, I'll be forever grateful." He handed the servant a coin, which produced a small—a very small—smile.

Max traveled lightly. His trunks were stored at the dock in Leith. But he had a clean shirt and drawers in his pack, and he could steam the wrinkles from his coat and trousers. If he couldn't persuade the librarian to his way of thinking, he'd be on his way before dinner.

Recognizing his mother's fancy stationery, he closed the folder.

It made sense that a cantankerous old bachelor would mostly have male servants. Max could relax a bit here, as he could not in his mother's home of husband-hunting maidens.

By the time he had scrubbed and shaved and felt almost human again, he had half a plan to persuade the old coot to agree to Max's choices.

Finding his host was another matter entirely.

He wandered the halls with no servants to guide him. The dust-covered parlor obviously wasn't the place to locate anyone. The scent of bacon drew him to a small breakfast chamber where a slight repast awaited—boiled eggs, cold toast, beans, and crisp, cold bacon was better fare than he'd had lately. He liked company with his meals, but no one made an appearance.

No one came to clear his place. Out of curiosity and a bit of spite for being thus abandoned, he carried his utensils through the nearly-hidden servants' door and downstairs to the kitchen. Camping in the outposts of nowhere had taught him self-sufficiency.

Only the old crone he'd seen earlier occupied the echoing stone hall. She glanced up without curiosity and nodded at a pot-filled basin.

"Where might I find Mr. Cadwallader?" he asked. At least here, he could expect the natives to speak some form of English.

The woman shrugged. Had she not understood? Or meant she didn't know?

Had he fallen down a rabbit hole? Would he meet a dormouse? Perhaps Mr. Carroll was holed up inside these walls somewhere, writing of weird wonders. Max had enjoyed the bursar's reading of the new novel on the long sail over here.

Wondering where to find a White Rabbit, Max returned upstairs to explore. Using the architectural changes he could discern in the walls, he decided the breakfast room and parlor had been carved from the original great hall. A magnificent medieval double helix staircase in the center of the great hall led the way to extensive apartments above. Judging by the dustcovers, none seemed occupied.

Returning downstairs, Max went outside and located the door he'd entered that morning. It had probably once led to a now empty stable. How did the librarian get about?

He was almost diverted by a door he thought might lead to the tower's cellars—or dungeons. The foundation definitely had a tilt, but it wasn't his job, he reminded himself. He might have a gift for solving engineering problems, but he couldn't fix the world.

Max studied the tower from the outside. Heavy draperies covered one set of windows. The panes were open on another set at the top. Traveling around the circumference, he located windows with gauzy curtains blowing outward.

Before he could find his room, a gray-cloaked figure stepped out of a hedged garden.

Ah, at last!

He strode toward his host, who waited for him by the garden gate. "Mr. Cadwallader, thank you for your generous hospitality. I—"

"Have you read the letters your mother sent?" the librarian asked sternly.

"I will hire a solicitor," Max said impatiently. "You asked me to bring my journals. I need to explain—"

"That you haven't written them." A dismissive hand appeared briefly from the cloak.

The librarian wasn't as old as Max had thought, judging by the smooth skin of that almost. . . feminine. . . hand. Distracted, he didn't respond immediately to the accusation.

"My gift is sensing Malcolm journals." The husky voice persisted as the hand returned to the cloak folds. "Yours is incomplete."

That set him back a little. "Well, yes, you see. . ." How did he explain his inability to read or write? He was a successful businessman and engineer—one who had never graduated school.

"Other members of the family have had difficulty with writing," the librarian abruptly continued, as if reading his mind. "They dictated their journals—as you've had your correspondence dictated."

Amazingly, Max heard no disapproval of his grievous, humiliating disability. With relief, he poured out his need. "I can't dictate my journals. They're supposed to be private. Which is why I am here. I ask your privacy, please. Do I have your promise of that?"

The cloaked figure remained remarkably still. "A Malcolm librarian keeps all the family secrets. Your journal will not be revealed to anyone but the librarian while you still walk this earth."

Max grimaced. It wasn't the promise he wanted but close enough. "For all intents and purposes, I'm dead. I've spent this past year letting people believe I'm gone. It's much simpler that way. But I've learned my son has lost his mother, and I'm facing the unanticipated task of preparing him for school. He'll be arriving any day. It's not something I can explain to my mother."

"You have a son?" There was the disapproval again.

"Three, actually. I do not apologize for their existence. I could live like a hermit in a cave on a mountain and women would find me. And spending months in the company of only men, I occasionally succumb to weakness when presented with temptation." More than occasionally, but that was neither here nor there.

"Women just fall into your bed?" his host asked with what almost sounded like amusement.

"Actually, yes." Irked at having to explain himself, Max paced. "If I were lodestone and they were nails, the magnetism couldn't be stronger. But I always leave a mail office where they can reach me. I take care of my responsibilities."

"Not if their mothers are raising them alone." The disapproval was back.

Max accepted the justice of that accusation. "You have not seen the parts of the world I've seen. I've made them wealthy with only a few spare coins. They marry well. But Bakari's mother fell ill and died, and her husband does not want the boy. He insisted on shipping him to Edinburgh, so I've come back to meet him. Bakari is six and old enough for school. I have some friends who might take him in the rest of the year. I can't be seen in the city, so I've arranged for him to travel here."

"Here? The boy is coming *here*?" The librarian sounded incredulous.

"I didn't know how else to arrange it. I hired an agent at the train station to watch for him and bring him up here. This place is well known, and I knew of no other. If you have a horse or some form of transportation, I could go back to town and make other arrangements, of course." Max had really been counting on a stable.

He had to wonder what kind of income a librarian had. He'd believed that the man was wealthy, like many Malcolms. Perhaps he should be offering payment for services rendered?

"Will someone be traveling with the boy?" the librarian asked sternly, disapproval clear.

"Yes, of course. He's coming from Egypt. The new canal keeps thousands of Brits employed. I paid passage for one of them to accompany the boy. He'll not be staying, if that's your concern. I mean to remove him to school immediately. We'll not trespass on your hospitality," Max promised.

He had survived all these years by studying his surroundings, analyzing reactions, and finding ways to work with others. He had a strong suspicion that the librarian was clenching his fists beneath that overlong cloak. Admittedly, books and librarians were out of Max's scope, and he was on edge in this unfamiliar environment as he wasn't in rough mining towns or ports, where money bought all he needed. He wasn't certain what it would take to gain a booklover's cooperation— particularly one who was a hermit.

"I don't know how to repay you for your hospitality," Max hurried to add, when the man didn't immediately respond. "But I can take a look at the tower's foundation, see if it can be shored up before it falls over."

Clutching the cloak, the librarian swung to examine the edifice. "It could fall?" he asked in what sounded like shock.

"You might consider removing the tower's contents to the main block of rooms," Max said sympathetically. "I daresay there have been underground shifts that have dislodged crumbling stones and walls."

"The *library* is in the tower," his host said hoarsely. "It would take years to move and arrange and build shelves and. . ."

"The weight of those books is probably responsible for the foundation's sinking. You'd be better off carrying them to the cellars and using them to prop up the walls."

The librarian practically hissed in outrage. Without another word, he strode through the garden gate, slamming it behind him.

Max whistled and wondered if he should start hiking back to town.

THREE

THE LIBRARY COULD COLLAPSE!

Lydia had spent her entire adult life cautiously calculating how to climb over one obstacle after another without unnecessary kerfuffle. In less than one day, Maxwell Ives had thrown her normal equanimity into turmoil and confusion.

When her father had died, leaving the vicarage to others, she'd seen the necessity of moving on. Her younger sisters were married and had families of their own. Her mother wished to retire to her sister's home. Not wanting to be the maiden aunt, Lydia had packed her bags, taken her small savings, and traveled from Northumberland to Edinburgh. There, she'd asked the ladies at the School of Malcolms if they could use a housekeeper or secretary with no talent except an affinity for books. They had perceptively sent her to Mr. Cadwallader. She had slipped into his life quietly and been content with her role of assisting his voluminous correspondence and researching requests.

Once he'd become ill. . . she'd assumed the responsibility of maintaining the castle and library and a minimal role of librarian—when she hadn't any gift for it. Weeping and wailing at the fates wouldn't pay the servants or answer the letters pouring in from around the world. So far, she'd stuttered along with Mr. C's limited aid and her photographic memory.

But losing the library entirely. . . Her heart nearly stopped at just the thought.

How could she possibly move centuries of fragile journals, hand-written by thousands of Malcolms, volumes with aging papers and fading ink that needed special care? And to keep them in order. . . the task was Sisyphean—even if she knew where to move them! Which she didn't.

And Maxwell Ives wanted to use those precious volumes to *shore up a tower*! He might as well ask that her bones be ground to dust and used to fill the carriage road. She just might be ill. She held her aching middle as she hurried up the library stairs.

The books whispered and called to her, but she could not understand the words as Mr. C did. She was afraid to misplace even one volume for fear it would upset his ability to locate the exact book needed. He could still find his way around the books, with aid. Perhaps he knew the answer to the tower problem?

Lloyd was just cleaning up after breakfast. "Mr. C is a little agitated this morning, miss. I think he senses our visitor."

Lydia heard the question in Lloyd's voice. "Mr. Ives has been corre-sponding with us. He's here to deliver his journals." His *unwritten* jour-nals, she recalled with disapproval. The man had used that excuse to hide away up here.

She glanced at her employer, who wore a dressing robe over his shirt and trousers. Mr. C was alert and listening. He was physically frail, but his mind was unharmed. If anyone had the knowledge needed, it was the librarian. She addressed him directly. "Mr. Ives says the tower foun-dation is crumbling, and that we need to move the library."

It was impossible to tell his reaction from his sagging facial muscles. But he dropped the pencil in his fist to the wooden floor and watched it roll.

Lydia watched it too. The pencil rolled all the way across the—appar-ently slanted—floor. "How long have you known?" she asked in dismay.

In answer, he pushed himself from his chair with the use of his one good hand and a cane.

Lloyd grimaced. "It's too much to ask that he climb those stairs."

"I know," Lydia said in sorrow. "But he has the answers and cannot give them without the books."

She shook back her hood and opened the hidden doorway so she could descend first, holding firmly to the metal rail. Lloyd held up Mr. C as best as possible. Should the frail librarian fall, she would break his descent. These days, he weighed less than she did.

The ancient tower had once been a medieval keep. The stone stairs for archers were on the outer wall. Chambers for knights had been converted to servants' rooms. Mr. C occupied the solar on the top floor.

But behind the seemingly solid walls of those servants' rooms was a whole different world accessed only from Mr. C's parlor at the top and the office on ground level. In the unseen interior of the tower, a spiral gallery spooled around the circular shelves of books lining the walls. The vast Malcolm library was merely an arm's length away from any point of the walkway.

The trick was knowing where to find the tomes one wanted. Only Mr. C knew for sure. Lydia had memorized the placement of the various books he'd given her to research, but those were only an insignificant number among the murmuring pages filling the tower's center.

Mr. C didn't attempt to reach for the volume he wanted. He merely pointed the cane tied to his hand and let Lydia pull it down.

She knew the routine. She opened the spine flat on her palms, letting the pages riffle in the draft until Mr. C steadied himself. He abandoned the cane to flip pages until he found the passage he required.

After that, she was expected to understand what he wanted. He couldn't communicate otherwise. He tapped the open page and turned around to shuffle back up. Lydia waited where she was until he was safely in his room again.

Then she memorized the writing on the pages indicated, the writer and date, the location of the volume if she needed it again, and returned the book to the shelf.

He'd chosen a volume from the 1700s so she could at least understand the English, except for a few words in Gaelic and mathematical formulas that she didn't comprehend. Her education had not been very scientific—not because she was a woman but because her father had been her teacher.

She hurried down the stairs to Mr. C's private study. Sliding open the concealed door, she stepped into the exterior office where the servants expected to find her. She folded the cloak and tucked it beneath the desk so their guest wouldn't see it.

It was wasteful writing out what was in her head, but she had a feeling Mr. C wanted her to show the pages to Mr. Ives. Did he know Mr. Ives couldn't read? It was a curious phenomenon that turned up occasionally in the males of that family. But their superior intelligence was seldom limited by their inability. Wealthy people could hire all manner of people to read for them.

She had the pages written by the time Mr. Ives finally found her. She'd thought about it and decided she simply wasn't good enough at deception to hide her existence *plus* Mr. C's condition. So she'd have to see how he would react to a female as Mr. C's assistant.

After Mr. Ives' comments about women and magnetism, Lydia awaited his response when he entered. He'd obviously bathed. He smelled of pine soap and that male scent all his own. She didn't feel physically drawn to him as a nail to a magnet, but he was an admittedly attractive man.

Given her own size, she appreciated a big man. He wasn't burly, by any means, but broad of shoulder and muscled like a man accustomed to physical activity. His gold satin waistcoat fit elegantly over a flat abdomen. His black suit was rumpled. So was his hair. His attire certainly wasn't his attraction—it was his air of suppressed energy.

He gazed around the office as if suspecting it hid secrets, but then homed in on her. His eyes widened—they were a rather startling topaz. She didn't meet many men, so she wasn't certain if that look meant approval or disdain or just surprise at discovering a woman in a man's lair.

"I'm sorry for the intrusion, Miss—?" He waited expectantly.

"Lydia Wystan, Mr. Cadwallader's assistant. How may I help you?" She used a higher, more direct voice than the husky one she used when imitating her employer.

He kept a wary distance. "Miss Wystan, pleased to meet you. Is there any chance I might have a word with Mr. Cadwallader?"

"No. He sometimes spends days with his research. Apparently you have requested information he asked me to transcribe for you." She held up her sheaf of papers. "It appears to concern this tower. Should I read it to you? I do not understand all the terms."

"Yes, if you would. May I?" He indicated the chair furthest from her.

Trying not to feel like a pariah, Lydia nodded and began reading. He translated the Gaelic for her and frowned at the mathematics.

"The circumference of the tower is less than its volume? That's not quite possible, is it? Is he saying the center holds up the exterior? Odd, but workable. Does this mean Mr. Cadwallader would like me to take a look at the tower foundation?"

Ever cautious, Lydia had not dared make that leap, but she reluctantly agreed. "Yes, I believe it is so. Marta has all the keys. You'll find her in the kitchen."

Did the library actually need saving? A rolling pencil did not necessarily mean much. She should probably inspect the foundation herself to verify the problem. Really, she was giving this stranger too much credit just because she liked his mother.

Mr. Ives didn't leave but rested his elbows on the chair arms, clasped his fingers over his torso, and fixed her with that penetrating stare she felt certain measured and weighed and found her lacking. She had the urge to see if her hair had come undone, but she resisted.

"Did he mention that my son will arrive shortly? I hope he will be welcome."

"Of course. Our staff is limited, so there is no nursery, but a cot can be brought to your room. Will you be staying for a while?" *Did he mean to repair the foundation* was her real question. He'd seemed in a hurry to leave for Burma, wherever that was. She waited anxiously.

Uncertainty didn't suit his strong features. He smoothed them into a smile. "A cot is perfect, thank you. I am curious about these notes. If I can find a solution to the foundation problem, I may linger longer than anticipated. Did Mr. Cadwallader mention that I need to preserve my privacy?"

Lydia prayed to all the powers that be that Mr. Ives could avert the disaster of having to move books. In hopes that all would be well, she very nodded, making mental apologies to Lady Agnes and adding mental limitations to her promise. "I follow Mr. C's orders. As long as he approves of your requests, I am at your disposal."

A grin briefly flitted across his curved lips. He rose. "You should word your offer more carefully, Miss Wystan. Not all men are gentlemen. I promised Mr. Cadwallader my journal. It is incomplete. Is there any chance you might take dictation?"

Lydia had no mind for nuance or insinuations and didn't grasp his warning. She fastened on the question that held her interest. "Mr. Andrew Blair has kindly sent us his version of the new typewriter machine. I've been training myself to use it. I can try typing your dictation if you go slowly."

His heavy dark eyebrows arched in surprise. "A typing machine? I've missed a great deal in my travels. I will be honored to experiment. I am not terribly gifted, and you'll find I have little to contribute to the library. I will attempt to keep my dictation to what may apply to others like me and not take up too much of your time. Would before or after dinner suit best?"

Lydia's heart pounded a little faster at the thought of spending hours in the company of an exceedingly attractive man. It would be safer if she could do so as Mr. C but not reasonable. "Dinner is served early so as not to waste too many candles or oil. Afterward, perhaps?"

"I'll pay for as many boxes of candles and barrels of oil as needed, of course. Would it be possible to work in a room larger than this?" He rose from his chair but lingered in the doorway while waiting for her answer.

What an odd question. But the promise of candles and oil overcame any of Lydia's objections. It had become increasingly difficult to pay the bills as the small sums she was able to access dissipated. Mr. C was too frail to travel to his banker and couldn't sign his name to request funds be transferred. She'd been forging his signature these past months on the castle's housekeeping accounts, but she refused to use fraud to request more, if there was more. She did not have permission to ask the librarian's solicitors.

"I'll have the typewriter carried to the guest parlor," she promised.

"Most excellent," he said with a broad smile. "That dusty desert should suffice."

On that puzzling remark, he departed.

DAMN, BUT THAT HAD BEEN AWKWARD.

Max hadn't realized the castle held any female but the old cook. His whole intent in staying in this out-of-the-way place was to keep his distance from marriageable women of any sort.

Curvaceous, sunset-haired Miss Wystan with her big blue eyes was just the sort he feared.

She had a sultry voice that rang familiar somehow. Had she been one of his mother's hopes for a daughter-in-law? One of the ones he'd run from as fast as he could go?

He just needed to keep his distance. Maybe he could talk through walls. He snorted at the ridiculousness.

He hurried down the kitchen stairs to find the cook with the keys. Studying a dungeon made more sense than puzzling out the librarian's secretary.

But he couldn't stop thinking about her, which was unusual for him. Usually, women appeared in his life and hung around while he worked, until he found them in his bed. This time, he'd deliberately asked her to work with him. Why in all the blazing fires of hell had he done that?

True, Miss Wystan was unlike any woman he'd ever encountered. The women he attracted tended to be of the seductress sort—beribboned and coiffed to the extent of their society's expectations. In Africa, that might mean plaits and paint. In California, it had been bonnets and bustles. In barren minefields, anything from calico and rouge to layers of lace petticoats and colorful skirts had prevailed. Whatever they wore, the women had petted and coddled him as if he were the only man they'd ever met. They suffocated him.

How did he include that in his journal? He couldn't. His weird magnetism was more curse than gift.

Miss Wystan, on the other hand, wore baggy old wool to conceal her voluptuous curves and barely acknowledged his existence. He'd been in this lonely castle an entire day, and she hadn't made any attempt to seek him out. She had the most glorious red-blond hair he'd ever had the privilege to set eyes on, and she'd pulled it tight and jammed it with unsightly pins. And she treated him as if he were little more than a bug on the wall.

He'd actually felt safe in offering to spend hours in a room alone with her.

Now that he was out of her presence, he realized he was out of his friggin' mind.

Once in the fascinating dungeon that supported the tower, Max forgot the world outside. In awe, he studied the amazing structure his ancestors had created—because there was no question that an Ives had built this. He'd known the castle was one of the many Ives' residences constructed over the centuries by his scientific family, but he had never actually seen one this old.

The foundation rose up out of what appeared to be an old mine, built on solid rock, supported by a maze of walls to confuse any invader. He might spend a lifetime exploring this subterranean cavern and never know all its secrets.

He almost missed dinner in his fascination.

After a hasty wash to remove the cobwebs and a mental note to send for his trunk so he didn't look like an uncivilized heathen, Max found the breakfast room again.

He should have asked where the meal would be served, but he'd guessed correctly. The small table had been set for three. The older man Max had originally assumed to be the librarian's assistant was already seated.

Accustomed to the egalitarian habits of mining towns, Max helped himself to the buffet and took a seat across the table. "Max Ives," he introduced himself. "Will Mr. Cadwallader be joining us?"

He had been torn between hoping to see Miss Wystan again and fearing the intimacy of dining together. Perhaps this older man was her father?

"Hamish Lloyd," the fellow said, answering that question. "Mr. C seldom joins us. Miss Wystan does upon occasion, but she's most likely to take supper in her office."

Max had the urge to pick up his plate and find her, but that would be rude, and Lloyd might hold secrets Max could use. He applied himself to ferreting them out.

By meals' end, he wasn't much wiser than he'd started. The librarian's staff was as close-mouthed as their employer.

But he'd learned the puzzling Miss Wystan had arrived here years ago and now practically ran the castle on her own. Extraordinary. A woman as steward and secretary. He'd like to know her story.

The fare was plain but hearty, and Mr. Lloyd was a reasonably competent conversationalist. Max appreciated the reminder of civilization.

After the servant excused himself to see if his employer required anything, Max poured a sip of fine Scotch malt from a decanter on the sideboard and set out for the dusty parlor.

Sitting behind a makeshift desk, Miss Wystan was waiting for him. He'd never seen her standing, but he could tell she was not a small woman. He liked his women sturdy.

Max surveyed the changes to the parlor since his last visit and raised his glass in toast. "You have been busy, Miss Wystan. Do you have an army of energetic brownies at your command?"

With surprise, she glanced up from her study of a mechanical contraption. Following his gaze to the uncovered and polished furniture, she shrugged dismissively.

"It's but a minute's work to remove covers and run a cloth about. Marta has a long-handled duster for the corners. The draperies and carpets still need beating and the windows washing, but I did not think that necessary for our purposes. I will also need to send to the stationers for paper. Do you have any idea how much will be needed?"

Amazing. Not one flapping eyelash or flirtatious smile. Miss Wystan was all business.

A single red-blond curl dangled at her elegant nape. The bit of lace about her throat clung to the enticing curves of her bodice. Max almost lost track of the question, except the nagging familiarity of her voice held his attention.

When she waited with her fingers posed on the keys, he jerked himself back to the moment. "Buy whatever paper you need for a year, and I'll pay for it. I should offer you a salary as well. This is beyond the bounds of hospitality."

"Mr. C pays me well," she said stiffly. "But the paper will be welcome. The household budget is not large."

"He pays people before things, admirable. I am not often at a loss for words, Miss Wystan, but I find myself in a quandary. I'm not at all certain my tale is suitable for feminine ears."

Returning her hands to her lap, she met his gaze frankly. "The Malcolm library was once an exclusive realm of women. Generations of Malcolms tracked their gifted relations and stored their private journals to help the next generation. Men referred to the journals as spell books and witchcraft—until over a century ago, when Malcolms began marrying Ives."

"And producing gifted males, I understand." Enjoying the sound of her voice, even her disapproval, Max wandered the room, studying the curiosities. "How many Ives journals have you accumulated?"

"Not many," she admitted honestly. "Men refuse to believe their gifts are unusual. Ives men, in particular, are more interested in building and destroying than in paperwork. As a man, Mr. C is better able to make demands of the Ives gentlemen. He's added an excellent collection of more recent volumes. They have been quite invaluable. I do not find them in the least shocking. I believe the transcript I read to you this afternoon came from a Malcolm/Ives descendant."

Her face became animated as she spoke. Max sipped his whisky and allowed her melodic contralto to flow over him. He avoided genteel ladies for excellent reasons, but this one had almost a hypnotic effect.

"If I am to trust you with my deepest, darkest secrets, Miss Wystan—"

"Lydia," she insisted. "Isolated as we are, it is easier to behave as family. As we are," she added hastily. "At some point, we all have Malcolm ancestry."

Max nodded agreement. "Then I am Max. As I was saying, Lydia, I'd like to hear your deepest darkest secrets in return for mine. After all, if we are all family. . ."

She frowned. "I have no secrets. You will be very disappointed in my life story."

"On the contrary, my dear Lydia, your name is etched on the ancient stones beneath the tower. I'd say the reason for that is a fascinating secret."

FOUR

LYDIA DIDN'T KNOW HOW SHE'D SURVIVED THE EVENING AFTER THE astonishing revelation about her name on the tower foundation.

Sitting at her office desk the next morning, writing the supply list to be ordered, she could scarcely concentrate.

Her name was on the foundation?

She thought Max couldn't read. How had he read her *name*? On a place where no one ever went. Surely, he was mistaken. She should have questioned him then, but she'd been too befuddled, and had let him control the conversation. She had little experience in controlling anything.

After posting her order for supplies—Marta's uncle picked up and delivered the mail—Lydia took the stairs up to Mr. C's chamber. She hated making him walk the stairs. She hated that she couldn't locate the volumes as he did. Books had always called to her, any kind of book. She read indiscriminately. That didn't make her a librarian with a catalog in her head.

She was nothing more than a clerk or secretary. If she believed Mr. Ives about the writing, could she be more? Nervously, she preferred thinking he was teasing her. Surely he wouldn't outright lie, would he?

Or perhaps there had been a Lydia Wystan in the past who had carved her name into stone.

Mr. C was sitting in his chair, waiting for her. He held his book closely in his good arm. His hand wasn't firm but his left arm was. The feeble one rested on the chair arm, unmoving.

"Mr. Ives is investigating our tilting foundation," Lydia told him. "In return, I am to transcribe his journal. I believe he's censoring his narrative because I am female."

The librarian's distorted lips turned up at one side, and he nodded agreement.

"Is there no way you can tell me who inherits the library? Whoever it is really should be learning the books. They could start by helping Mr. Ives find volumes on the tower's construction. There ought be a whole *school* of scholars cataloging against a time when there is no librarian. Malcolm gifts are never guaranteed." Lydia hid her desperation with scolding.

Mr. C wrinkled his nose in disagreement. She'd spent months learning these tiny signals. She simply didn't know which point he disagreed with.

He tapped his book as he always did when she brought up the library.

"But I cannot read your words until you're gone, and *I* could be gone by then," she protested. "I cannot read the journals with my mind as you can. I have tried and tried, but there is nothing except vague whispers."

Lydia liked to believe she was akin to a sturdy piece of furniture, always there, always useful, with no concern for human drama. But Mr. C's disability frustrated *her* even more than it frustrated *him* some days.

Mr. C slumped unhappily in his chair, unable to argue. It was unfair of her to expect more.

"I think I will investigate to see if the tower really needs work," she decided. "I'm not entirely certain Mr. Ives can be trusted. Anyone who hides from his own mother—well, I cannot approve."

When Mr. C did no more than let his chin fall to his chest as if he wished to sleep, she stomped back to her small room where she'd returned her cloak. It was a bit warm for a summer's day, but the tower cellar would be damp.

And she wanted to speak with Mr. Ives—Max—as a man and not a woman.

She should probably be insulted that he saw her as male, but she'd accepted her size early on, when even the promise of a small dowry hadn't interested the local fellows.

Well, she hadn't been much interested in them either. She liked books and far rather spend her time reading than flirting. Or whatever it was one did as courtship.

Which was why Max's appeal was such a conundrum. He wasn't a book. He couldn't even read. His tale last night of quitting school at fifteen to sail the seas—definitely appalling. And fascinating, she had to admit, like a good book. She wanted to know his story. She was hopeless.

Wrapped in her cloak, she took the stairs down to the wine cellar below the kitchen. The unused vault smelled of must and stale air. With the promise of more oil to come, she turned her lantern up as far as it would go and studied the walls as she descended.

The stairwell had been plastered and once painted white to better reflect candlelight. The walls were riddled with cracks because they were *old*. They could be plastered again.

She scanned the perimeter of the nearly empty cellar. If she had endless wealth at her disposal, she might ask that the walls be better shored up and maybe whitewashed. With new gas lights for illumination. . .

Other than a few kegs of ale and whisky and an ancient rack of wine, they didn't use this room, so that idea was ridiculous. And if there had ever been a means of accessing the tower's underground rooms from the kitchen, she couldn't locate it.

Fine. She knew where to find the tower's outer door. It had been built wide to allow in cattle at one time. The gardeners used to keep tools down there.

Pulling her cloak over her hair, she hurried upstairs and into the sunshine, drinking appreciatively of the scents of earth and greenery after the musty cellar.

The kitchen garden had once flourished at this time of year, but Marta didn't have time to tend vegetables along with all her other chores. Some potatoes grew back every year from small ones left in the ground. Marta had a few herbs she clipped. Lydia brushed her fingers along the plants to stir their fragrance as she located the cellar door—which stood open.

She entered the cool damp expecting to see Max, but the byre appeared empty, except for the now-unused gardening tools. The packed dirt floor held faint boot prints, but they could be a hundred years old for all she knew. The air was fresher here than in the wine cellar, but she didn't like being underground.

Intent only on verifying their guest's claims, she raised her lantern to study the walls.

More primitive, cracking plaster. Other than a rolling pencil, which meant nothing except the floor wasn't even, how did one discern a tilt?

She'd never explored the byre. She tried to imagine moving the library down here and shuddered. The place crawled with spiders—and probably mice.

In a dark, back corner she found another open door. Was this the back of the wine cellar? Where did this other door lead?

Did she really want to know? Well, she'd like to see if her name was written somewhere. That seemed fantastical. But she needed to see a tilt or a crack or something that looked dangerous. Maybe outside. . . ?

She was retreating to the outer door when she heard footsteps.

"Mr. Cadwallader, excellent timing. Come along, let me show you what I've found."

Covered in filth, Max strolled from the interior door, beaming as if he'd discovered gold.

"YOU HAVE A FASCINATING STRUCTURE HERE, MR. CADWALLADER," MAX said, holding his lamp up so the librarian could follow safely.

He'd always had the impression that Malcolm librarians were ancient, but this one followed him with strong, youthful strides—although he was about as talkative as the monk he appeared.

"It seems that you have a structure within a structure." Max led the way through a maze of empty storage rooms, probably for grain and munitions. "I would say the core of the tower was a primitive peel watchtower originally, except it appears to be circular, not square. And the dry stone construction behind the cracking plaster is similar to a *broch* I heard about in the Orkneys. The engineer who'd seen them was fascinated by the unique design. Apparently, the structures date back to the iron age. The brochs he'd seen had spiral staircases on the inside, simply amazing for that period, but I can't find a way into this thing to find out."

"The *iron age*?" the librarian rasped in a low voice. "As in the first century, before even peel towers were built? But this is far from the Orkneys." The librarian ran his cloaked hand over the walls and studied them as they walked.

"Exactly. Maybe the engineer who built this one took his talents north. Or he was a Norseman who brought his talents south. Who knows? Or maybe it is just a very early, very primitive peel tower. Archeology is not my field." Max shrugged. He might be interested in the past, but it didn't pay for the future. "At some point, probably when the fortress was expanded in the 1400s or 1500s, they constructed your outer tower around the original watch tower. You're walking through that part now."

"Does this have anything to do with the tower leaning?" the librarian asked with the usual hint of disapproval.

"That's what I need to find out. Early plumbing required water—a moat, a stream, a river—not just for drinking but to carry off waste. If there is an underground stream, it might be causing subsidence. This newer, outer wall. . ." He gestured at the heavy timbers overhead. "Has protected the inner core from the weather and deterioration."

"But if the inner wall fails, the whole tower falls? The main tower may be held up by a fourteenth century watchtower? Or something even *older*?" The librarian sounded incredulous.

"It's possible, yes. It requires further study. The ten-foot thick walls dissecting the space between the inner and outer towers are the support." He pointed out the depth of the arch they passed under. "Peel towers normally only had three floors. You have four, indicating the outer tower was built over the inner. The design is brilliant. Are you certain an Ives didn't originally own this land?"

The librarian snorted inelegantly. "Your scientific family and my psychically gifted Malcolm family have a long history together. Have you seen our family castle in Northumberland?"

"The seat of the earls of Ives and Wystan—now the marquess of Ashford? Is that your assistant's ancestral home? I've heard of it, of course, but I left home at fifteen. I haven't seen much of the isles except Scotland." Max regretted that, but his inability to read history prevented learning anything useful.

"The Ives and Malcolms have been neighbors back into the mists of time." The librarian stopped to examine a fissure forming in one of the stone walls. "They married, built castles and towns together. A century or two ago, a war over the Northumberland castle led to a long break, but chances are that this tower may have preceded it. Imagine both a mystical Malcolm and a scientific Ives designing a defensive fortress. For all we know, they could have stored ghosts in here."

Ah, the librarian could speak—like a book Max should have read. "My parents never told me the tale. My mother watched me for Malcolm traits. My father simply expected me to follow in his footsteps, increasing his Ives fortune. They weren't much on family history."

"Is this crack the reason the tower tilts?" his companion asked in a low, husky voice.

He wished for the hood to fall back so he could see the librarian's expression to see if he spoke with disdain or disapproval.

"It is evidence that the ground is settling, no more. I'll show you my concern." Max took another zigzag in the maze of chambers created between the supports, bringing them to the final corridor. He patted the patched, ancient, dry-stone wall lovingly. "The original watchtower. Our ancestors probably painted themselves blue and stood at the top, spears in hand, ready to fight off the Romans."

"Your idea of history is a touch conflated if you think the Romans were here in the fourteenth century," the librarian said with amusement. "But if you truly believe it is from the first or second. . ."

Max circled to the northeast, holding up the lantern until he found what he wanted. "There, that's the entrance to the original watchtower. It's been closed up with stones and masonry. There ought to be a byre on the other side of that arch. If it's a peel tower, a ladder might have led to the first floor. It's possible they filled the byre with stone as support when the new tower wall was built." He patted the old walls.

The librarian studied the ceiling. "They built a frame around the watchtower to support the newer tower. Surely these inner walls should last forever."

"Nothing lasts forever. See where the beams are separating from the foundation? More soil settling. All this excavation may originally have been part of a mine."

"So, the core might sink, pulling down the rest of the structure?" the librarian asked sadly.

"Possibly. I need to run tests, experiment with loads. Sinking piles to repair it. . . could be prohibitively expensive. Here, look at this." He held the lamp up to the smoother stones creating the arched doorway. "See the etching?"

The librarian's elegantly long fingers traced the carved stone. "Well worn. It's been here a long time."

"We wouldn't see the writing at all if not for the new tower protecting it from the elements. The bottom names are the most weathered, so they're probably from early days, before the new castle. As you reach the top, they're more legible. That is the one that says Cadwallader, I believe." Max pointed at one of the chiseled, flat arch stones at head height. "It's still old, etched well before our time, I'd say."

"Extraordinary. Although I suppose this could be the name of an ancestor." The librarian looked higher. "How are you able to read the names, especially with this odd lettering?"

Max shrugged. "I know my letters. I simply can't see them the way others do. But I can *touch* these since they're carved in stone."

Max pointed out the barely visible secretary's name above the librarian's head. Feeling those letters hadn't been easy since they were so faint. "It would be hard to imagine two ancestors with similar names listed together. Is Miss Wystan the next librarian?"

"She does not have the gift. I see nothing on the stone above hers, which might mean there will be no more of us. I shall research these names and see if there might be another meaning." The librarian lowered his lantern and turned back. "Have you written your solicitors about your mother's finances?"

"You know I have not," Max said in irritation. He'd wanted more excitement over his amazing discovery, not nagging and depressing tasks he couldn't carry out. "I'd have to go into the city, and I am disinclined to do so."

"Have Miss Wystan write for you. The matter is too critical to be ignored." Evidently done with the tour, the librarian walked away.

Max uttered a few mental curses. He was supposed to let the beautiful secretary know the location of his secret ally? Any Malcolm worth her salt would tell his mother the instant she had a name.

LYDIA HAD CHEWED HER NAIL DOWN TO HER THUMB BY THE TIME MAX finished his dinner and arrived in the parlor. Playing the role of taciturn, reclusive Mr. C was wearing on her honest nature. But she was quite certain the engineer would not have led a woman under the tower or shown her the magical archway.

Her name had been listed after Mr. C's.

She would be a useless librarian—and apparently the last one if the stones were to be believed. Her incompetence could be the end of the library! If Mr. C lived a lot longer than the doctor said—perhaps she might *memorize* locations and hope someday to be useful.

That might only take a century or two.

The library may have been built centuries ago! It was amazing understanding the age of the walls supporting what had seemed like a perfectly ordinary library. It was hard to imagine the generations of librarians carved into those stones. Might they go back to the first century or even earlier? Did they even have books then?

Perhaps she was meant to find a new library and librarian! That was an immense feat but not as impossible as using gifts she didn't possess.

Lydia eyed Max warily as he entered the dim parlor. He hadn't brought much luggage, and his day's endeavors had left his only suit a disgrace. He didn't seem to mind as he considered the stack of neatly typed papers on the table in front of her.

"That's my journal?"

"It is. I had to retype. I made too many errors. I've decided it is more economical if I attempt notes with a pen, then type them later." She picked up her pad of paper and a pen, ready to take down the rest of his tale.

When he merely paced the far side of the parlor, she spurred his memory. "You were saying that you left school to take sail with a ship of engineers on their way to India."

"And they taught me more in a year than I ever learned at school." He made a dismissive gesture and studied a soot-blackened painting on the wall. "I think I should have some of *your* story."

"I keep a journal. It will go in the library and be available to the next librarian and to everyone upon my death. There is extremely little in it. I have what Lady Phoebe is calling a rare photographic memory. I can remember any written page I see. It's not a particularly exciting gift, but it's useful in a library. That's all there is to know about me. Whereas, you've traveled the world and seen and done things I can never hope to."

"Huh, photographic memory." He turned to study her but kept his distance. "Your mind is a printed page I couldn't read even if I could read minds. Interesting. I wish I had my mother's knack for reading thoughts, but I just do equations in my head."

"I suspect your mother has an intuitive ability to read faces and gestures like any good fortune teller, although she does possess a fair bit of prescience about family members, perhaps through a spiritual connection. It's just difficult to sort out what she knows and what she *guesses* based on what she knows. If your equations are proved accurate, then you have real evidence of your abilities. That's important." Lydia made a note in the shorthand she'd developed for taking Mr. C's wandering dissertations, back when he answered his own correspondence. "Where did you go after India?"

"Home," he said curtly. "My father died when I was eighteen, and I sailed home. He'd always counted on me to take over his business and investments. He knew I could do mathematics in my head. He wouldn't accept that I couldn't read contracts. So I went home, prepared to honor his wishes and do my duty."

Lydia could hear the disaster in his voice. "You could hire people to read contracts for you," she suggested.

He paced to the back of the enormous parlor—far away from her, she noted. It was a good thing she had excellent hearing, and the acoustics in here were perfect.

"My uncle and cousin can read contracts just fine. They simply needed my signature. But I was *eighteen years old*. I not only knew nothing of business or society, but I'd spent three years on ships, in the company of men. I was dazzled by the discovery of women. Boys that age aren't capable of thinking about the future, just what's in their—" He stopped and Lydia wondered what crude word he might have said had she been Mr. C.

He continued with irritation. "I was frustrated that I couldn't do what was expected of me and willing to be distracted by the ladies who knew I was heir to a fortune. And I do not think it is proper to explain what happened next." He swung to face her from a distance. "May we skip to the part where I sail away, never to return?"

"It's your journal." She looked up from her notes. "But it seems you're telling me that you have a *talent* for engineering but a *gift* with women. Don't you think it might be best if you let any other men with your gift know how you deal with it?"

He rubbed his big hand over his big nose but his grimace was still evident. "At that age, very badly. The only lesson there is in what not to do."

"Then approach it from that direction," she advised.

"Don't believe innocent-looking females aren't harpies. Don't believe they won't dig their hooks in any way they can, then fight over which one claimed you first. Don't believe taking your own rooms and a mistress will remove you from the cat fight. Is any of this of value?" he asked in disgust.

Lydia stared at him, her notes forgotten. "You are blaming all your problems on women?"

He threw up his hands. "No, I'm blaming them on *me*. I went to a boy's boarding school, remember? I knew *nothing* about women. I barely even knew my own mother. And all of a sudden I was surrounded by frilly young things who flirted and teased and made me feel like a giant among men. They offered walks in the garden and kisses, then expected proposals. I didn't know that. I just kissed them because it was fun. And because I badly wanted what they seemed to be offering. I told you this wasn't a suitable topic."

Lydia tried very hard to see this big, confident man as a young, confused boy, but her imagination wasn't that good. "I have read a great many books," she reminded him. "I may live outside society, but I'm aware of everything you describe. There are no surprises here. I assume you became too entangled with eligible young ladies and removed yourself to a period of decadence."

He sent her an amused, almost relieved look. "Something like that. Boys that age have a lot of energy. I found a good way of expending it until I found it easier to settle down to one mistress, but even that couldn't last. Whatever this is that draws women to me continued no matter what I did. I couldn't walk down the street without women I'd known slapping me or confronting me or flirting with me. I threatened to become a monk."

"And then you realized a ship full of men was even better than a monastery," she suggested, trying not to laugh. "I can't say I've ever read about anyone with that much magnetism. Perhaps it has worn off? I do not feel compelled to attack you."

"Which is a relief beyond measure," he said, not coming any closer. "I just like to believe I've become wiser in avoiding the problem. I gave up and left Edinburgh after my first son was born. He's sixteen now and will be attending the university in the fall. I'm supporting two others, at last count. The youngest is six. He's the one coming to me from Egypt. Perhaps I've learned to be more cautious with age."

"You have a son right here in Scotland and you weren't planning on seeing him?" Shocked and appalled, Lydia wanted to heave a heavy book at his empty head, but he was too far out of range.

A large man gesturing helplessly was an impressive sight. "Richard has a mother and stepfather. He doesn't need me. I provide for him with my travels. It's not as if I know anything about raising children."

He was probably right. An only child, growing up in boarding school, expecting nannies to take care of the young. . . Lydia almost felt sorry for him and others like him. But he had a son who needed him now, and he needed encouragement to do the right thing.

"I should read you the journals of some of your ancestors," Lydia said. "You are not the first and will not be the last of the Ives to raise a cadre of bastards. Of course, in earlier times, they were far more callous about them than you seem to be."

He ran his hand through his hair. "Oh, I'm still a callous bastard, all right. What I want to do right now is invite you to my room so I can see if your hair is as hot to the touch as it looks."

FIVE

MAX CURSED HIS PENCHANT FOR SPEAKING TO THE RED-HEADED SECRETARY as if she were a man. Her sensible suggestions and prosaic tone had relaxed his guard. When he had his back to her, he could almost believe she was Mr. Cadwallader listening to his tale.

And then he'd turn and those haunting, deep blue eyes would fix on him and that voluptuous figure beckoned and. . . He turned into a monster not fit for polite society. He'd made a lewd suggestion to a lady!

And the truly odd thing was that he never said things like that to other women. He'd never had to. They simply took his arm and went home with him, no encouragement necessary.

He might as well be eighteen all over.

After his indecent proposition escaped his mouth, the lady's eyes widened in shock. Then amazingly, her brow puckered in thought. Lydia Wystan was a work of art comparable to the Mona Lisa when she fell still like that.

He waited for the scathing blast he deserved.

Instead, a little V formed between her eyes. "That is a very strange suggestion, Mr. Ives. I am not a ravishing beauty. I do not flirt or tease. I merely sit here behind this typewriter like a tool meant to be used. You complain of women who throw themselves at you, yet when one does not, you are disappointed?"

"Even I cannot analyze my behavior, Miss Wystan. I take it we are back on formal terms? I am very good at analyzing most situations, but somehow, you've . . . No, I can't blame you. You're right. You've done nothing to give me any notion that you'd be receptive to my suggestion. It just fell out of my mouth, bypassing what I've always considered to be a formidable brain. I'll go now." He started for the door on the far end of the parlor where he didn't need to pass by her.

"Mr. Ives."

Her tone brought him up short.

"Perhaps while you are analyzing your behavior, you might consider that your mind scrambles women the same way that your eyes scramble letters. You need focus."

"Thank you for that thought, Miss Wystan. I deserved it. If you will excuse me, I mean to soak my head in water to see if that cleans out my filthy mind."

Max didn't, however, go to his room. He went outside to wander around the tower, hoping to prove his mind had better purposes than insulting maidens.

He was quite sure that Miss Lydia Wystan was a virgin who had probably never been kissed.

What on earth was the matter with him? The first woman who hadn't used her big blue eyes—

Malcolm eyes. Max thumped his head—hard—at his stupidity. Lydia Wystan's name was on that foundation. She was working in a Malcolm library. Her family name was on a friggin' Malcolm castle.

She was a Malcolm, just like his mother. He'd known that. He just hadn't comprehended the consequences.

He was an Ives, like his father.

Like magnetism, they attracted and repelled with equal force.

He needed to get the hell out of here first thing in the morning. He'd stay in town, meet the boy at the station, and take him directly to school. He had plenty of time to catch the Burma ship.

To hell with journals and intriguing towers and an even more intriguing woman. He needed to make a living, and he couldn't do it here.

But he had tonight to explore the tower just a little more. For the sake of his more educated relations, he'd like to know the library was safe.

Lighting a lantern, he easily found his way through the maze of rooms. He admired the builders who had made it almost impossible for invaders to access the stronghold of the upper floors from the ground floor entrance. They would even have difficulty bringing it down with fire since all the supports were stone, and the stone center was completely inaccessible and probably magicked somehow, if he believed his mother's nonsense.

He found a long augur in the tool pile and carried it with him, looking for cracks, under the theory underlying mining excavations or streams may have caused the ground to shift.

Since the inner tower seemed to be the central support, he started there.

He had the augur almost all the way up to the hilt in the dirt floor without finding any sign of a shaft when he became aware he wasn't alone. Strange. How could anyone walk back here without flashing a lantern like a warning signal?

Straightening, Max wiped the sweat from his brow and glanced around.

A white-bearded figure shrouded in gray watched from the shadows.

"Mr. Cadwallader? Did I disturb you?" Max asked, fearing Lydia had run straight to the librarian with her tale of insult.

Oddly, the old man wore the cloak over the front of him, with the hood hanging down his chest so Max could finally see his face. Letting his long white hair brush his collar, the librarian tilted his head as if he might be studying Max. "You have disturbed me in many ways, yes. You are not what I imagined. In other ways—you relieve me. The burden has been heavy, but I believe Lady Agnes's surmise might be correct."

All Max made out of that was that the librarian had been corresponding with his mother, not unusual. His mother had a teacher's affinity for libraries. Her house contained an entire floor of books.

"And what did my mother surmise?" he tried to ask politely, and not with the exasperation he felt.

His mother's all-female school of Malcolms was one of the many reasons he'd never go home.

"That you would return when you are needed. Take care of Miss Wystan, please. She is far more valuable than she understands."

The gray-shrouded figure turned and walked away—straight through the sealed-up stone arch.

LYDIA WAS IN HER OFFICE, UNABLE TO SLEEP. SHE'D WRITTEN OUT EVERY word she remembered Max saying, including the bit about analyzing his behavior.

She didn't write about the offer of his bed.

The idea had so unsettled her that she couldn't think straight. She had no experience in these matters except what she found in books. And she didn't know what journals to look in for matters of carnal relations without asking Mr. C, and she wasn't about to do *that*.

A man of the world like Maxwell Ives thought she was attractive? Or was that flummery he offered because he was bored, and he missed his mistress?

How was a woman supposed to know these things?

She couldn't, which was why marriage had been invented. That settled it. No beds without marriage. He'd already proved his procreative ability and didn't need her or more children. As entertained as she might be by the notion of a man finding a large lump like her attractive, she refused to be another notch on his bedpost.

Lloyd knocked on the doorframe, looking for permission to enter. Mr. C's manservant didn't entirely approve of women and seldom sought her out. She was instantly concerned.

"What is it? Do you need a hot toddy to settle him down?" she asked, knowing Marta had gone off to bed.

Lloyd shook his head, his basset-hound face even more mournful than usual. "He's going, miss. I thought you might like to say your farewells."

"Farewells?" Stunned, Lydia sat up straight. Was Lloyd saying what she thought he was saying? "What do you mean, *going*?"

"He still breathes, but he's not there. I tried to wake him for his dinner, and I can't. It's only a matter of time." He looked lost and sorrowful.

She'd had one too many shocks this evening and couldn't absorb another. "But he was fine earlier." Fearing some misinterpretation, she hastily rose. "Stay here. I'll go up and see for myself."

She took the concealed door and inner stairs up. Lloyd knew all Mr. C's secrets, so she wasn't revealing anything the servant didn't know.

Carrying her lantern, holding her skirt, Lydia almost flew up the spiral staircase to Mr. C's chambers. She'd never given the tower's construction a single thought until Max had described it to her. He hadn't seen the top floor, but the engineer had known it was there.

Mr. C's suite sat on top of both towers. Mighty beams supported the roof. The walls of the different chambers on this level might be supports also, for all she knew. She had never seen more than the room where the stairs opened out. Mr. C used that room for his bed these days. After his stroke, he'd wanted to be closer to the library.

Lydia caught her breath as she entered and *felt* the emptiness. Mr. C's energy had always consumed this space. It was gone. Setting the lamp down on a dresser, she approached the bed. A candle burned on the table, illuminating the gray bulge beneath the covers.

Lloyd was right. The librarian still breathed. Praying anxiously, she took his gnarled hand. It was cold. Lloyd had laid an old cloak over him for extra warmth. She checked the grate, but the fire burned steadily.

He breathed. She had to bring him back from wherever he'd gone.

Pulling up a chair, she sat beside the bed, holding Mr. C's hand and offering muddled prayers to the universe and any gods who might be listening. She didn't even know she was weeping until a teardrop fell on her arm. Mr. C didn't move.

She brushed his bearded face, tucked his overlong white hair behind his ear, and whispered words of encouragement.

For one brief second, she thought he squeezed her fingers. And then his chest stopped moving.

She didn't need a physician to know he was gone—his journal was already whispering to her.

He'd left it on the table instead of holding it.

∙ ∙ ∙

ROYALLY SPOOKED, MAX SEARCHED THE STONE ARCH FOR ANY SECRET opening he might have missed and found no means of entering. Determined to find answers, he returned to the darkened castle in search of his elusive host. Walking through solid stone was just not done. He needed to know the trick. He wanted inside that tower.

Entering through the side door Lydia had first shown him—did no one ever lock doors here?—he saw no light burning downstairs. Since there were few servants to lock doors or light lamps, those tasks were probably neglected. He liked that there wasn't a bevy of maids hovering, so he wouldn't complain.

He checked the office where he'd found Lydia once before. Embers glowed in the grate. She or her employer must have been here recently.

Mr. Lloyd was slumped in a chair beside the fire, fast asleep. That seemed ominous.

A gray cloak hung on a hook behind the door. Did that mean the old man had returned here by some secret passage?

To hell with looking for secret passages. Max started up the narrow stone tower stairs. He couldn't see beyond the next bend as he climbed , but when he reached the final turn, he saw light under a door at the top.

It looked like a good hiding place for a reclusive librarian. If the old man could startle the daylights out of Max, Max could return the favor.

He raised his fist to knock. The door swung open with the brush of his knuckles. "Mr. Cadwallader?" He didn't like entering without permission.

A soft sob greeted him.

Max knew he wasn't a demonstrative man. Weeping women caused him to turn on his heel and head the other way.

But the door opened wider to reveal Lydia curled in a wing chair, weeping her heart out, and he couldn't bear it.

She didn't even look up. Momentarily flustered, unable to shed the fear of women flinging themselves at him when he entered a room, Max warily studied his surroundings.

The gray-cloaked, white-bearded figure he'd seen below lay in a small bed against the wall. The room was almost overheated, but the man was buried in covers.

Max tried to correlate the figure he'd seen in the cellar with the one he saw here. He was very good at sizing up situations, but this one added up to the impossible.

He crossed the room to check the old man's pulse. There was none. He was cold to the touch, which meant the librarian had been dead for a while. The chances that Mr. Cadwallader had run down a set of stairs to warn Max and run back up to die—zero.

He was wearing the cloak over his chest like a blanket, just as the. . . apparition. . . in the cellar had.

He'd seen a ghost. Max shivered a little, but he was a pragmatic man. The living came first.

He turned to Lydia. She clung to one of her ancient tomes, hugging it to her chest as if it were a child. He hated emotional scenes, never knew what to do, but he couldn't just abandon her.

"Should I bring up Mr. Lloyd?" he asked tentatively.

She shook her beautiful sunset curls, sending a few more tumbling. "There's nothing can be done until morning."

"Would you like me to sit with him so you can get some rest?"

She shook her hair again.

At a loss, not wanting to mention ghosts at a time like this, Max drew up a chair in front of hers. The apparition had said to take care of her, that she was more valuable than she thought. If that was a man's dying wish, he should listen. "Is that a book you can read to me?"

That startled her. Her liquid blue gaze jumped from him, to her dead employer, and down to the book.

"It's Mr. C's journal. It's calling to me," she whispered. "It never did that before. That's how I knew he was gone."

"Books call to you?" he asked, trying to hide his skepticism.

His doubt flew right over her head. The curl near her ear bounced as she nodded again.

"Mr. C's journal never spoke to me before, because he was alive. Your. . . journal. . . isn't really a book and you're alive, so I don't hear it. But all those volumes in the library. . ." She gestured helplessly. "They whisper, but I can't hear the words."

"Is this one talking any louder than those?" It didn't matter if he believed her. She'd stopped weeping. That was a good thing, wasn't it?

She thought about it, then reluctantly nodded again. "But it could just be me wishing it was saying 'open me' because I want to so badly."

Out of curiosity, Max pried the book from her elegantly long fingers. She released it without a fight, watching him as if he held the secrets to her heart's desire.

"It's all right for me to open the journal now because he's no longer alive?" At her reluctant nod, he opened the first page to see how badly the words swam.

Pretty badly. The librarian had written in a precise, ornate script, with so many loops and swirls they threatened to make Max's head pound. He flipped through to see if there was any interesting formula or drawing of the tower. The writing deteriorated as it progressed. Near the end, he discovered shaky but large square block letters.

He handed the book back to her. "Start there."

Her thick, reddish-brown lashes flapped in surprise. Gently, as if the old leather was a precious jewel, she took the book back.

She traced her name—Max had been able to read that much clearly in the plain print. Then she took a deep breath and began to read, *to herself*.

Fair enough. Max waited impatiently.

After a few minutes, she glanced up at him in astonishment. "He says the books tell him we need an engineer to save the library. And I can be the next librarian as long as the books live. I'm to write his solicitor for anything I need."

Her eyes darkened to indigo with hope and despair. "I want to be the librarian more than anything on earth. Can you save the tower?"

SIX

LYDIA KNEW HOW TO BURY DEEP, ABIDING SORROW. SHE'D DONE IT AFTER HER father died by handling all the practicalities that her weeping mother and sisters had been unable to deal with. She'd turned herself into an impervious tower shielded from emotional drama so she could see her way through disaster.

Afterward, out of sight of her family, she'd wept all the way from her home to Edinburgh.

She didn't have the option of fleeing now. She had to stay and sort through Mr. C's affairs and try to establish her own position somehow. If she trusted Mr. C's journal, this was her home—or could be, she thought, maybe.

She could be the librarian—if she saved the tower. She'd never had the ability to control anything in her life, but Mr. C had left her one thin thread of hope.

That slender thread held her together. She'd had a few hours of sleep in the chair beside Mr. C's bed. Then Marta had come to sit with him while Lloyd rode with Marta's uncle into town to seek the local minister. They needed pallbearers to carry Mr. Cadwallader to his final resting place in the vault beneath the castle chapel, with the other librarians. The list of things she must do kept growing.

Mr. Ives made her nervous, so she avoided him. She needed him to stay, but the thought worked on her very few nerves, so she didn't *think* about him either. It had been kind of him to help her through last evening. That's all she would admit.

Mr. C's journal gave her the instructions she needed. She had Lloyd send a telegram to ask the solicitors to settle his affairs. The castle was apparently in a trust and had monies for maintenance. Mr. C's journal assured her that she was named as the executor. She didn't know how much money was available, but now that she might eventually have access, she could hire back the servants. Confined to the tower, Mr. C had never noticed their absence. When she'd tried to talk to him about funds, he'd fallen asleep.

Apparently money hurt his damaged brain, so Lydia had given up and started using her own savings to pay those accounts requiring more cash than was in the study drawer.

With the journal to give her confidence, she made lists of what they needed to be functional again.

Unfortunately, Max Ives was on the very top. If Mr. C believed the tower was in danger, then it only made sense to have an Ives engineer fix it.

Mr. Ives had not agreed. Not last night, leastways.

He wanted to go to Burma. She had to stop him.

She hadn't seen him this morning, probably because he'd gone into town with Mr. Lloyd.

The first inkling of change arrived with light footsteps and a familiar sing-song voice. "Miss Lydia! Miss Lydia! I'm here. Old Tom says as you'll be needing us back."

Beryl. With a smile, Lydia ran into the corridor to signal the cheerful housemaid. "Beryl, I'm so glad you're free to return! I missed you."

Lydia had basically been an independent employee on the par with a steward. She still wasn't certain of her current status except she'd always been able to hire staff. She'd simply lacked funds. So the lower servants treated her with a degree of familiarity as well as respect. She returned the favor.

"I helped Pa with the shearing and Ma with the youngers while she was breeding," Beryl said breezily. "But I'm ready to be on my own again. Is that nice lad, Young Tom, returning? I should have asked Old Tom, shouldn't I have? But I was so excited that I ran off to pack my bag, and he went on."

"I told Old Tom to pass the word that everyone was welcome to return, if they wished. I don't know Young Tom's decision. It should be exciting to have everyone together again, even if the occasion is a sad one."

Beryl had a round face made rounder by a frame of wiry brown curls, but her expressive mouth obscured any flaws. It dipped downward now. "It's so very sad to not have Mr. C about, but it was sadder still to see him crippled up. He'll be happier with his ancestors."

"I like to believe that too. But we have a lot of work ahead of us, and I don't know when I can promise payment. Will that be all right? I'll try to do right by everyone, whatever happens." Lydia knew the merchants of Calder would send supplies on account, so everyone would be fed and dressed. It was just coin she lacked, temporarily, she hoped.

Beryl nodded enthusiastically. "It's like going back to school and waiting for everything to settle out. Where should I start?"

"Marta is in Mr. C's room. Why don't you ask her? She'll be happy to see you."

Beryl laughed. "Marta is never happy, but she'll know what needs doing." She practically skipped away.

Just that little bit of joy helped Lydia to navigate the first day of her new life. She lived in dread of it all being ripped from her hands as soon as the solicitors received her telegram, but until then, she'd take her happiness where she could find it. Knowing she'd never talk to Mr. C again. . . But then, they hadn't actually *conversed* in almost a year. Beryl was right. His spirit would be glad to move on.

Servants trickled back throughout the day as word spread. Neighbors arrived bearing small contributions like cheese and oatcakes so Marta didn't have to scramble to feed visitors as well as all the new staff.

To Lydia's relief, Laddie returned with his mule and cart and settled into the stable. She could go into town again! Unlike Mr. C, she wasn't a hermit. She loved the library and could spend an entire wintry day in it, but she loved people as well.

Well, maybe not all people, all the time, she thought, listening to the arrival of a carriage and team. The only person arrogant enough to take a carriage up that rough, hilly path was their neighbor, Lord Crowley.

Mr. C had usually refused to talk with him, leaving Lydia to endure the baron's tirades and his improper proposals—most of them monetary, thankfully, and not personal. Although she suspected if she had not towered over the cad by some inches and a few stone, the personal part may have required evasive skills she did not possess.

She almost wished Max were here. She prayed he hadn't run off to Burma. Or Siam. Or whatever the farthest place was from here.

Deciding she needed some symbol of authority, she added Mr. C's key ring to her skirt ties. She didn't own pearls or silk gowns, so she needed a pretense of authority if she were to step into Mr. C's very large shoes.

"Lord Crowley to see you, mum." Beryl curtsied in the doorway.

So Zach the footman hadn't returned yet. Jingling her keys for reassurance, Lydia held her head high and sailed down the corridor to the small—newly clean—parlor. They'd have to uncover the great hall for the funeral service.

"Lord Crowley," Lydia said with a haughty nod as she entered, the way she'd seen Mr. C do when he'd been persuaded to talk with the man. "Please do not smudge the glass."

Probably five-five, with all his weight in his bulging belly, Crowley was fingering an antique crystal clock on the mantel. It was a work of art in gold and bronze with a crystal cover that Mr. C had prized and kept running, and Marta polished lovingly.

Crowley took his grimy hands off the crystal and wiped them with his handkerchief as if the clock had contaminated them. "Miss Wystan," he said curtly. "I have come to extend condolences."

"The household thanks you." She did not sit down, forcing him to remain standing. "I fear we're at sixes and sevens today. We hope to hold services tomorrow."

She would not lie and say he would be welcome.

He patted his forehead with the handkerchief before tucking it back into his pocket. "Unfortunately, I have business in Edinburgh tomorrow. I thought I might inquire if you will need transport. My carriage is more comfortable than the train."

Lydia forced her eyebrows from reaching her hairline. "That is very kind of you, sir, and I appreciate the offer." She'd rather take a fast train than a slow ride with Mr. Crowley. She summoned courage she didn't know she possessed to continue. "But I am Mr. Cadwallader's executor and the current librarian. I won't be going anywhere soon."

She tried not to cringe when she called herself librarian. If Mr. C believed it. . .

"Executor?" Crowley harrumphed. "Women can't be executors. They have no legal rights. I knew Cadwallader was losing his wits. You'd best go with me and talk to his solicitors directly."

Lydia felt a chill but refused to give into it. "Times are changing, my lord. I am quite certain his excellent solicitors would not have drawn up his papers and filed them if they were not legal. The castle is in a trust, and I am executor of that trust. I hope you have a safe journey. Good day." She marched out. Or retreated. She wasn't entirely certain except she'd been abominably rude—for good reason.

Lord Crowley wanted to buy the castle.

Mr. C had said that would be over his dead body.

They were burying his body tomorrow.

MAX RETURNED TO THE CASTLE ON THE BACK OF A BROAD-BEAMED HORSE Old Tom had assured him had once belonged to Mr. Cadwallader before his apoplexy. The horse swayed like an ox, but the mare bore Max's weight up the rutted path without breathing hard.

She was also wide enough to hold a six-year-old boy who wordlessly clung to her mane.

Max was fairly certain Bakari spoke English. The boy's mother had, quite volubly, if Max recalled rightly. But he hadn't seen Bakari since he was a wailing infant.

Max was as terrified as the boy.

To his relief, a lad actually popped out of the stable when Max dismounted. He lifted his son down and unbuckled his saddle bags. "We'll have trunks arriving," he warned. "I'm Max Ives, by the way." He offered his hand to the scrawny lad taking the reins.

The stableboy gaped at him in awe. "Yes, sir, Mr. Ives. I'll carry the trunks in." He didn't shake Max's hand.

The British class system was more structured than the American. He should remember that and not make the servants uncomfortable.

Not if he planned to stay, leastways.

That part remained undecided. His feet itched to be off, but Lydia's pleas last night—had completely unnerved him. And his son's silence. . . made him itch all over. That was the only way he could describe it.

"Come along, lad. What did your mother call you?" Max knew the boy's formal name, of course. He'd abide by it if necessary. But a good old-fashioned Bradford would go further in these climes.

The boy didn't answer. His huge brown eyes had fastened on the towering castle.

It was a great stone heap, like all others of its ilk, except no one had thought to turn this one into a Gothic horror of turrets and arches. Yet. It had once been a square crenellated fortress with an enormous, disproportionate tower from earlier times attached. A few more impressive blocks of stone had been added over the centuries, some of them even dressed up to look vaguely Georgian. But it was a hilltop fortress, nonetheless.

"Shall we go in?" he asked the boy, pointing to the side door nearest the stable.

Wide-eyed, the boy nodded. So he did understand English. Max led the way across the stable yard and tested the door. Still unlocked. He pushed it open and let the boy step in first.

The first thing that struck him was a strong odor of vinegar and lemon oil. The second was the sound of voices. *Voices*, in a tomb with all of three people in it? They could inhabit different territories and not see each other from one week to the next.

Gazing at the towering walls of this back corridor, the boy had frozen in place. Max hadn't given the walls a second glance. They were full of the usual sorts of portraits of musty ancestors, aging hunting paintings, a few blunderbusses, a few claymores. . . gruesome, not awesome. But he supposed nothing in the boy's home of Egypt would compare except maybe a museum. Or a mausoleum.

What did he do now? Just install the boy in his room and find Lydia to tell her he was here? Find Lydia first? That could take a while. And if he found her, did he tell her about the ghost in her cellar?

Not any time soon, he resolved.

Her office wasn't too far away. He needed to see if his half-Egyptian son was welcome. Nudging the boy to keep moving, he led the way to the room where he'd first seen sunshine. Lydia Wystan lit a room without need of a window.

He had to quit thinking like that. He stopped at the office door and admired the stack of red-blond tresses bent over the desk. She was so absorbed in her task that it took a second before she looked up.

Her whole face lit, but she wasn't looking at Max. She was looking at Bakari.

"Your son has arrived! What a pleasure to meet you." She came around the desk and crouched down to Bakari's height, to the best she could. "I am Miss Lydia. How do you do?"

The boy burst into tears. Max panicked.

Lydia cast him a glance of annoyance, then took the boy into her arms, gently patting his back. "It's been a long, long journey, hasn't it? You must be very hungry and tired. Shall we see if the kitchen has a cake or sweet you might like?"

Bakari nodded half-heartedly. Lydia swept him up in her arms and carried him into the corridor.

"Here, let me carry him," Max said, annoyed. It had never occurred to him that the boy might be exhausted. He usually pushed right through his own fatigue, but he wasn't a child. "He's heavy."

"No heavier than my little sister used to be when I carried her about after she broke her leg. And this poor lad is positively scrawny. Have they not been feeding him?"

There was that tone of disapproval he expected from everyone, although Lydia hadn't used it as much as others. She sounded like her late employer. She'd start nagging about his mother next. Maybe that's what librarians did.

"Jones said he was seasick most of the way." So the lad was probably starving now. And Max hadn't given it a thought. He'd never taken care of anyone or anything except himself in his life. He'd never even owned

a pet. More proof that he needed to send his son off to school immediately.

"Oh, my, you poor boy!" Lydia cuddled the lad against her curvaceous bosom, and Max felt a stab of envy. "What's your name?"

"He doesn't seem to talk," Max replied after an awkward silence.
"His name is Bakari Ives Elmahdy. We should probably call him Brad or
Bob."

She sent him another look that smacked of disapproval. "He's lost his
mother and his home and you wish to take away his name too?"

"I'm only trying to be helpful," Max protested as they descended to
the kitchen. "The other students will poke fun at him enough as it is. You
have no idea what those schools are like."

"And knowing that, you mean to send him to one?" she asked in scorn
as they emerged into a kitchen containing actual servants besides Marta.

The kitchen contained *females*. Reflexively, Max backed up the stairs.
One of the younger girls hurried toward them, wearing a bright smile.
He had to get out of here.

"Mary, welcome back," Lydia said, oblivious to the danger. She
handed her burden over to the young maid. "We need to see what
Master Bakari likes to eat. Have we any oatcakes left?"

"I'll fetch some, miss." A second young maid curtsied, while sending
Max a fetching smile. "We have some berries and cream too. Would the
gentleman like a pint to wet his whistle?"

Max shook his head and backed up another step. Unlike her servants,
Lydia's attention was entirely on his son—and not him—he'd never
become used to that. She failed to notice his retreat.

"Berries are an excellent idea. Mary, set Bakari down at the table and
see what else is in the pantry that might tempt a growing boy. Cheese,
maybe?" Lydia finally turned to Max. "Is he vegetarian by any chance?
Lady Phoebe has a friend from India who does not eat meat."

Max hadn't thought about his eccentric cousin in ages. He rolled his
eyes. "Phoebe collects oddities. His mother ate meat. The last time I saw
him, he was still drinking mother's milk, so I can't say if that changed."

"Shall I help Mr. Ives set up a cot for his son?" a third smiling young
thing asked, stepping forward.

"Don't be silly, Sally. Beryl can handle that. You need to be scrubbing pots." Lydia sat down across from the boy as oatcakes and honey were placed in front of him. "Break off a piece and dip it. It's fun and messy."

"Beryl?" Max asked warily, easing up another stair when Mary returned her predatory gaze to him. Usually, he could count on distance halting whatever this thing was that possessed him, but staying out of sight worked best.

Lydia frowned at him, puzzled, rightfully so. "I've asked all our former servants to return if they're available. I am very much hoping that the trust has enough funds to pay them. Mr. C used to deposit money in his desk drawer every quarter for wages—until he became ill and couldn't go into town. I am hoping I will have use of the same funds. A place this size cannot be maintained without an army."

"If you don't entertain, why does it matter? You seemed to be doing fine without help." Max didn't want to embarrass himself even more by arguing from his own perspective—an army of women was dangerous to his vow to never father another bastard. He might be stronger than he was as a youth, but when women offered, it often seemed rude to say no. He was a man, after all. He wasn't averse to pleasure.

She gestured at Mary to go back to work. "Half the town will be here tomorrow for Mr. C's funeral. And we once had lots of visitors. Any Malcolms traveling to the area used to pay their respects. Others wanted to research. We've had to turn them away this past year. It wasn't as if Mr. C needed much."

Mary didn't return to her work. Sally wasn't cleaning pots. The unidentified one was heading toward him with the pint he'd refused and a gleam in her eye. Max backed up two more stairs.

Lydia eyed his retreat warily. "Are visitors a problem? You needn't attend the service."

With a degree of panic, Max glanced at the three young women circling the table, drawing closer. "If you don't mind, I'll leave you to feed the boy while I see if our trunks have arrived. Tell this Beryl I'll take care of my own room. I don't wish to be burden. We'll leave in the morning."

He fled.

SEVEN

Nonplussed, Lydia watched Max flee as if the hounds of hell were on his heels. What on earth had set him off?

Mary abruptly returned to mixing, Sally to scrubbing pots. Lydia frowned, trying to remember what they'd been doing while Max was present. She looked to Marta for answers. The cook merely raised a questioning eyebrow. Lydia wasn't good at reading non-verbal communication. She wanted to ask *What had just happened here?* But she felt ignorant in asking.

Shaking her head, she turned back to Bakari. The boy was hungrily shoving down oatcakes and honey and ignoring his fruit. She spooned some berries on the oatmeal rounds with the honey. He liked that too. "Maybe some milk?" she suggested.

Mary set down a full glass. "My little brother likes sausage. Shall I fetch some? And maybe take something up to Mr. Ives?"

"Mr. Ives will eat when everyone else does," Marta said sharply. "Finish that pudding before it's ruined."

Lydia cut off a piece of cheese. The boy eyed it skeptically but apparently trusting her, took a bite. He nodded, then dipped it in honey too.

She'd need to hire the beekeeper back to look after the old hives. She needed someone with authority to handle servants. "Does anyone know if there is any chance Mr. and Mrs. Folkston will return? Or should I start looking for a new butler and housekeeper?"

While Marta suggested the older couple might have retired to their cottage or gone to relations, Mary sulked. The other two maids kept glancing at the stairs, as if expecting the arrival of good King Wenceslaus.

Or Max.

Surely not. He was a guest. He shouldn't have been down here at all. That was her fault. But these were good girls. They weren't the kind of women who hung about mining camps, looking for trouble.

But just in case, she wiped Bakari's chin when he finished his milk and led him upstairs herself.

She found Max pacing in his room.

"I didn't know you'd have servants!" he practically shouted. "I'll *have* to leave now."

That caused Lydia a pain too great to analyze. Not that she wasted time analyzing anyway.

"Mr. Cadwallader said I would have privacy—" Max halted as he realized what he'd said. "You promised to follow his orders for privacy."

"I'm sorry. I wasn't thinking about you when I hired them back. I just knew how much their families need the money. And I wanted Mr. C to have a proper service. I hadn't realized *servants* bothered you." She helped Bakari out of his suit jacket.

He was a beautiful little boy with a thick mop of dark hair like his father's and lovely bronze coloring, presumably like his mother's. He would grow up to be a heartbreaker.

"*Civilization* bothers me," Max said grumpily. "I don't fit in here. I'm not much of a father either. I didn't even think he'd be hungry."

"You have no practice at raising children and I do. I've been told growing boys are always hungry. You should know that better than I, though. My siblings were girls." Lydia helped the boy between the covers. The child's lids were so heavy, he could barely keep them open. "We should step outside and let him sleep."

"Thank you for helping with him. I know I've been a curmudgeon." Visibly disgruntled, Max held open the door.

Lydia had to brush past him to reach the corridor. She tried not to notice his male aroma of horses and shaving soap and something more. . . primal. . . but it appealed to her senses.

"Experience has taught me my limitations," he said with a male growl that tingled her down to her toes as he closed the door.

What on earth was wrong with her? She never noticed men, but this one felt as if he were inside her skin. "You'll need to stay with your son so he doesn't wake up alone," she warned.

Max was standing much too close, but they were whispering, and she couldn't back away. His chest looked so broad and sturdy— She tucked her hands behind her back.

"I'll lock the door and hide in my room until we go," he muttered. "I really wanted to take another look at the tower before I left. I could swear I saw Mr. Cadwallader down there last night. He walked straight through a stone wall."

"Mr. C? That's impossible! He couldn't walk—" Lydia swallowed hard. She wasn't good at deception. Did she tell him he'd never spoken to Mr. C? "A ghost?" she asked weakly. "You saw a ghost—in our cellar?"

"He couldn't walk where?" Max demanded.

Of course he'd notice that misstep, drat him. If she told him the truth, he'd think she was just another woman tricking him into staying. But she was so bad at lying! "Very well, he couldn't walk well. Do you really think you saw a ghost?"

"I don't normally believe in ghosts, but last night, after lecturing me, he walked through a stone wall! What do you mean, he didn't walk well? When he accompanied me through the cellar, he walked as well as you walk—" His voice trailed off, and he studied her with suspicion. "The *ghost* was shorter than you. The Mr. Cadwallader I spoke with was as tall as you and walked like you. How ill was he?"

"Very," she said with a sigh, giving up. Max was much better at figuring out puzzles than she ever would be. "He couldn't talk. He lost most of the use of his hands. And one leg was paralyzed. He refused to see anyone, and most of the time, he just slept. I'm hoping he's in a happier place now. He was a very good man. If his ghost talked to you, you heard more than I have in a long time. What did he say?"

"He said you were more valuable than you know. I can't believe I'm saying ghosts give warnings." Max pressed the base of his palm to his forehead, as if forcing himself to focus. "*You're* the one who has been nagging me to see my mother, not Mr. Cadwallader." It wasn't a question. "And you're the one who told me to trust *you* with my journal. That's not fair, you know." He didn't sound angry, just tired. Or maybe resigned.

Mr. C had said she was valuable? Or Max's odd hallucination had said it. She found that a bit hard to accept.

"I only said what Mr. C would have told you, if he could," she said defensively. "You cannot let your mother lose her home and school."

"If we're to believe the phantasm, he was corresponding with my mother," Max said, anger apparently building. "So I telegraphed a friend while I was in Calder today. He has the head for business I don't. I have no idea what he can do, but I asked. I had hoped to stay here until he replied, but if you're bringing in servants, that will be a disaster. Do you have a remote cottage, by any chance?"

She didn't think Max was a lunatic or making up his fear of women. The problem apparently seemed very real in his mind. She supposed she was so large that he thought of her as a man and wasn't afraid of her, which made her feel ugly, but that was nothing new.

What mattered was that he seemed to sincerely believe the maids would sneak into his bed like the loose women he'd known, and he was angry and unhappy. She needed to placate him if she meant to have him stabilize the tower. *If* it needed stabilizing.

"I'm not aware of the extent of the estate's property," she admitted honestly. "I believe Mr. C leased land to farmers, but his bankers and so forth handled all that. I only manage the household."

Max frowned. She could almost feel him packing his bags and running into the village. Or to a train and a ship and. . .

She glanced at the tower stairs just down the corridor. "This is the oldest part of the house. I put guests in your room because it's convenient to the public part of the library, where most of our guests spend their time." She nodded at the book-lined chamber directly across from his—the one he'd never set foot in to her knowledge. "But there are small cubicles with cots inside the tower, and the downstairs tower door locks."

His expressive face lit up with curiosity. She'd finally caught his interest. He strode toward the tower entrance. "I could lock the whole tower and not be disturbed?"

"Mr. C has been removed to the chapel, so it shouldn't be a problem," she said sadly. "I'm not sure what to do about Lloyd, though. His room is up there. Once he cleans out Mr. C's effects, perhaps I could ask him to stay as a footman."

Max snorted as he examined the ancient wooden door at the foot of the tower. "Lloyd's not tall and good-looking. Isn't that how footmen are chosen?"

He started up the stairs, apparently in search of the cubicles.

Lydia ran after him. "The rooms are very small. I don't think there is space for both you and your son. And they're farther from the bath. Shouldn't you at least wait to see if anyone disturbs you?"

"Is there anything else at the top besides that chamber I saw last night?" he asked, glancing into the first cubicle and moving on.

"It's all Mr. C's suite. I've never seen more than the front parlor where he made his bed this past year. Lloyd tends it. You can't stay *there*!" She rushed after him.

"We should at least take a look. It might hold clues to the tower's listing." He continued up, taking the narrow, winding steps two at a time. The late afternoon sunlight illuminated only the west-facing stairs, throwing a pattern of dark and shadow.

Flustered, Lydia ran after him. "Your son can't climb all these steps!"

"Have you ever watched small boys? They never sit. They run up and down stairs and hills and will climb anything within reach. He'll love this. That doesn't mean we should occupy the suite. I simply want to take a look."

She hoped he knew what he was talking about. He hadn't known much about feeding small boys.

She really wanted to hear from the solicitors before being so presumptuous as to enter Mr. C's chambers. She hadn't even read his private thoughts in the journal except those last pages with her name on them. She preferred to move cautiously.

Maxwell Ives on the other hand, preferred flipping his world upside-down. He didn't even seem to be aware that he was doing it. He had this amazing confidence that everything he did was right. Or if he did it wrong, that he could fix it. Maybe that was the key.

She didn't have that sort of confidence. She hadn't once fixed anything. At best, she held things together to prevent them from falling apart. Which was what she was trying to do now—keep the tower from falling apart.

THE ARROW SLITS DID NOT PROVIDE SUFFICIENT LIGHT FOR A GOOD examination of the walls. Max vowed to come back later with lamps and look for damage. He was just excited at studying a different part of the tower. The idea of an eyrie above the household, accessible only to him, and the boy, of course, was an equal enticement.

Lydia was right, dammit. His son wasn't ready for school.

He'd telegraphed his investor friend, Hugh Morgan. He'd ask Hugh about schools. Right now, the tower had his complete interest.

Not true, he realized a moment later when Lydia's lavender fragrance joined him on the top landing. Every nerve tingled with awareness as she unlocked the door with her chatelaine of keys.

"We never lock the bottom door," she said pragmatically. "But this one works well."

"Let's take a look at this place. It was too dark last night to see anything." Except Lydia, weeping, but Max didn't mention that.

Lloyd or Marta or both had apparently straightened the sick room he remembered. The cot was gone. The stacks of ancient tomes had disappeared. An old horsehair settee was centered on one wall. Wing chairs flanked the fireplace. A piecrust tea table held knickknacks. The room looked fussy and unused.

Lydia gasped in shock. So, she hadn't ordered the removal of her employer's effects.

"If the servants are allowed to move things, then we should be allowed to investigate the suite," Max announced. He had a feeling Lydia would simply have turned the room into a shrine.

If she was the new librarian, this suite should probably be hers.

"Where is your room?" Max asked when she didn't respond. He paced, studying the high-ceilinged chamber.

The windows overlooked a rolling hillside. A tapestry covered the wall that should be the inner tower. He wanted to see the confounded inner walls. He crossed to the door he assumed led to a proper bedchamber.

"We passed my room on the way up," Lydia replied, sadly touching the settee. "I needed to be near Mr. C and the study."

"You live in one of those cubbyholes?" He stopped to stare at her in disbelief. "Where do you put your wardrobe?"

She glanced down at her shapeless gown. "I hang my gowns on hooks, as I've always done. It's not as if I need evening gowns or walking dresses and whatnot." She chuckled at the notion.

She was even more gorgeous when she smiled. Max replied without thinking. "You would look spectacular in an evening gown. If I were on speaking terms with my mother, I'd curse her for sending you to this remote outpost with only a hermit for company. You should be adorning ballrooms and dinner tables."

If she reacted to his insane declaration, Max couldn't tell. He was really bad at this flirtation business.

He opened the door and stepped up—into another damn library. How many libraries could the place have?

The Malcolm *librarian* lived here. Of course the castle spilled over with books. . .

As well as several globes, a telescope, a ship's compass, a celestial mobile. . . Max drank it all in. If he had a home, this would be it.

Lydia touched the map globe as if fearful she'd burn her finger. "I've never seen anything like this. How do you find anything?"

Happy to have an excuse to stand close, Max leaned over her shoulder and spun the sphere until he found the British Isles. "This is where we are, in the upper half. Your school didn't have a globe? How did you learn geography?"

He longed to kiss that long neck or nibble her ear. She'd probably plant a noser on him if he tried, and he rather enjoyed the notion. She was a challenge like no other woman he'd ever encountered.

"I didn't," she said, shrugging. "My father was my teacher. He knew Latin and Greek and how to write sermons, among other literary things, but nothing scientific. I lived with his books. I didn't fit in well at school.

After I memorized all the school's textbooks, the teacher didn't know what to do with me. And when I outgrew everyone else. . . I learned more at home."

Max wanted to fling all those idiots out windows. Instead, he squeezed her shoulder and leaned over to show her Burma, on the southern hemisphere. "That's where my next job is."

"It's on the other side of the world! How do you not fall off?" She tilted the globe up and down to measure the distance.

"There are millions of people there, and as far as I'm aware, none have flown off. Here's where Bakari lived." He pointed out Egypt. "We sail through this sea here, out to the ocean, and straight up the coast to home."

"It almost looks easy," she said with uncertainty, edging away from him.

By all the gods, he wanted her. Max wanted her with a desperation he could scarcely control and certainly didn't understand. He had so little experience with wooing, that his limitations were frustrating. Unlike every other woman in his life, Lydia barely acknowledged his existence.

She drifted away to examine the telescope and compass.

Shelves of books hid the inner wall in this room—and they were square like all the other walls. How did that work? The outer walls were obviously curved with lots of windows. He could practically see Edinburgh. With the telescope, he might see the ocean.

"The journey is not easy. From Egypt, it takes months, even with a steamship." Max crossed the Turkish carpet to the next door—another step up, odd, as if the suite was a spiral staircase. If the roof covered both towers, then this suite could very well reflect what was under its floors.

He threw open the next door— a small valet's chamber. He crossed the closet of a room, took the steps, and opened the next door— a bath similar to the one downstairs. "Is there a cistern on the roof?"

She looked more comfortable with this topic. "There is, and a well in the cellar on the castle side, near the kitchen. I believe there is also a cistern on the roof of the main block, but it's a warren of closed-off rooms."

He glanced up. The timbered ceiling continued through here, but it wasn't as high as in the parlor. He knocked on the windowless inner wall. It sounded solid, but then, there was probably five feet of stone behind there. "This has to be an Ives castle. I don't understand how it became a Malcolm library."

"The families intermarried way back when," Lydia reminded him. "And there's no reason someone couldn't have simply hired an Ives to make improvements."

"I know the history. I live it. Malcolms married Ives for their fortunes and titles. I'm reasonably certain that's why my mother married my father. They were in no way alike, but her father was a bankrupt earl, so she brought connections." Stepping up to the next door and glancing in, Max blocked the entrance to the librarian's private chamber.

"Your maternal grandfather owned property that he rented out," she argued. "The earl wasn't bankrupt. I saw the journals. He left Lady Phoebe's mother an entire tenement when he died. His brother inherited a considerable rural estate."

"And my mother and her sister inherited those crumbling medieval townhouses, I know. The old earl never improved what he owned or invested in anything new. My maternal uncle, the current earl, doesn't either. That's why my mother married an Ives, a progressive who understood that time marches on."

"Are his brother and your cousin like your father?"

"Uncle David is only my father's stepbrother and not an Ives, but as far as I'm aware, he and my cousin George were on their way to owning half Edinburgh when I left. So, yes, I'd say peas in a pod."

Max finally stood aside so she could see inside the librarian's bedchamber. "Apparently the elves have not only carried off Mr. Cadwallader, but magicked his chamber, Miss Librarian."

Inside this final room, gold and blue hangings adorned the enormous tester bed. Lavender scented the air, as if Lydia had been living here all along. A delicate blue and gold teapot, still steaming, waited with a set of cups on a tea table before a grate already set for burning.

Slippers and a robe waited on the bed, along with a lacy frilly nightgown that gave Max way more ideas than he needed.

EIGHT

AT SIGHT OF THE CHAMBER MADE UP FOR HER, LYDIA COVERED HER MOUTH to prevent a cry. Shoving past Max, she ran back through the suite to Mr. C's room. His journal was gone. She hadn't moved it.

They'd erased all signs of Mr. C. Fighting tears, she tried to compose herself while waiting for Max to follow. He did so slowly, studying the tower's architecture.

Should she show him the library? Mr. C had never told her that the inner tower was a secret. There just hadn't been any reason to tell anyone else about it. And well. . . concealed doors seemed secretive to her.

Lloyd knew the inner stairs were there. That's how he and Marta had performed miracles without anyone noticing. They'd moved her into Mr. C's room—as if they expected her to be the new librarian!

For any hope of that, she *needed* Max to stay and verify the tower wouldn't tumble. Or prevent it from tumbling. That was imperative, far more imperative than the servants she'd promised to hire back. She should have been more conscious of his fear of his weird gift or magnetism and not invited them to return yet. But they were so happy. . .

The deed was done. It was apparently now up to her to make all the decisions, even if they were wrong. She took a deep breath—and felt Max's gaze on her.

Lydia swung around and saw his frankly admiring look. She wanted to smack him for making her self-conscious when she needed to think clearly.

"The suite should suit you and Bakari while you stay here. There is a lock on this door." She could almost hear Max's question, so she forestalled it. She didn't know how to lie properly, so she had to tell him about the library, somehow. "Marta and Lloyd, however, have keys."

"And they turn invisible and climb the stairs right past us to set up teapots and fires?" he asked with humor, nailing her problem at once.

"You're a guest," she muttered. "You're threatening to leave tomorrow. I'm still learning what the librarian must do, and I'm following Mr. C's example as best as I can. I don't know how much leeway I have until I find an instruction book or something useful. I don't know how much to tell you."

"This should be *your* suite," he said emphatically. "You do not have to tell me anything. Maybe there's a door on one of the corridors in the main block I can lock. I'd explore, but you said I need to stay with the boy until he wakes. If I stay, I'll need to hire a manservant to look after him while I work—I could hire Lloyd!"

She looked at him with suspicion. "Lloyd as a nursemaid?"

He shrugged and studied the tapestry concealing the library door. "He'll be wanting a position. Would he make a suitable tutor?"

"You're staying?" she asked, still not quite trusting him.

"I don't want to," he admitted. "But it seems my responsibilities are growing greater than my itchy feet can carry. Bakari isn't ready for school," he admitted with a sigh. "I was twice his size at that age and could defend myself. And I had my Ives cousins to step up when the taunting became unmerciful. I have no idea if he has Ives cousins near his age. I've not kept in touch."

She nodded, breathing a little easier now that one uncertainty was almost arranged. "I can check your family tree. Bakari should know his cousins—and his brothers." She shouldn't have said that, but she'd been raised in a closely-knit family and couldn't imagine not knowing them.

She gestured at the parlor. "This suite is ideal for your purposes. We could move the cot up here. You'd have privacy. Lloyd is used to sleeping in the valet's room. I'd hate to put him out. He could act as your valet and perhaps tutor Bakari a little."

Max frowned and lifted the tapestry. "If we do this, it will only be for a very little while, until I learn what's happening with the tower and figure out what to do with the boy."

"And your mother," she insisted. "How long will it be until your friend answers your inquiry?"

That would give her a little breathing space. She could stay in her usual routine for a little while, add tasks to her list as they came up, not leap into anything like this beautiful suite which should belong to the *real* librarian. Despite Mr. C's promise, she didn't think she qualified.

She watched uneasily as Max tapped on the wall. He knew. He was an engineer. He knew the other tower was behind there. He had no use for books, so it shouldn't matter one way or another if she let him in.

"Morgan? He's usually pretty prompt." Max began pushing against an unseen seam. "It just depends on what else he's doing and how much time he has. How long will it take for you to determine if Bakari has cousins his age?"

"It depends on how complete Mr. C left the genealogy before his illness. Push two blocks down and one block over from the painting." If he stayed in the tower, he'd find the door sooner or later.

Max shot her a smile that nearly brought her to her knees. No wonder women flocked to him. With that large nose, he wasn't really handsome, just. . . compelling.

"I was wondering when you'd trust me." He pushed the designated block, and the wall slid to one side. He stuck his head through and grunted in disappointment. "More books. I should have known."

Lydia almost laughed. "Light the lantern on the stand. You'll enjoy the architecture."

He studied the high ceiling in the parlor, ducked through the door, and stood upright on the landing on the other side. "Holy flying monkeys," he said in awe.

The books whispered and beckoned, like a wind whistling through leaves. Lydia couldn't translate whispers any more than she could wind. She was aware of how disastrous it would be if she couldn't find the books people needed. The family would realize she wasn't a real librarian. A call would go out and others would come to take her place. She shivered and stepped through the doorway to join him. In her mind, the library breathed like a sentient being. She simply couldn't communicate.

Lloyd had left Mr. C's stack of journals on a table evidently set there for this purpose. The servant didn't know how to file them. Books waited for her to shelve.

Unless she'd seen them removed, she had no idea where they belonged.

"They improved on the original *broch's* spiral staircase and galleries," Max said in awe, studying the wrought iron galleries and stairs. "This place is completely protected from the elements. Your chamber must be right over the ceiling." He leaned over the rail to see upward. "This inner tower is the ideal place to store books."

"There are other libraries," she said diffidently. "I think the oldest one is in Wystan Castle in Northumberland. There's another, newer one, forming near the Highlands. I'm not exactly certain of its location. I believe there is one forming in China as well. I've had a letter from them and replied, but that's all I know."

"China." He whistled in surprise. "Chinese Malcolms. I cannot imagine. . . They speak English?" He took several stairs down.

"The librarian does, at least."

"I'd like to know if there are books about the building of these towers." He stopped to study the journals on the nearest shelf.

As if passing straight from Max's thoughts, some of the whispers grew louder, clearer. *Tower. Spiral. Broch.*

Lydia's head spun. She staggered and gripped Max's arm for support. She curled her fingers around the rail as well. *Tower. Spiral. Broch.* Steadying herself , she concentrated on the clearest whisper.

Max slid his arm around her waist and held her upright with a look of concern. His support let her breathe a little easier as she tried to orient herself and the odd vibrations in her head.

She scanned the library, locating the closest source. "There." She picked up one of the books on the table. It felt right. It felt similar to the one Mr. C had showed her the other day. Pulling free of Max's grip, she started down the stairs. The oldest books were near the bottom of the tower. The more contemporary ones were nearby. She reached for another calling to her.

With Max trailing behind, she continued downward, occasionally halting to determine the direction of a call and adding another book to her collection. At one point, she handed the stack to Max. By the time she had another pile, they had reached the hidden study at the bottom.

"Books mentioning towers and brochs," she told him briskly, as if she did this every day and wasn't secretly screaming with joy. She proceeded past Mr. C's study to the door that would take them to her outer office. "We'll put them in the guest library where we can work on them."

"It's easier for me to take tower measurements than read journals," he grumbled. "I thought you couldn't find books?"

"I can't. I couldn't. I don't know what happened." Exhausted, head spinning, she hurried through her office and down the corridor to the library where guests worked. The glassed bookcases held reference books, not Malcolm journals.

She dumped her load on the long, polished mahogany library table and Max did the same. "I know you don't want to read these. I can. I don't know if I can go directly to the right page or not. But just being able to find the books. . ." She closed her eyes and offered a prayer of gratitude to Whoever was watching over her.

"Combining resources," he said in admiration. "I like it. I hate taking up your time. I saw all that correspondence on your desk. . ."

She waved away the thought. "I read quickly. You need to go back to your son, while I look for Lloyd and see if I can persuade him to be a temporary tutor. Tomorrow will be a busy day, and there will be visitors everywhere. You might want to hide beneath the tower or in your suite."

Max caught her waist and spun her around. Without any warning, he dipped his head—

And kissed her.

BLISS, ABSOLUTE BLISS. MAX SAVORED THE SWEET TASTE OF LIPS THAT HAD nibbled on oatcakes and berries, inhaled the spring freshness of lavender, and fell into a cauldron of desire before he knew he was tipping over. He pulled the librarian tighter, relished feminine curves crushed against him, and ran his hands over her unencumbered backside. He hated bustles. She was all woman beneath his hands—a woman who melted into him as if she belonged there, who didn't push away his whiskered jaw or complain that he stank of horse, which he probably did. She kissed him with enthusiasm and with every appearance of enjoying the moment as much as he did.

A loud harrumph brought him back to his senses. Cursing, Max glanced over his shoulder—a large, bespectacled business man stood there. That could only be Hugh Morgan.

"Perhaps we should wait in the parlor, Mr. Morgan." A feminine voice confirmed Max's supposition.

Lydia shoved away, brushing her hair from her face, and ducking her head to hide her blushing cheeks. Max wanted to smack his associate and whisk Lydia away and. . . He rubbed his forehead. "Yes, Morgan," he snarled. "Maybe you should wait in the parlor."

"Don't be rude." Lydia straightened her gown and her shoulders.

Stepping past Max to greet their guests, Lydia looked like a regal queen—Elizabeth came to mind, with all the royal red hair. A relation to the Tudor dynasty might explain his hostess's ruthlessness in emerging from an abyss of pleasure with no evidence of the confusion Max felt.

"Hugh Morgan? I've heard of you from Lady Phoebe. Pleased to meet you. I'm Lydia Wystan." She held out her hand.

Morgan took it. Uncouth Glaswegian that he was, he didn't look certain whether to shake or kiss it.

Lydia shook his hand and turned to his companion. "I don't suppose you'd be Miss Trivedi? The ladies have told me of you and your admirable mathematical expertise. Perhaps if we return to the parlor, I can call for tea. You must have traveled quickly!"

"Back to the parlor," Max muttered, punching Morgan's shoulder. "And thanks for bringing a female with you. You might as well have brought my mother and her entire contingent."

"Miss Trivedi isn't a Malcolm. She's an accountant. And you need an accountant who can explain things better than I can. You're in bigger trouble than you know." Morgan turned and followed the women, taking no umbrage at Max's accusation.

"And you ascertained that in what, a single day? You've developed my mother's prescience?" Max stopped and peered into his room, where his son slept soundly, his pillow scrunched beneath his face. He left the door open so he could hear if the boy called.

"I've been looking into your mother's affairs ever since Lady Phoebe mentioned a problem. I just couldn't do anything while you were gallivanting the world. Everything is tied up, and you're the only one who can step in. Have you decided to return from the dead?"

Max hadn't decided any such thing, but Morgan had loyally kept his secret all this time, so he shouldn't begrudge the question.

Lydia pulled the bell rope. Max cringed, hoping Lloyd or a footman would heed the call.

He waited until the ladies had taken their seats. He'd been yanked from bliss to hell in a few short seconds. He needed time to regroup. Lydia spread her skirt on a settee. After waiting to see where Miss Trivedi sat, Max took the seat beside Lydia on the opposite side of the fireplace. He needed her solid proximity to remind him the world wasn't entirely insane. He had a wild hope that she might act as his magnetic shield.

Morgan settled his large frame beside Miss Trivedi. That lady studied Max with interest, but she seemed firmly affixed to Morgan. It happened that way sometimes. Max breathed a little easier and warily watched the door for maids.

"I'm sorry you've come this distance at a time like this," Lydia apologized. "Mr. Cadwallader passed away last night, and we're making funeral arrangements. We're not at our best, I fear."

To Max's relief, Marta appeared with a tea tray as if she'd been lurking close by.

"Is Beryl busy?" Lydia asked her cook in surprise. "You shouldn't have to be waiting on us."

"I had a moment, miss, and thought it best." The servant cast Max a glance, and he vowed to tip her well.

Apparently, older women didn't fall under his weird spell. Maybe he could arrange to live in a house with old crones and never go outside.

At least he hadn't had to answer Morgan's question yet. It seemed forgotten over the traditional distribution of cups and cakes. He could see Lydia fretting and surmised it was over where to put their visitors for the night.

"I should check to see if my trunks have arrived. I'll carry them up to the tower, as you suggested," Max murmured as he took his teacup. "Morgan can have my room."

"I don't wish to put Miss Trivedi in a cubicle," she whispered back. "I need to have another room opened and cleaned."

She turned to Marta. "Do we have anyone who can open up a couple of rooms in the main house? Our guests will be spending the night."

Marta nodded. "Mr. and Mrs. Folkston just arrived. They came for the funeral and said they'd stay to help awhile. They'll see to the rooms."

Max had a feeling Morgan and Miss Trivedi would prefer a room together, but of course, one couldn't say that in front of the servants. He was re-learning the customs of civilization.

"I should greet them." Lydia rose.

Max suffered a moment's panic but shoved it deep down inside. He didn't think Miss Trivedi or Marta would be attacking him. He stood up with Lydia. "I know I'm taking too much of your time, but I hope you'll help me with the books when you can."

She had reacted so well to Morgan's arrival that he hoped she'd excuse his earlier abysmal behavior. But for a brief moment, he saw her confusion and knew he'd done that to the intrepid librarian.

She squeezed his hand, nodded, and sailed out after Marta.

With their departure, Morgan instantly returned to his subject. "You'll have to return from the dead, appear in court, and testify that David and George Franklin are fraudulently having you declared dead in order to cover up the theft of your estate."

Max felt as if he'd been punched in the gut.

NINE

HE'D KISSED HER. MAXWELL IVES HAD *KISSED* HER—AS IF HE REALLY meant it.

And she'd liked it. She'd liked it a lot.

Had he liked her kiss? How would she know? Why was she even thinking about it?

Lydia hurried down to the kitchen to greet the returning butler and housekeeper. She enthusiastically welcomed them back and apprised them of the current financial situation. They assured her that money didn't matter for this week of mourning. They had their little nest egg and a cottage elsewhere. But they would enjoy working again if matters turned out right.

The couple immediately set the maids to cleaning rooms for guests. Lydia felt almost giddy at the idea of visitors. Or was that the result of Max's kiss?

She approved Marta's menu, then located Lloyd polishing the silver.

"I'm thinking of temporarily putting Mr. Ives in Mr. C's room. He needs privacy and time to study the tower from inside and out." She made that part up to ease the frown of disapproval forming on Lloyd's brow. "Perhaps you could act as his manservant?" she asked tentatively, waiting to see how the man accepted these changes.

Lloyd continued polishing while he pondered. "It's the only home I know, miss," he finally said. "I reckoned I'd have to move out of the tower when you moved in. I wouldn't mind keeping my little room a while longer. Mayhap it will make it easier to accept Mr. C's absence?" he asked, sounding uncertain.

"I'm not sure anything can help with that," she replied unhappily. "But the little boy should brighten our days a bit. You wouldn't happen to know anything about teaching, would you? The poor child can't be sent to school until he's a little bigger and knows his way around better."

Lloyd pondered and polished some more. "Seems to me, the lad being a foreigner, that he needs a little education in being a Scotsman. I might help with that. Show him his manners and such. And Laddie could teach him to ride a pony."

"Or a mule, since we don't have a pony," Lydia agreed with a smile. "That's a truly brilliant idea. Once Bakari has a little more confidence, and he's more comfortable with Mr. Ives, then we can decide what he needs next."

"Roughhousing," Lloyd said succinctly. "Boy that size needs to defend himself."

"That, I will leave to you and Mr. Ives. I know nothing of fisticuffs. Thank you so much, sir. And know you will always have a place here. We're family." She thought Lloyd's normally gloomy expression brightened just a little.

"I'll move your things back to your room," he agreed reluctantly, setting down the polish.

Lydia knew she was putting off the journals waiting in the library. She didn't understand why she'd suddenly started hearing words instead of whispers. Well, she heard the whispers, too, but the words Max needed had just appeared in her head. And she'd located the volumes by following the sound. It had been an extremely odd experience.

How would she summon the words again? Was that how Mr. C had heard the books?

The voices had been more unsettling than Max's kiss, which had been glorious and a memory to treasure for a lifetime. She should certainly never engage in such seductive activities again. His friend was in the parlor right now, either driving Max to flee or luring him back to the city. For Lady Agnes's sake, she hoped it was the latter.

For her sake. . . She needed to pretend to be The Librarian, the dispenser of all Malcolm wisdom.

If she could not hear the voices again, would the castle revert to the Crown, like a lost title? She shuddered at the thought.

She wished she could excuse herself from dinner as Mr. C often had. Zack, the footman, had finally returned, so she had a man who could serve so Max needn't fear the maids. But it didn't feel right to isolate herself when Max's friends had come to his rescue so swiftly. She needed to encourage him to do what was right, didn't she?

Of course, standing in her tiny cubicle, looking at her three plain gowns, she thought maybe her place was in the library, going over the books she'd pulled from the shelves, like the drab assistant she was.

She'd spent most of her life being overlooked, considered a workhorse who simply kept households running. Once her daintier sisters found husbands, Lydia had gladly helped with their wedding arrangements. She'd even made herself available whenever one needed her to help during their lying-ins. She had never resented their married status in the least—because she had the library. Once she'd discovered the library, she'd found her place and been content.

But now. . . she fretted. Mr. C had never dressed for guests, but she sort of wanted to look like she'd tried. At least everything she owned was already dark so she needn't worry about buying mourning. With a sigh, she added her bit of lace and rummaged in a drawer for her father's gold watch. Perhaps she could wear it as she had the keys. It was gold anyway—almost like jewelry.

And then she worried that lace and gold weren't appropriate for mourning. . .

Rolling her eyes at herself, Lydia brushed out her hair, curled it into a chignon, and fastened it tightly. Her hair had a mind of its own and bits and frazzles would eventually pop out all around her face, but at least she could start out neat. She pinched her cheeks, bit her lips, took a deep breath to be certain her buttons would hold, then marched down the stairs to the dining room.

Except everyone had gathered in the small parlor, and she stopped there instead.

"I'm sorry the drawing room isn't quite ready," she said, uncertain why everyone was here. "Did you find your rooms satisfactory?"

"You're not a hotelier, Lydia," Max said. "You're the Malcolm Librarian. Let your housekeeper tend us. She and Mr. Folkston have been very helpful."

"A librarian can be a hostess," she corrected defensively. "Did your trunks arrive? Are you and Bakari settled in? I had a talk with Lloyd—"

"Yes, he told me. He's with the boy now. And yes, our trunks arrived, thank you. I simply have to decide whether to work on the tower or go into the city and fight for my money." The usually affable Mr. Ives almost snarled that speech. He took her hand and placed it on his arm. "Let us go to dinner before I start gnawing on the furniture."

Lydia sent a helpless glance to Mr. Morgan and Miss Trivedi. They set down their half-empty glasses. Mr. Morgan wordlessly took his companion's arm, but Miss Trivedi gave Lydia a sympathetic look and smiled.

"The warriors are arguing over battle plans," she explained. "It makes them disagreeable."

Did she even wish to ask what battle?

"I SHOWED THE BOY THE STAIRS UP TO THE TOWER," MAX TOLD HIS HOSTESS as they strolled toward the dining room. "He's thrilled with every part of this fortress. We'll probably never see him again. Lloyd can't possibly keep up with him."

Max was actually pretty proud of the boy. *People* apparently terrified his son, but exploring castles was a fun game.

"Up until this past year, the place has been well maintained. I don't think any part is truly dangerous." Lydia hesitated in the formal dining room where plates were laid out. "And it's usually easy to find the great hall and the way back to the tower. He should be fine."

Max could think of a dozen ways a boy could find trouble without getting lost, but he refrained from mentioning them. He shouldn't be taking his ill humor out on a woman who was trying to help.

"A round table, just like King Arthur's court!" Approving of this setting, Max pulled out a chair for Lydia against the back wall so she could watch the door, then appropriated the seat beside her. If maids were to be leaning over his shoulder. . . He wanted Lydia as shield.

Morgan set Miss Trivedi in the next chair and took the one beside her. The table was fairly large, but the plates had all been set on one side. Max wiggled uneasily at having a woman he didn't know this close, but Miss Trivedi didn't seem to notice.

Huh. Did that prove his theory that she was loyal to Morgan?—an interesting new angle to his preposterous gift. Could he detect which women were inclined to wander?

"Do we dispense justice like King Arthur's court?" Morgan asked, indicating the round table. "Or do we need more knights?"

"More ladies," Miss Trivedi said demurely, settling her napkin in her lap. "That's the problem with all governments, they're male. They only ever have one thought in their heads at a time and cannot perceive the ramifications of their decisions with any clarity."

"It's easier to make decisions if we don't have to consult a thousand different opinions," Max argued, using his own predicament as an example. "If we all agree someone is a usurper, we simply decide on how to remove him. We don't care if his family suffers for it. That would stand in the way of decision-making."

Lydia sat silent, pushing her soup around with her spoon.

"Both your uncle and your cousin have families," Morgan pointed out the obvious. "If you have them jailed for fraud and take away all their assets, their families will suffer. And some of the assets may rightfully be theirs."

Max couldn't see Lydia's expression, but he was pretty certain she was frowning, albeit still silently. The librarian didn't like to express her opinions without a great deal of thought, it seemed.

"I will benevolently grant the families of my usurpers an allowance, as they have my mother." Max was still furious and not ready to be rational.

"Do not most men of finance, particularly avaricious ones, keep books that show how much they have earned?" Lydia finally spoke, albeit slowly. "Would that not be a starting place in dividing what belongs to whom?"

"It won't matter much if Max doesn't stand up in court and accuse them," Morgan said grumpily.

"And once investments are sold and the funds intermingled, it's not quite that easy," Miss Trivedi added. "But yes, there is probably a foundation that both families started with. And profits could be divided to some degree by applying a percentage based on what each family contributed. It would not necessarily be a fair division, only a means to start a conversation."

"I'll just cut off their heads and leave others to work out the money." Max tucked into his excellent lamb broth. "If I have to expose myself to the city again, I want them to pay. I *counted* on those bastards to take care of my mother and my inheritance!"

"I do not understand your dislike of Edinburgh," Miss Trivedi said, not eating the soup.

Lydia whispered to a young footman and had him take the lady's bowl, leaving Max to try to answer. As if he could explain the impossible and not sound vain while he did so.

"Do you know anything about magnetism?" he asked.

"Lodestone and iron and such? Not a lot," Miss Trivedi admitted.

"They are working on forms of electromagnetism now," Morgan said. "It's a fascinating science with a great deal of potential."

"There is research that shows the earth itself is magnetic, which is why compasses point north," Max added. "I don't think I contain lodestone or electricity, but I seem to possess a form of paramagnetism that, let us say, is extremely uncomfortable in crowds."

The footman returned with a plate of mixed greens and set it before Miss Trivedi. The lady sent Lydia a grateful look and dug in with what appeared to be pleasure at eating weeds. Max glanced at his perceptive hostess. She knew a lot about people, simply from reading.

And listening—she had been paying attention even as she directed the servants. She looked up from her soup now. "Paramagnetism? You did not use that word earlier. Is this a scientific concept?"

"Scientists have discovered a number of elements can become magnetized if placed in a magnetic field," Morgan explained. "But once that field is removed, the magnetism disappears."

Lydia turned her huge indigo eyes to Max, and he twitched uncomfortably.

"*You* are the magnetic field?" she asked. "Ladies are the elements? And if they are removed from your presence, they forget your existence?"

"Possibly." He applied his attention to his soup rather than the uncomfortable conversation.

"Ladies are drawn to you?" Miss Trivedi asked in amusement. "And this is a problem?"

Max gritted his teeth, but once the footman removed his bowl, he had to reply. "If I may sketch a mental picture. . . Have you been inside my mother's School of Malcolms?" When she nodded, he continued. "Imagine if you will what happens if a magnetic field that attracts females enters those doors."

Miss Trivedi's fork hovered over her plate as she considered this. "I am not a particularly imaginative person, but I can recall what happens when one man has too many wives. It is sometimes very ugly."

"In that case, at least, the wives know why they're jealous of each other. In my case, there is no logic to the catfights. Do not ask me to repeat the experience, please. Women aren't as docile as they are portrayed in literature." Max sat back so the footman could set a nicely browned pheasant with accouterments in front of him. Grateful for the distraction, he said, "Marta is brilliant. Does she always cook like this?"

Lydia studied her plate with interest. "Most generally, we eat from a buffet and it's nothing more than soup or stew. I didn't know she had this in her." She gave him a mischievous look. "Maybe she's fallen under the spell of your magnetism and wishes to keep you here."

"Go ahead, laugh, but it's a good thing courtrooms are run by men. If I'm to sue my relations, we have to keep women from the courtroom audience. And I need to avoid my mother's house, preferably by not letting her know I'm here. I might manage a courtroom, nothing more." Disgruntled, Max hacked at his dinner.

Miss Trivedi tucked into the potatoes and other vegetables she'd been served.

Morgan hummed in appreciation, apparently of both Max's decision and the bird. "We might manage a closed courtroom. But we'll need to pry the books from your uncle's hands to prove his guilt first. I can't do that. You must."

Max grimaced and conceded. "Fine. I will give you my power of attorney. You may tell my mother that I am on my way home. I'll give you a letter asking her to sign a power of attorney to you as well. Take it as far as you are able without me."

"What about Bakari?" Lydia asked. "Will you be sending him to school?"

"Not yet." Mentally saying farewell to his Burma job, Max stabbed a potato. "I'll stay here and study your tower and try to figure out what he's good at. Maybe if he starts school with some talent that gives him confidence, he'll feel better. And we'll know by then if he has cousins to help him."

"He needs to meet them first," Lydia warned.

"Which means meeting their mothers," Miss Trivedi added, obviously enjoying his predicament.

Because meeting young ladies had worked so well the last time he'd been here, Max thought gloomily. But he'd been only eighteen then. Running away had been the only solution he'd known. Although he'd spent most of these past years in sparsely populated areas, he'd learned a few tactics. He simply despised the necessity of hiding.

He glanced at Lydia, who was studiously picking apart her dinner without looking at him. If he had to go out in civilized society, he needed a shield of respectability. How could he go wrong with a woman who looked like a queen and kissed like an angel?

All he had to do was persuade her to leave her tower of books.

TEN

AFTER DINNER, LYDIA LEFT MAX WORKING WITH MR. MORGAN AND MISS Trivedi on plans to pry financial information from his uncle and cousin. She had a funeral to plan, guests to prepare for, and a stack of books calling to her.

The staff knew what to do. They simply needed to be reassured about the change in circumstances and that Lydia approved of their work. She was a vicar's daughter, accustomed to church social gatherings, not aristocratic assemblies. Anything the servants suggested was fine with her.

With that task accomplished, she returned to the library, swept up a few tomes from the pile she'd found for Max, and retreated to the hidden study inside the stacks. She didn't want Max catching her by surprise. She didn't want to be *kissed* again—much. She just wanted to be left alone to explore whether or not she might be able to fulfill the librarian's duties sufficiently to scrape by until she either learned how to hear the books or a more qualified person could be found.

But the tomes meant little to her. She listened to the whispers, found pages mentioning the tower, and marked them with the supply of bookmarks she'd created for Mr. C. She would have to read the pages to Max to see if they meant anything to him.

Discouraged, she set the books aside and wandered into the stacks, concentrating on the words *librarian* and *instructions*, to see if that stirred the whispers enough to hear. It didn't. *Ownership* did nothing either. She flipped through the ancient directory but mostly it listed the authors of the journals and occasionally made reference to the author's gift. Nothing screamed *This is how you find a librarian*. She'd have to hope that the solicitors knew more than she did.

She settled on a step near the shelf containing Mr. C's journals. Perhaps if she started with reading how he became the librarian. . .

Descending from his tower suite, showing his son the secret passage, Max discovered Lydia sound asleep on the library stairs. One well-turned ankle dangled from below her skirt, a book rested precariously in her lap, and her temple reposed on a stack of tomes. If he could paint, he'd paint Portrait of a Beautiful Librarian.

"She'll hurt herself," his son whispered in concern.

It was a long way down if she tried turning over on a circular iron stairway.

Max didn't know where Lydia's room was. He supposed he could go down the outer stairs, opening doors to see if any looked likely. But it was far easier to deposit her where she belonged.

She stirred when he lifted her, but she had to be terribly exhausted. She didn't wake.

Max was unaccustomed to taking care of anyone but himself, but it was becoming obvious that the librarian needed someone to take care of her. She couldn't do it all—be the librarian and her own assistant and steward of all she surveyed. They'd have to work that out in the morning. For now, he carried her up the stairs and deposited her on the spacious bed obviously intended for her.

"Where will you sleep?" the boy asked, again with concern. The lad had more compassion than Max would ever learn.

"I've been sleeping on the ground and on ship decks for years," he assured him. "I'll sleep in the other room with you, if that's all right."

They caught Lloyd just entering the parlor from the outer stairs, apparently ready for his own bed. Max grimaced. There was a snag.

"I put Miss Wystan on the big bed," he informed the valet. "She fell asleep on the stairs, and I didn't know what else to do. If you can direct me to her chamber, I could sleep there, but I don't know how she'll react if she wakes up to you and my son in the suite."

Lloyd nodded and squinted his eyes in thought. "She really does belong here. It's expected. I can take one of the cubicles. They're all furnished. I'll just need to remove my things." He looked at Max expectantly.

Max could take the guest room he'd been using. It was perfectly adequate. Morgan and Miss Trivedi had been given rooms elsewhere.

But he'd already caught one of the maids turning down his covers and leaving a bottle of whisky on his night table. He really wanted an entire locked tower between him and the household. Besides, their trunks were here.

Max gestured vaguely at the parlor. "I'll sleep with the boy in here tonight. We'll work out better arrangements in the morning."

Lloyd didn't seem fond of that idea, but ever the obedient servant, he gathered up his few personal articles, carefully locked the door to the little closet leading to Lydia's bed, and departed. As soon as he was gone, Max picked the lock and opened the door so the boy could use the washroom. Max knew he was an honorable man, in his own way, but he respected that not everyone else appreciated his ability to resist a beautiful woman.

Almost resist—he opened the chamber door and verified that the lady slept soundly.

"She's like a beautiful princess," Bakari murmured in awe. "Like in the fairy tales."

With her golden-sunset hair tumbling over her porcelain cheeks and lace collar, Lydia did indeed resemble an untouchable princess. For perhaps the first time in his life, Max felt regret at walking away.

LYDIA BLINKED AWAKE AT HER USUAL HOUR OF DAWN. SHE FROWNED AT THE ceiling that had suddenly developed delicate flowers and colorful birds. Finally realizing it was a canopy and not a ceiling, she hurriedly scrambled from a bed almost as large as the room she'd been sleeping in.

How did she end up in Mr. C's room?

She'd been reading his journals. She'd learned Mr. C's mother had been a librarian, so he had simply inherited her position. She must have fallen asleep before she read further.

The funeral! She had so much to do. . .

She cast a longing glance at the bath, but she didn't know how she'd got here or who was on the other side of that wall. She'd run down to her chamber and find fresh clothing. . . except both sets of stairs were in the parlor. Drat. She should have told Lloyd to leave her gowns here. . . except she'd meant for *Max* to use these rooms while they had guests. Had he even unpacked? She peered into the ornate clothes press, but it was empty.

Fluffing out her skirt as best as she could, she inched open the bathing room door, then crossed to Lloyd's chamber. The large form in the valet's bed was quite unmistakably not Lloyd. What was Max doing in here? At least he was wearing a nightshirt and had the covers almost pulled over him, but it was hard to resist looking. He badly needed a shave, and he dwarfed that tiny cot. She'd never been this close to a man in dishabille, and the heat his muscular form engendered embarrassed her.

Covering her eyes from temptation, she tip-toed past and into the study, then safely to the parlor, where Bakari slept on the cot that had been carried up for him. He tossed restlessly, but she sneaked past without disturbing him.

Back to normal! She rushed down the stairs, happy to be in the safety of her own little world again. Her world did not include beds fit for a queen and men who could be kings.

She bathed in the downstairs tub, donned her best black silk, added the gold watch and lace collar, and took a deep breath. Today, she must behave like the Malcolm Librarian for all the world to see. It had been easy enough to do with a man who knew nothing, like Lord Crowley, but in front of perceptive Malcolms. . . She prayed they wouldn't question on a day like this.

That would happen when they started seeking answers she couldn't provide.

She rushed down in time to see Miss Trivedi and Mr. Morgan off to the early train heading into the city. Services wouldn't be until the afternoon, after the return train arrived. Guests needed time to take carts and horses up the rough road to the castle from the train station.

Downstairs in the kitchen, Marta produced a delicate black lace mantle for Lydia to wear. "It was in the wardrobes we cleaned and looks as if it's meant for you."

"It's lovely, like something a real lady would wear," Lydia exclaimed, wishing she could kiss the cook. The mood in the kitchen lightened considerably as she threw the lacy confection over her shoulders and showed off her new acquisition. "I feel special now, thank you."

After ascertaining that Marta and her staff were fine, and Mrs. Folkston had the guest rooms in the main house under control, Lydia finally retreated to the guest library to finish working through the books that Max needed.

Max was already there, sipping from a mug of coffee and studying the array of volumes she'd left on the long library table. He contemplated her with what appeared to be interest at her entrance but merely nodded a greeting.

Embarrassed that she'd crept past him while he slept, Lydia nervously held out the oldest volume. "This one has a sketch that appears to show the outer wall being built, but the text is in Gaelic. I can attempt pronunciation but I cannot translate."

Setting down his mug, he took the volume and examined the drawing. "Nice. They sank the stones deep, so the mine isn't directly under the foundation as I feared. Attempt pronunciation, please. One of the engineers who taught me spoke Gaelic."

To her surprise, the words seemed to roll off her tongue as she read the page. She even almost understood them, as much as she might understand anything involving angles and diameters and so forth. It did not appear to say much.

Max frowned in thought but drew some diagrams on a blank piece of paper. "Did a woman write that?"

Lydia verified the title page. "Yes, but she seemed to understand the terms. Or she copied down what someone told her. This is from the 15th century, so it was unusual for women to write, but Malcolm women have always been educated."

"Which is why they were called witches. Women aren't supposed to have brains." He offered her a big smile that almost brought her to her knees. "Men have been idiots for ages. What else do you have in this array of boring tomes?"

Grateful for the table's distance between them, Lydia settled in a chair and picked up the next volume. "This one is Latin. Do I need to translate as I read?"

"Definitely. I haven't met any Romans on my journeys. Should I send for tea for you?" He looked around for the bell pull.

"No, don't. They're in a tizzy in the kitchen right now, preparing for guests. And neighbors are at the back door with offerings, even though this place has more food than their poor larders can hold. So there will be a crowd well into the evening. You'll have to stay out of the way. There's even a chance your mother and aunt might be here. I think they're the eldest Malcolms in the area."

He grimaced. "Bakari and I stand forewarned. I assume the city guests will be staying the night. So feed me as much information from these books as you can, and we will make ourselves scarce until we're told the way is clear."

"You may have your bed back tonight. I'm sorry I somehow usurped it. How did I end up there?" Lydia tried not to show her anxiety over the question.

"You fell asleep on the stairs, and I didn't know where to take you. But this works out well. Have Lloyd carry up your clothes and leave him in a cubicle. We won't disturb you. That chamber is rightfully yours."

"But I have to go past you to reach the stairs," she protested. "It's not at all proper. I'll have Lloyd remove me to the guest room at the bottom that you were using, and then if I fall asleep again, you'll know where to put me." She attempted a smile, waiting to see if he corrected her assumption that he'd put her in the bed.

He didn't.

He'd carried her up the stairs. . . Lydia's mind went blank. No one could carry her. She wasn't small. Those stairs were narrow. Max had *carried* her. Her heart almost fluttered out of her chest.

Max frowned but didn't argue with her choice of beds. "At least that's better than a hole in the wall, I suppose. And we don't have time to argue. Let's read through the rest of this." He gestured at the array of volumes. "My head is likely to explode before we're done."

They were hurriedly finishing the last volume just as Bakari ran into the room to warn that carts were coming up the drive. Max had a page of sketches and notes apparently only he could decipher. He shoved the paper in his pocket and pushed back his chair. "I really want to kiss you right now but realize it's inappropriate."

He flashed a wide white grin that left Lydia stunned and unable to speak as he ambled out, trailing his son.

How was she supposed to even *think* after that declaration?

ELEVEN

"The service was perfect, Miss Wystan." Blond and compactly rounded, Mrs. Olivia Blair, formerly Lady Hargreaves, almost made Lydia feel like a towering giant.

Except Lady Phoebe stood between them. A beanpole with a high stack of chestnut tresses, the lady never seemed uncomfortable with her height. "The heather was a lovely touch. I'm amazed the stained glass has held up so well all these years. I had never thought about how old this place must be."

It was on the tip of Lydia's tongue to discuss what Max had told her about the tower, but then she'd have to reveal how she knew, and it all became too complicated. She settled for social niceties instead. "I didn't expect your aunts to send you in their place. They are always so interested in the library."

Lady Phoebe waved a dismissive hand. "Aunt Agnes is certain that Max will arrive any day, and she wants to be home when he does. She said it's time for the younger generation to step up now that we're all marrying."

"It's so sad to see her disillusioned," Lady Dare added. Newly married to Viscount Dare, who had just come into his title, the viscountess was a dark-haired beauty from India—about the same height as Olivia.

Lydia hadn't met her before. But Azmin, as she was known, had brought her photographic equipment and had been memorializing the occasion. Lydia pondered whether the future library should contain photograph albums.

Phoebe sipped her tea and shook her head. "No, Lady Agnes will be proved correct. Mr. Morgan has sent letters all over the world, to every place Max has ever worked. One of them will reach him."

"Unless he's dead," Olivia pointed out.

They all seemed to wait for Lydia to respond. She tugged the lacy black mantle tighter and steeled herself. She loved talking to other Malcolms. It was wonderful having guests to ease the sorrow of Mr. C's passing. But she had to be the official Malcolm Librarian and say nothing. No wonder Mr. C had given up entertaining.

She simply couldn't label herself with that fraudulent title and had to reply from his perspective. "Mr. C kept anything he knew in confidence, and you know your cousin won't write journals. I can tell you nothing." Which was completely the truth.

"It's always good to know our confidences are being kept," Olivia acknowledged. "I'm thoroughly relieved you are here to step into the position. The twins are reaching an age where they'll want to know more about their abilities. I'll need a guidebook on how to keep them from shocking the neighbors."

The discussion evolved into the rest of the family and their various abnormal gifts, and Lydia drifted away to greet the neighbors and encourage them to enjoy the buffet.

The guilt of knowing she could ease Lady Agnes's mind ate at her. Should the lady ask her directly about Max—Lydia didn't think she could lie. It was a relief knowing Max's mother had stayed home.

She watched Lady Dare and Mrs. Blair wander off to explore and prayed Max had figured out how to lock the tower door.

Sitting in the tower window seat overlooking the castle drive, Max watched his family ride off to the train station early the next morning.

From this distance, he didn't think he could identify any of them except Lady Phoebe. She'd only been about ten when he'd left home that last time, but she'd been a beanpole with a head full of hair even then. She'd been too young to be involved in any of the catfights surrounding him.

Lydia had explained who the others were last night, after everyone had retired. He supposed he vaguely remembered the brown-skinned, scrawny child Azmin had been in some of the family summer gatherings, but she hadn't lived in Edinburgh as Phoebe had, so his memory wasn't strong. And Olivia had apparently wandered with her parents throughout England most of her life, so he didn't know her at all.

He was just thoroughly relieved that his mother and aunt hadn't chosen to attend the funeral.

Since he'd spent the better—or worst—part of his youth in boarding school, he didn't know any of his family well and hadn't particularly missed them. But he was curious about them.

He'd love to meet his eldest son someday too, although the boy would probably try to lay him flat for being absent all his life.

He set Bakari to work adding sums after the boy had proved he already knew his numbers and letters. So far, he hadn't persuaded the boy to take a suitable nickname, but Max was growing accustomed to the foreign one. He still worried about the boy attending school, but at least he didn't show any tendency to Max's disability.

Working on sketches of what he'd learned of the tower's construction, Max waited for Lydia to let him know the house was clear of guests.

After the last cart had been gone half an hour or so, he heard footsteps on the outer stairs. Lloyd had delivered breakfast earlier, but Max was ready for a mug of tea and company. He wasn't much used to isolation. He eagerly opened the door before anyone could knock.

Lydia looked a little startled and a trace frazzled, but she beamed in relief. "You're here. Good. There's been a telegram from Mr. Morgan and one from the solicitors. I am to present myself to their offices as soon as possible. I had hoped that they might come here." She frowned worriedly as she handed over his telegram, then realized what she was doing and took it back.

Max waited as she unfolded his message. His mind was already ticking though. He couldn't let Lydia face a cadre of dour solicitors who would disdain a woman as executor of anything. She needed her own man with her. Would Morgan go?

Uncle filed request to declare you dead, she read. Her expression echoed the dread he felt.

"What will you do?" she whispered.

Max rubbed his face. "We discussed this. Morgan says I must appear in court with witnesses to declare I'm alive and that I am who I say I am. And it's not as if I can ask my cousin or uncle to do so."

"You can't have your own solicitor simply charge them with fraud or theft? Wouldn't that stop them?"

"Not if I'm dead," he pointed out with warped humor. "I believe that's the whole point. I can't sue if I'm legally dead. The dead have no rights. And I've been gone long enough for them to have a case, although Morgan can produce my letters to prove I'm alive. But he can't prove the letters come from me, because, of course, they were written by other people."

She folded the paper and creased it with her fingers. "How did you meet Mr. Morgan? Would that count if he saw you in person at some point in those years?"

"Good thought but not workable. Morgan owns shipping firms. I had my assistant correspond with him over supplies we needed while I was in Egypt. He had some sensible suggestions. We continued corresponding. We became friends and business partners, but I never met him in person before the other night." Max wanted to pace, but his son was watching him worriedly, and he didn't want to upset the lad.

He could see his hostess fretting, and he hated that he was adding to her burdens. "We'll go into the city together," he impulsively suggested. "Morgan will arrange to keep everyone clear of the courtroom when I arrive. And after, we'll talk to your solicitors. Perhaps Morgan will have a lawyer willing to accompany you. Will that help?"

The relief on her fine features was so enormous that Max actually felt a little proud of himself for a change. Now all he had to do was figure out how to make this happen.

"If you wouldn't mind. . . if you would. . . oh, please, yes. I'm terrified they'll tell me things I don't understand or make demands I can't carry out. If I can't keep the castle running, I'll have to send everyone home again." She looked as if she wanted to hug him.

Max *wanted* her to hug him. Huh. He usually backed off at this point, but his arms were feeling empty. But he could not, would not, use this admirable woman as he used others. "If they take away the castle, you'll lose your home and the library as well." He pointed out the obvious to show he grasped the problem. "We can't let that happen."

Her smile was positively beatific. "Thank you for understanding. I can have Laddie harness the mule to take us into Calder. I'll have to hire a carriage there. We won't have another train coming through until tomorrow, and these messages seem urgent."

Now? Today? Max almost panicked. He had hoped to dally a little longer, work on the tower. . . Avoid any chance of seeing his mother, who would take his head off, then introduce him to every female in her damned school. . .

At his hesitation, Lydia looked worried. He wanted the happy look back. She was an intrepid female who would keep marching forward, doing what was right, even if she had no idea what she was doing and was too terrified to speak. She'd go into the city by herself if he didn't go.

The Librarian's ghost had said to take care of Lydia, that she was more valuable than she knew. Max knew damn-all about specters, but the advice seemed sound.

"I'll start packing. Do you think Lloyd would mind watching after Bakari? If we leave within the hour, we might reach the city by lunch, but I don't imagine we'll accomplish everything in an afternoon. We'll have to take rooms." Rooms somewhere no one knew him and wouldn't immediately report his presence—a gentleman's club maybe. Could he join in one day?

"Lloyd and Laddie will help with Bakari. He can ride a mule and polish silver or whatever. I'll telegraph Lady Phoebe to let her know I'm coming. She'll arrange. . ." She caught his look and sighed. "I'll simply tell her *I'm* coming, and I need a place to stay. You can make your own arrangements."

"An hour then. We'll send telegrams from Calder to let them know we're on our way." At her worried look, he remembered what she'd said about having no funds. "I'll take care of the telegrams and carriage. It's the very least I can do given all you're doing for me."

She nodded uncertainly. "I'll repay you if I can. I'm reasonably certain Mr. C had funds. I simply don't know if I'll be allowed access to them."

She left to pack her bag.

Max studied the tidy nest he'd made of the tower and the boy watching him with worry. For the first time in his life, he wasn't eager to hit the road. He must be growing old.

He crouched down to meet his son's eyes. "I will be back, I promise. I'm your father now, and I hope to be a good one. Is there a book or game you'd like me to bring back?"

Max felt pretty adult when the boy threw his arms around his neck as if he actually were a father worth holding onto.

LYDIA WAS GLAD THAT IT WAS A LOVELY SUMMER DAY AS LADDIE DROVE THE open cart down to the village. In her effort to look like a lofty librarian, she'd left Mr. C's old cloak behind.

"Do you think I could ask the trust solicitors to reimburse me for the money I took out of my savings to keep the castle running?" she asked as the wheels rattled down the rutted path. "It would be nice to buy one or two things I need since we'll be near shops."

"I'm appalled that they didn't make the arrangements a year ago," Max grumbled.

He wasn't in a happy mood, she knew. She hated that he had to worry over family he'd trusted. She wanted to pat his hand and tell him all would surely be fine in a day or two, but that seemed. . . presumptuous. And he might feel as if she were an encroaching female like all the others.

"After his illness, Mr. C couldn't write well. And I was afraid if I told anyone how helpless he was, they'd put him in an institution. I couldn't bear that. So it's my own fault that no one looked into matters," she admitted.

"Your loyalty and your frugality are to be admired. Whereas I left *family* in charge, men who owed me loyalty, and they have either frittered away an entire fortune or stolen it, leaving women and children helpless. I should put *you* in charge." He crossed his arms and glared at the horizon.

He really was unhappy about going to the city. Lydia sighed. "Well, I had to send away servants who relied on their wages in order to protect a man who was presumably wealthy, so I'm not exactly *admirable*. We do what seems best at the time and learn the error of our ways. Are your sons relying on the estate you left behind?"

Max snorted inelegantly. "Let my family know I had sons and no wife? I set up separate funds for each of them in the countries where they were born. Lawyers look after them." He smacked his forehead as she'd seen him do before. "Damn—what if *those* lawyers are as greedy as my family? I'll have to write. . ."

"Just tell me what to write, and I'll do it for you," she finished for him. "I'm not sure how you write a lawyer and ask if he's cheating though," she said with a trace of humor.

"I'll think about it. If I weren't so perfectly wretched about these matters, I'd do it myself." He slumped into gloom again.

"You cannot do everything," she admonished. "You taught yourself engineering despite your inability to read. You have evidently made a fortune all on your own, without need of your father's estate. You put people in charge you had every reason to trust. The harm is theirs, not yours."

He shrugged. "Other men manage. But I suppose they stay in one place so they can oversee in person. I thought I could walk away and live on a desert island."

"You could have been right here in the city and your uncle might still cheat you. You don't possess your mother's prescience. Do you have any Malcolm traits at all?" she asked, re-directing the topic to prevent him from beating up on himself more.

"Besides animal magnetism?" he asked with a chuckle. "Not that I'm aware. I'm pretty certain my ability to do calculus in my head is from the Ives' side."

"Animal magnetism—charming. Ladies are not *animals*. And if you're such a magnet to women, why am I not in your lap right now? Perhaps your charm has worn off." She primly crossed her gloved hands in her skirt.

He twined his fingers and stretched his arms in front of him, exposing the grand magnitude of the muscles beneath his tailored coat. The cart hit a rut and lurched, but he swayed and stayed upright as if he were a sailor at sea.

Lydia had to clutch the side to prevent falling into him.

Max noted the gesture with a quirked eyebrow. "You were almost in my lap just now," he said with a naughty leer. "But I take your point. Other than age, I perceive few differences between any of the women who are drawn to me. The very old and very young mostly lack interest, but you don't fall into that category. I've noticed some women, like Miss Trivedi, are so firmly attached to their men that they resist my magnetism. Do you have another man in your life that I don't know about?"

"Hardly," she said with a sniff. "Unless you count Mr. C, but he's dead."

"Then it must be reverse magnetism," he decided, flashing her that smile that turned her insides out. "I'm very attracted to you. You have reversed my poles."

Hot lava coursed through her middle. Lydia forced herself to look at the back of Laddie's head. "That's ridiculous. We'll see how well that works once we're in the city, and you're surrounded by beautiful ladies."

"I have no intention of being surrounded by anyone. We'll go directly to Hugh Morgan's office. He's just recently moved from Phoebe's lair to a proper building where no one will know us. The only other female likely to be around is Miss Trivedi, who is happily attached to Mr. Morgan and barely acknowledges my existence, as it should be. We can hope that by the time we arrive, he'll have arranged to meet a judge and keep the courtroom clear, since it's a private matter. And I'll find a gentleman's hotel for the evening."

"And Mr. C's solicitors will certainly have no women about. Perhaps, if all goes well there, you can take the train back to the castle, and I can stay in the city and do a little shopping." Since it was hard to speculate more, Lydia chose to admire the landscape she had seen so rarely this past year. She drank in the fresh scent of heather, absorbed the sun's heat, and noticed Max smelled of sandalwood today. She'd added it to that last batch of soap Marta had made. She clasped her hands tighter.

She would not, could not, be one of the ladies he despised so much.

TWELVE

"I CANNOT SUMMON WITNESSES TO MY EXISTENCE IN AN *HOUR*," MAX protested, pacing Hugh Morgan's unassuming office. He tried to maintain his normally unflappable demeanor, but the pressure had him roiling like a steam boiler. "It's been nearly twenty years since I was in school. I can barely remember the names of fellow students and certainly don't know where they reside. And if my mother's family can't testify because they're not objective, I'd need my Ives relations, and they're all in the south of England as far as I'm aware. Dare is the only one close. He really isn't an Ives, just a relation by marriage, and if we ever crossed paths, I don't recall it. My cousin George knows me, best, damn it."

Estes, the portly barrister Hugh Morgan had hired, crossed his hands complacently over his belly. "Then we'll present Mr. Morgan's evidence that funds have been misappropriated, demand the investments be held by the court until you can produce witnesses, and threaten the miscreants with criminal action for fraud and theft. They'll either have to admit that you are who you say you are or fight a long legal battle to regain control of their monies."

"There's enough evidence in those files?" Max asked. Morgan had explained the papers to him, but paper was just that to him—expendable fuel for fires.

"The judge won't understand them," the barrister said dismissively. "I have documents prepared that simply need his signature to freeze the funds. That means you can't access them either, but it's a delaying tactic. We need to be going." Using the chair arms, Estes hauled himself up.

"What about Lydia?" Max inquired anxiously.

The librarian had been sitting quietly in a dark corner, listening. She had to be going mad with worry about her own problems, but she sat patiently through this meeting, absorbing it all, reading any document he handed to her so he knew he could trust what he was being told.

"Estes is a barrister," Morgan reminded him. "Miss Wystan needs a solicitor. The meeting with the judge has been scheduled, so that takes precedence." He turned to Lydia. "Miss Wystan, would you be comfortable speaking with the trust's solicitors with Miss Trivedi in your company? If not, then do you think the meeting might wait until we find a suitable attorney to accompany you?"

Max wanted to crawl under a desk at her look of panic. He *needed* to be there for her.

But the truth was, his aid was rubbish. The whole reason he'd left the estate to his uncle and cousin was because he was useless in these matters and only made himself look like a fool. Lydia didn't need a fool to accompany her.

He needed to hug her, to tell her everything would be all right, that he would sue the trustees into perdition the instant he had his hands on his money. . . But that did not help her now.

He felt like a total cad when he saw her accept that he could not help. This was the reason he could never be the man his father had been. He was only useful in uncivilized areas that needed his crude abilities.

Lydia clenched her fingers in her lap and nodded at Morgan. "I would appreciate Miss Trivedi's accompaniment, thank you, although I dislike taking her away from her tasks."

Hugh Morgan almost managed a smile. "Miss Trivedi lives to take apart presumptuous gentlemen. Let us all hope your trustees are reasonable men or they're likely to be left in shreds on the carpet."

"Thank you, I think." Lydia tentatively returned his smile. "Where will I find her?"

"She works here most afternoons, in the office next door. I warned her that you might need her help, so she is ready any time you are."

Max stood up when Lydia did. He took her hand as she passed. "If it doesn't go well today, we'll have alternatives. Just remember—you are the *Malcolm Librarian*. It's like being a duke, I think. Think of yourself as a duke and the lawyers as ignorant peasants. You can do it."

Her bottom lip trembled slightly, until she bit it, squeezed his hand, and nearly broke his heart with her courage. "A duke, thank you. Or a duchess. I think I'd like being a duchess. I'll see what I can do."

She bravely left, leaving Max no choice but to grit his teeth and do the same. He tapped on his hat and held the door for the portly barrister. "Thanks, Morgan, and if I ever pry those funds loose, you'll be the one I turn to for investing. You'll be worth every farthing of your commission."

The taciturn broker saluted with a finger to his brow and returned to work.

Max swallowed hard and set off to make an ass of himself. After which, he'd have to visit his mother. He wasn't sure which was worse.

"IT IS BEST IF YOU PRESENT YOURSELF AS A PERSON OF AUTHORITY," KEYA Trivedi told Lydia as they entered a building not far from Mr. Morgan's, off elegant Prince's Street in the new part of town. The area was exceedingly respectable, and there were lovely shops nearby that Lydia wished to peruse.

She had never been a person of *authority*. Shopping and reading she understood, not managing. How did one handle the responsibility of an entire estate, especially when one was only pretending to be what she was not?

Mr. C had wielded a great deal of authority in his own quiet, hermit-like way. His journal had said he'd left her in charge. He must have had confidence in her, confidence she didn't feel. Max had said she must be a duchess, however unqualified she might be. People more experienced in the world relied on her. She had to listen.

"Do I pretend you're my servant?" Lydia asked doubtfully. "When you know everything and I know nothing?"

Keya flashed a brief, mischievous smile. "Let them think me a servant. Surprise can be advantageous. Of course, if they are broad-minded men willing to listen to a small, brown female, then we've lost the element of surprise, but we will still be far ahead. Just think of this as an informational meeting."

"Informational, right." Lydia straightened her rather broad shoulders, adjusted the lace mantle she wore for luck, and tried not to be intimidated by the soaring ceilings, gilded walls, and marble floors of the foyer they traversed. She started up the stairs. "I am a duchess, and you are an insignificant companion."

Thinking like that did not come easily to a vicar's daughter. Lydia automatically reached for the office door knob. Keya stopped her by touching her glove and opened the door for her.

Right. Duchesses had servants. Duchesses did not lift a hand to help themselves.

"Miss Lydia Wystan, the Malcolm Librarian, to see Misters Dobbs and Henry," Keya announced to the startled clerk, while holding the door for Lydia to enter.

Head high, chin up, towering above Keya and the seated clerk, Lydia refrained from glancing about in curiosity but merely waited to be shown to the peons controlling her money. She tried not to laugh too hard at that whimsy—or weep in abject terror.

The clerk, a pallid, skinny man in spectacles, blinked in surprise. He rose to his short height and bowed uncertainly. "Miss Wystan, welcome. I . . . uh . . . if you'll wait one moment. . ."

"We don't have time to wait," Lydia said in her best commanding voice, having no idea where the words came from except an overactive imagination. "Lead on and let us be done with the formalities. I need to return to the library posthaste."

She started toward the corridor the clerk had glanced toward. He ran ahead to warn his employers.

"Most excellent," Keya whispered with what sounded like laughter. "I had not thought about height as a factor in this battle. Let us hope the solicitors are very short men."

Lydia bit her lip to hold back a terrified chuckle. "I fear that makes me a bully."

As it happened, only one of the solicitors was short, the older one, Dobbs, if his name plate didn't lie. Assuming the other suited gentleman was Henry, he wasn't tall for a man, but he matched Lydia in height. They both rose at her entrance, looking vaguely cross, and bowed perfunctorily.

The office was all polished dark wood except for a window over-looking a park. Lydia longed to be outside walking through the green grass. Instead, she took the largest leather chair she could find and settled into it, wishing she'd thought to bring a parasol with a large point on it. She would buy one the instant she had her money reimbursed.

Keya hovered at her elbow, looking the part of apologetic servant in her drab brown gown.

Sitting down again, Henry, the younger man, located a file amid the confusion of books and papers scattered across both their desks. "You have brought the parish records showing Mr. Cadwallader's death?" he asked in a voice that sounded as if he did not expect it.

Except Mr. Morgan and Keya had prepared her for this. With relief, Lydia nodded imperiously and Keya opened a leather carrying case. She silently produced the document.

Both men had to inspect it, as if they'd recognize the preacher's signature.

Lydia was dying to ask questions, but she decided a duchess wouldn't be bothered.

"And you have identification proving you are Miss Lydia Wystan?" the older man, Dobbs, asked suspiciously, looking over his gold-rimmed spectacles.

Again, she'd been warned. Lydia supposed it was good common sense and a sign that the solicitors were performing their duties. Keya opened the case again and handed over copies of Lydia's own parish record of birth and a "to-whom-this-may-concern" letter from Mr. Morgan assuring the recipient that he knew both Mr. Cadwallader and Miss Wystan and verifying her identity.

Their delaying tactics failing, the solicitors harrumphed and took their time. Finally, the bespectacled Dobbs sat back and examined Lydia, perhaps to see if she might turn into a toad and hop away, she thought spitefully. She glared back, as surely a duchess would.

"Very well, Miss Wystan. Mr. Cadwallader has said you are an excellent assistant and capable of running his household. He wished to leave you in charge if you were still with him at the time of his demise."

Lydia remained frozen. She wanted to make demands, but she didn't like his tone. It sounded as if there might be a very large "But. . ." at the end of this speech.

"As it happens, we have had a most excellent offer for Mr. Cadwallader's property that will remove the burden of the estate from your shoulders," Mr. Henry continued with barely concealed eagerness, pushing a paper forward. "We have negotiated an excellent deal. You would be left with a sizable trust for your services and would no longer have to worry about a crumbling—"

Red rage roared through Lydia.

Normally cautious and implacable, she didn't know how to control the fury boiling up. As if yanked by angry gods, she rose from the chair to tower over the men at their desks. "Over my dead body will I *sell the library* to that snake Crowley. I am the *Librarian*!" She roared this with all the vehemence she'd heard Mr. C employ, and for this moment, she actually believed it. Perhaps she channeled her former employer.

Dobbs and Henry scrambled to stand. "Miss Wystan, it is an honest offer from a gentleman who can better. . ."

"Am I, or am I not, executor of the Malcolm Librarian's trust?" she demanded in a voice she scarcely recognized as hers. Except she'd used it on Crowley and had made him go away. She'd make these termites go away too.

"Of course, of course, Miss Wystan," Henry said nervously. "But you are a woman, you see, and a woman cannot. . ."

Lydia tried not to turn purple. Her sisters had called her an old cow who harmlessly munched her way through the field until all the grass was gone. But right now, she was a raging bull about to trample annoying vermin.

Duchess. She had to be a duchess, not a bull. She was the *Malcolm Librarian*. With what she hoped was a sufficiently evil smile, Lydia turned to Keya. "Maharani, would you care to explain what a woman can do?"

Keya grinned at the purely fictional title of princess, nodded obediently, and opened her case again. "I have with me orders to remove the Malcolm Librarian's estate trust to the offices of Morgan, Blair, and Trivedi. These are copies, you understand. The originals will be filed with the court upon the word of the librarian, who is, as we understand it, executor of the librarian's trust and currently represented by Malcolm Librarian Lydia Wystan."

Fictional titles abounded today. She was no more a librarian than Miss Trivedi was a princess. But explaining that would undermine what very little authority she possessed, and the castle would end up in Crowley's hands. That would never do.

The solicitors looked as if they'd swallowed toads. "I've never heard of the firm," Dobbs muttered. "This is outrageous. Our office has handled the trust for a century. We are simply carrying out our duties by offering the best possible—"

"Your duties are to the *librarian*, sir," Keya said without the fury Lydia would have spilled. "The librarian's duties are to the library. The property you wish to sell is the *library*. If you fail to see the importance of a library to a librarian, then you fail to understand your duties."

"I will not be lectured to by a female over a pile of ancient books," Dobbs said irritably, taking the papers and examining them closer. "Miss Wystan is only an *executor*. An emotional female cannot possibly understand business—"

Lydia lost her patience. "The Malcolm library was established by *women*, has been collected by *women*, written by *women*, and run by women for centuries. It is only recently that a man has set foot inside it, and only because his *mother* was the Malcolm Librarian, and he had the affinity for it."

Dobbs, the older man, glared back. "According to the trust documents, the librarian must *prove* that she is worthy of that position. To be perfectly clear, you are merely a caretaker until then."

Lydia swallowed her terror, wrapped her fury around her like a shield, and held up her hand when Henry opened his mouth. "The Malcolm Librarian *knows* when she is librarian, as do the rest of the family, not outsiders like you. You are merely appointed to manage money."

Then she pointed at Keya. "Miss Trivedi is heir to both the Trivedi and Yedhu fortunes, making her one of the wealthiest women in the kingdom. And it is her wise investments—a *woman's* investments, mind you—that have grown those fortunes. Do not tell us women cannot understand business."

Looming over them, Lydia glared. "If you cannot accept a woman as executor, then you are no longer suitable as the trust's solicitors. Am I clear?" She turned and blithely smiled at Keya. "If you will persuade these gentlemen to reimburse me for the funds I have personally expended upon the estate, you may continue this argument or leave with me to file your papers. I have some shopping to do."

Feeling as if she waved a flag for women and librarians everywhere, Lydia marched out.

She wished she also felt victorious, or at least like a real librarian, but she didn't. Despite her bullying behavior, she was simply a foot soldier in this battle, not the general.

The very real possibility that she'd be revealed as the fraud she was would fuel Crowley's fight to steal her home.

THIRTEEN

"JUST STAND BACK, OUT OF SIGHT," THE BARRISTER ORDERED, POINTING AT the shadows of the courthouse chamber. "I'll signal you when I need you. Half of courtroom procedure is drama."

Max despised drama. He simply wanted to walk up, smash his fist into his cousin George's nose, spit on his uncle's polished shoes, and demand his money back.

He swallowed a sigh. Punching probably involved drama. Estes meant a quieter sort of theatrics.

Max simply wasn't a man who waved papers like swords. He needed action. Hiding in shadows did not suit him at all.

Leaning his shoulders against the corner wall and crossing his arms, he watched his step-cousin and step-uncle stroll in with their bewigged barrister, fully confident of their success. His Uncle David's once-golden head of hair was nearly bald these days. Paunchy in the gut, he still carried his wealth well with understated tailoring and glints of gold from his pocket watch and his tie clasp.

Cousin George was a bit of a dandy, flashing a heavily embroidered silver-threaded waistcoat and a fashionable single-breasted gray tweed cut loosely to conceal the fact that his youthful muscles were turning to flab. He couldn't put up a good fight if Max punched him.

Even though this was an informal meeting, the judge strolled in in full regalia of robe and old-fashioned long wig. He took a seat at the head of a table. His clerk took a chair at his side. He did not indicate that anyone else be seated.

His uncle's barrister presented documents to the judge in a bored tone, as if Max's death was a foregone conclusion, and Max was buried under a tombstone in some distant grave. The man had to know there had been an objection raised.

Standing in the shadows beside the doorway, Max almost smiled as he caught his thieving executors casting surreptitious glances to Estes, who stood on the other side of the table. They probably expected Max's mother to be in attendance.

Morgan had blessedly arranged a closed meeting. Max was safe from the females in his life for a little while longer.

The judge turned to Estes. "You object to this deposition, sir? It seems clear enough to me. The gentleman in question hasn't been heard from in over fifteen years. I'm amazed I haven't seen a petition sooner."

Wearing a short, neatly curled wig, Estes shoved a few documents toward the judge. "The trustees of the Ives estate received regular instructions from Maxwell Ives until this past year. As is documented here, Mr. Ives travels extensively, building projects such as gold mines in South Africa and canals in Egypt. He cannot be expected to maintain close correspondence with men he assumed had the ability to handle mere financial matters without his aid."

The judge studied the documents through wire-rimmed spectacles. "This shows that a Maxwell Ives was involved in these projects but does not prove it is the same Maxwell Ives or that he is, indeed, alive. I should think the gentleman has lived an exceedingly perilous life, and it would be quite remarkable if he has survived these endeavors."

Max held back a snort. That was the comment of a man who never ventured further than his club.

"He has, indeed, survived, Your Honor." Estes nodded in Max's direction. "Mr. Ives, if you will kindly present yourself to the court."

Max decided the shock on his relations' faces as he ambled over to the table was almost as good as a punch in the snout. They recognized him all right. They looked flabbergasted. George's jaw dropped open briefly before he snapped it shut and forced a neutral expression. Uncle David couldn't hide his fury fast enough.

Max grinned and waved. "Hey, Unc, Cuz, most excellent seeing you again."

"That is an impostor," his uncle intoned, barely containing his anger.

The judge turned back to Estes. "Do you have witnesses proving this gentleman is not an impostor?"

"I would like to first ask that the trustees prove he is *not* an impostor, Your Honor. It is their word against his, is it not? I would like you to keep in mind that the executors of the trust are on the brink of committing fraud, perjury, and theft and are unlikely to admit to Mr. Ives' identification. Since Mr. Ives has just returned to these shores after fifteen years, it will take time to collect witnesses from his youth. I would like to ask the court to impound all funds until such time as Mr. Ives is able to bring forth testimony to his identity."

Max crossed his hands behind his back, rocked back on his heels, and donned an insouciance he didn't feel. At this very minute, he loathed and despised his father's relations. He clasped his hands to prevent bunching them into fists. He had to let the judge see that he was fully confident of his success, while the worms squirmed.

Who knew he could be good at drama?

He just prayed he wasn't asked to read anything.

The judge harrumphed. "This is highly unusual. I allowed this informal meeting assuming it was cut-and-dried. I did not expect to have to inquire into lists of investments, trust documents—"

Mr. Estes set another stack of papers on the table. "We anticipated your needs, Your Honor. Indeed, Mr. Ives has provided a great deal of information in advance of his arrival, which ought to indicate that he is who he says he is."

That was Morgan's doing, not Max's. He owed the man a fortune and gratitude beyond excess.

The judge picked up the top paper, then shuffled through the rest. The other barrister shifted uncomfortably, obviously itching to see the paperwork.

The judge pushed the stack toward Max's uncle. "This seems fair enough. The monies are in trust already. I'll sign these orders to see that

they remain so until Mr. Ives can bring witnesses. Will a week be sufficient, gentlemen?" He looked in anticipation at Max and Estes.

"A month, if possible, Your Honor. We may have to bring the
Marquess of Ashford, the Earl of Ives and Wystan, and the Duke of
Sommersville to the court. They reside in the south of England and are
busy men. It will take time to make travel arrangements."

Max was quite certain the judge had to clamp his jaw shut at those
grandiose titles. That was a ploy and no more. The lowly schoolboy he'd
been had scarcely been remarked upon by the marquess and never met
the duke to his knowledge, unless one of his cousins had come into a
title. And the duke was a Malcolm, not an Ives, although he certainly
had no reason not to be objective.

"A month then, granted." The judge began signing the orders to
impound the estate's funds.

"Your Honor," the opposing barrister objected. "If you impound the
funds, my clients will be unable to feed their families!"

The judge stopped signing and looked to Estes. "Are these all the
funds available? As trustees, have they been adequately compensated?"

"More than adequately, Your Honor, to the extent that they have
nearly emptied the trust's accounts. I have taken the liberty of adding all
the investments that once belonged to the trust in those orders. My client
wants a full accounting."

The judge nodded and returned to signing. "If they haven't saved
sufficient funds or made their own investments, then they will have to
ask Mr. Ives for an allowance. He seems well able to look after himself."

Max grinned and refrained from whistling. His worthy trustees
didn't even look his way.

"A month, Mr. Ives," the judge warned. "I expect you back here in a
month with a courtroom full of witnesses to your existence. We're
adjourned." Handing the orders to Estes, he stood and walked out, his
clerk on his heels.

"Now I guess you'll have to murder me to make me really dead,"
Max suggested cheerfully to his relations as they headed for the exit
without a farewell.

"Don't give them ideas," Estes said in an undertone. "As I understand it from Mr. Morgan, you have just impounded a fortune which

they have helped to build. I trust you will have plenty of witnesses lined up or you'll be dead one way or another."

Max's good cheer deflated instantly. Now came his punishment. In order to find witnesses to his existence, he'd have to face his mother and aunt. He wouldn't blame them if they pretended he was dead.

STEPPING OUT OF THE HACKNEY WITH LADY PHOEBE, LYDIA PROUDLY smoothed a wrinkle from her new lavender-striped skirt. It had been so long since she'd worn colors that she had to keep testing the fabric to be certain it was hers.

Pretending to be a duchess, if not a real librarian, she had left Keya dealing with the trustees. Lady Phoebe's home wasn't far from the solicitor's office, so she'd walked over. Once the solicitors had delivered Lydia's private funds, Phoebe had led her around to her favorite shops. Lydia now sported an elegant puff bonnet, with lace flutings and lavender and green flowers, from a shop where Phoebe knew the hat designer. Lydia touched it to be certain the confection stayed in place.

"Are you sure I shouldn't be wearing black?" she asked, probably for the thousandth time. Lydia was a wee bit dubious about Lady Phoebe's fashion advice since the eccentric lady tended to wear split skirts, battered straw hats, and ride penny-farthings, but she was the only aristocrat Lydia knew to ask.

"Mr. Cadwallader was not your immediate family. Lavender is perfectly suitable half-mourning. You need to *look* like our librarian and not a vicar's daughter." Phoebe led the way up stairs set in between two storefronts.

Lydia rather wanted to protest that she *was* a vicar's daughter, but that was not conducive to carrying out Mr. C's wishes. He had wanted her to take care of his castle for a reason. She was hoping Phoebe's aunts might enlighten her as to why he had chosen her, which was the whole point of this shopping spree to look like a proper Malcolm Librarian.

She was also hoping Max would be here, crowing of his courtroom success. If he wasn't. . . she simply couldn't lie to a despairing mother. She anxiously clasped her gloved hands and prayed.

The door at the top of the stairs was opened by a blond, blue-eyed adolescent nearly bouncing in excitement. "Lady Agnes told us you were coming. Welcome, our librarian!" She bobbed a curtsy.

Wondering if anyone had curtsied for Mr. C, Lydia had no idea how to respond. Did she curtsy back? If the girls were lying in wait for her, then that must mean Max hadn't arrived yet, or they'd all be surrounding him.

Phoebe tugged Lydia's arm, forcing her inside the foyer. "Celia, I'd advise you to gather up all the giggling girls hiding behind you and return to your studies. Miss Wystan may wish to visit with you later, but we need to speak with my aunts first. Off with you, now."

Giggles and flurries of skirts and petticoats followed as a gaggle of students ran out of hiding places and up the stairs. Lydia thought of Max walking through those front doors and almost turned around to stand guard on the doorstep.

Phoebe tugged harder, pulling her toward the parlor on the right. "You can't flee now. I can't take the Malcolm Librarian into my home without introducing you to the ladies. They would scalp me."

"I've already met them," Lydia whispered in weak protest.

"Not as our librarian. They need to be confident that you can handle the library or it will make them quite anxious."

And undermine her position, Lydia understood. She had to play her part.

Of course, if Max walked through that door, the ladies would forget her existence. Lydia took some comfort in that, although she was disappointed that he wasn't here.

Her new bustle wiggled as she walked. She wasn't entirely certain why she wanted her bottom to look any bigger than it already was, but the dressmaker had insisted it had to do with the gown's draping. And the lace-trimmed silk draping was very fine, finer than anything she'd ever owned. The skirt itself rather restricted her ability to stride quickly. She wouldn't be crossing any fields in a gown like this—but then, ladies did not stride fields.

The parlor she entered was even shabbier than it had been six years ago when she'd arrived at the school's doorstep. Crocheted doilies and woven shawls obscured fading upholstery and battered, ancient tables.

Amid the clutter of books and ornaments sat two gray-haired ladies in all their old-fashioned crinolines and bows.

"Miss Wystan, how lovely to see you again," the shorter, plumper one cried. "Sit down, sit down. Phoebe, ring for tea, please."

"I just sent the girls scattering, Aunt Agnes." Phoebe bent to kiss powdery cheeks. "I'll fetch the tea myself."

Lydia bobbed a small curtsy. "It is a pleasure to be here, my ladies. I hope my visit isn't disturbing your day."

"Nonsense, girl. Sit down." Dyed black hair fading to iron gray, the taller, stouter lady patted the sofa cushion beside her. "Have a seat. Phoebe was quite right to bring you here. We are so sad to hear of Mr. Cadwallader's passing. He was with us for a good long time. A very helpful man."

Lydia cautiously took the seat offered, hoping the aging furniture wouldn't collapse under their combined weights. Lady Gertrude was not a small woman. "Mr. Cadwallader was a brilliant librarian. He taught me a great deal. Do you recall why he was chosen? Isn't it unusual to have a male librarian?"

"Indeed, it is." Lady Agnes beamed as if she had chosen the perfect topic. "For centuries, Malcolms only had girls, so only women were librarians. The stacks were much smaller then, of course."

"And then Ninian Malcolm married the Earl of Ives over a century ago, and our world changed." Lady Gertrude polished her pince nez. "We finally have sons, even if they are ungrateful adventurers like dear Max. Mr. Cadwallader proved his ability, so we accepted that the son of a Malcolm Librarian might take her place."

Even Mr. C had to prove his ability? How? She didn't dare ask.

Lydia smiled weakly and was relieved when Phoebe hurried in with the tea tray.

They had worked their way through the teacakes and the ladies were questioning uncomfortably close to Lydia's weaknesses when the girls upstairs emitted a shriek and raced down.

"It's summer," Lady Agnes said apologetically. "Their classes are done early and they are excessively bored."

Knowing Max had meant to call on his mother once he was done at court, Lydia gnawed worriedly at her bottom lip. Unable to explain, she rose briskly and entered the foyer just as the girls flung open the door and squealed some more.

On the other side of the entry stood Max looking shell-shocked at the wave of femininity pouring toward him. He raised his eyes, saw Lydia, and shock turned to panic.

Wordlessly, he slapped his hat back on and fled down the stairs. Before the girls could follow, Lydia slammed the door and blocked it with her body to cover the sound of her heart breaking.

He thought she was running after him like the others.

FOURTEEN

MAX RAN AFTER THE HACKNEY AND CAUGHT THE DRIVER BEFORE HE TURNED down Cowgate. He had the urge to order the carriage straight to the port.

But he was no longer an eighteen-year-old coward.

He *felt* like eighteen, filled with rage and despair and not knowing where to turn. He'd *trusted* Lydia. He'd thought she was sensible, level-headed, and not inclined to escalate the conflict between Max's gentlemanly upbringing and his animal nature.

If Lydia chose to push herself at him, he would not be able to resist. He knew it right down to the marrow of his bones. And other places. That she was at his *mother's* house, waiting to pounce like every other female. . . His disappointment was immense.

Why was she at his mother's house? And where would he go now if he couldn't even keep Lydia at a distance?

Bakari was back at the castle. He'd have to collect his son and depart for parts unknown until he knew what to do with the boy. And himself.

He still needed to speak with his mother. How would he do that without being set upon by a pack of savages?

Leaning his head back against the carriage seat, Max ordered the driver to the nearest stable. This was insane. He had a tower with a key

to lock it. The tower belonged to Lydia, so he'd have to leave eventually
—after he figured out how to talk to his mother.

He could have Lydia send her a letter. . . Max laughed bitterly at that.
He could dictate a telegram, perhaps, asking his mother to come to him.
His mother might even know what to do with Bakari. Maybe he wasn't
too late for the Burma project.

By the time he'd purchased a steed suitable for mountain climbing
and was on the road, Max had talked himself out of panic and fury. He
was in despair that he could no longer rely on Lydia, but he'd managed
these last fifteen years without her. It was just. . . he felt as if his right
arm had been severed. How had he become so dependent on her in just a
few days?

He'd never had a woman he could count on before. He had to
acknowledge that he'd thoroughly enjoyed kissing Lydia, teasing her
until she blushed, waiting in anticipation for those moments they shared
over the silly books. Her research had been so helpful that he was almost
certain he knew the cause of the tower's tilt.

He had to stay long enough to organize the repairs. Damn.

He tried to revive his anger at seeing Lydia rushing to the door with
all the other females, but all he could summon was how beautiful she'd
looked in that fancy gown, with the foolish hat perched on her mass of
sunset hair. Her eyes had widened to enormous pools of indigo when
she'd seen him. Out of all the feminine pulchritude rushing for that door,
Lydia was the only one he could recall. Literally and figuratively, she
would always stand out above all others.

Which meant he'd probably have to picture her every time he took
another woman to bed. Imagining stripping off that fancy gown and
seeing what she wore under it carried Max out of the city and half way
back to the castle before the long northern day darkened. He stopped at a
tavern for food and to rest his nag, then decided he might as well go the
rest of the way. At least he wasn't walking.

He continued his fantasies as the horse swayed through the night.
Lydia had generous breasts. Would they have freckles? Would her
nipples be pert and small or rosy and large? Did she wear frills and lace
beneath her petticoats? And if he removed them, what color was the hair
below?

He wasn't entirely certain why he was torturing himself that way, but by the time he reached the dark castle around midnight, he was almost prepared to seduce the librarian just to satisfy his curiosity. He watered, fed, and curried his new horse himself, patted the old mare he'd bought for Bakari earlier, and tested the garden door. It still wasn't locked.

Shoulders relaxing for the first time all day, Max traipsed up the tower stairs to the safe and cozy haven Lydia had provided.

He had never thought he'd have to lock out Lydia as well as the maids.

WRAPPING HER CROCHETED SHAWL AROUND HER PLUMP SHOULDERS, LADY Agnes set her lips with determination as she stepped off at the Calder train station the next morning. Behind her gray ringlets and bows and dangling earrings, the lady was a force to be reckoned with, Lydia had discovered.

"I cannot promise he is there," she warned the lady again. "He may have fled for Burma for all I know."

Lydia had salved her conscience by knowing Max had *intended* to let his mother know he was alive, and that the girls had seen him, even if they couldn't identify him. She didn't think she was violating his privacy, much.

Lady Agnes nodded and fiercely regarded the mule wagon pulling up to the station. "My son is alive. That's what is important. I understand you can't explain what is wrong with him, but I appreciate that you told me he was on my doorstep. He came home. I'll learn the rest in good time."

"Only if he is here," Lydia was compelled to remind her. She couldn't mention that Max's son was here too, and that was her main hope for his return. Surely Max wouldn't abandon Bakari. "I had hoped he'd be on the train this morning, but I saw no sign of him."

"I'll wait," the lady announced as Laddie assisted her into the cart. "I know he will come here again. And you will need him. There's a dark cloud on your future."

Lydia shivered. The lady's prescience had proved correct in several small ways. She couldn't disregard her predictions, especially since she was almost certainly right about Max. He'd left his trunks in the tower along with his son. She hadn't told his mother that.

Did the lady know about Lydia's inability to find books? That was definitely a black cloud.

Laddie threw their hat boxes and satchels into the back of the cart. Holding her new parasol, Lydia settled on the seat beside Lady Agnes and leaned over Laddie's shoulder. "Do you know if Mr. Ives has returned yet?"

"There's a new mare in the stable," Laddie said. "Reckon someone rode it there."

Lydia sat back in relief. She would have hated raising Lady Agnes's hopes and dragging her up the mountain for nothing.

They arrived at the castle a little after noon. They'd seen no sign of Max fleeing down the narrow path, so surely he was still inside. Somewhere.

Once they arrived at the castle, Lady Agnes wanted to sit in the parlor until Max made an appearance. Lydia persuaded her to take tea in her room and rest a bit until he was located. She had Beryl lead their guest to one of the newly-cleaned chambers in the main block. She traipsed off to the tower's downstairs guest room, the one she had chosen for hers while Max was in residence. Musical bedchambers did not bother her so much as wishing she knew she deserved these privileges.

She'd ordered some new day dresses, but they would have to be delivered later. For traveling, she'd worn her old black wool. Studying the aging mirror in her new room, she decided she didn't look any different after this past week of turmoil. Her hair still escaped its pins. She brushed it down and pinned it again. To drape over her boring bodice, she'd bought a pretty gold scarf that looked well with her hair so she didn't look quite so matronly. But there was little else she could do to improve her appearance.

And she shouldn't be trying. The annoying man had made it quite clear that he didn't appreciate her looking after him.

She took the stone stairs up to Mr. C's chamber and rapped on the door. Lloyd answered it. She could read the expectant question on his dour features, but he'd never ask.

She hated lying, so she prevaricated, only slightly. "I am officially in charge, as Mr. C wished."

Lloyd appeared to release a sigh of relief. Before he could say more, she asked, "Is Mr. Ives in? He has a visitor."

Bakari waved cheerfully from the floor where he appeared to be working on a sketch of. . . the universe? "Hello, Miss Lydia. Papa says he'll teach me to ride!"

"An excellent notion, I'm sure, sir." Lydia waited for Lloyd to answer.

"He's down in the dungeon," Lloyd explained. "Said something about wells and plumbing, but I didn't grasp it all."

"I don't suppose Zach would know how to find him?" Lydia tried to remember if the footman had ever stirred himself to so much as descend to the wine cellar.

"He's got a voice and feet," Lloyd said. "Tell him to employ them."

Well, yes, that firmly put her in her place. If she must play the part of Malcolm Librarian, she must act as ruler of all she surveyed. Librarians ordered servants, not questioned them. Interesting lessons and challenges loomed.

Knowing Max was on the premises helped. He hadn't completely run away. He'd just rejected her and a school full of giggling girls. She couldn't blame him too much for that.

Downstairs in her study, she rang the bell for Mr. Folkston. A butler was supposed to command the household when there was no steward.

Mr. Folkston was a portly man in his fifties, not much taller than Lydia. His black suit and starched white shirt were impeccable but showing signs of wear. Recalling with satisfaction the legal documents Keya had sent around last night, Lydia felt the day improve incrementally. She had a bank letter and a larger allowance than before.

"If you would, send Zach into the tower cellar to fetch Mr. Ives. But before you do that, I'd like to assure you that I am now in control of the castle funds." Lydia watched the butler relax ever so imperceptibly, although all he did was bend slightly in acknowledgment. "I will pay everyone on first of September as always. I shall give them a full quarterly wage and a little extra for their loyalty. I hope to raise that wage by ten percent, if you will explain that to them for me, please."

She had told Keya that raising the household funds was absolutely necessary. At some point, she hoped to have some idea of the entirety of the trust, but knowing the castle's allowance had been increased was enough for now.

Mr. Folkston broke his reserve sufficiently to exhibit a brief smile. "The staff will be more than pleased to hear that, miss, thank you."

"They've earned every penny. Once I have a better understanding of our funds, I'll attempt to set aside enough to cover any more emergencies so this doesn't happen again. I still have a year's worth of repairs and maintenance to catch up, but I've been given the wherewithal to buy new uniforms and shoes for all. If you'll have Mrs. Folkston handle that, I'd appreciate it."

The butler bowed again, this time looking grateful. "Do we use our local merchants?"

"I'd prefer that. If you think the fabric quality is inferior, you might suggest that we are able to pay a little more and ask them to order what they need from the city. I trust your judgment." And she trusted the Calder merchants not to cheat their best customer.

After Folkston departed on his tasks, Lydia stared at the correspondence gathering on the desk—*her* desk now, not Mr. C's. The weight of responsibility—and her fraud—weighed heavily on her shoulders.

It was a good thing she had wide shoulders.

Even wide shoulders couldn't stop a tower from toppling—taking the library with it. She had to find a way to make Max stay.

FIFTEEN

Wiping sweat from his face with his filthy hands, Max traipsed from the depths of the tower cellar, following the shouts to the open entry. The young footman in his polished shoes and starched linen nervously stood silhouetted against the daylight. He actually backed up a foot when Max appeared, but apparently realizing ghosts didn't come covered in malodorous mud, he didn't flee.

"Miss Wystan has asked me to fetch you. And it is almost luncheon," the footman added, presumably as a bribe to ease the command.

Lydia was back. She must have caught the first train out. Max grimaced. He'd hoped to have proved his theory before they had a confrontation, but he'd only had a couple of hours to work.

"Tell Miss Wystan I'll be at lunch, although I may be late. I can't go in all my filth." If he'd been in Burma, no one would have cared if he traipsed in wearing a three-day beard and mud up to his knees.

Perhaps to prevent her from falling into his arms, he ought to remain filthy, but he couldn't insult his hostess.

Afraid Lydia might be heaving him out, if only out of mutual embarrassment, Max trudged through the garden door and up the tower stairs to scrub in his own private tub. The irony that the drainage from said tub might be undermining the tower did not escape him.

Bakari showed him the sums he'd done and the map he'd drawn. Max knew nothing about children, but he thought the boy was exceptionally smart and deserved a reward for his hard work and patience. At least, *he* would have appreciated an occasional reward when he'd been that age. Of course, reading a simple page of one-syllable words had been an achievement for Max. His teachers hadn't appreciated that fact.

"We'll take the horses out after lunch, shall we?" he asked. "I know they're not ponies, but let's see what we can do."

The boy brightened as if given all the gold in China. Max was a cad who didn't deserve a son like this. One more reason to find him a good school where he'd learn to be respectable and fit into society, unlike his father.

Bathing and hastily shaving, Max tried not to speculate why Lydia wanted to see him. If she decided his despicable behavior justified throwing him out, he couldn't disagree. If she'd suddenly been afflicted by his magnetism, it wasn't her fault. He should have just shoved past the students and found a room in his own home where he could have closed out everyone—except his mother. Who would have wanted his aunt and Lydia with her and asked for tea to be served and that he stay for dinner and. . .

Society simply wasn't for him.

Max traipsed downstairs in his favorite tweed coat, pleated khaki trousers, and unstarched linen cravat. Loose-fitting and comfortable, they'd served him well for years.

Remembering Lydia yesterday in her fancy bustle and ornate hat, Max thought maybe he should invest in slightly newer attire before he left civilization again.

He was late, he knew. Hearing voices in the small breakfast room, he assumed Lydia had started without him. He hoped it was the footman and not one of the maids to whom she spoke. Blithely striding into the parlor where the staff usually served a light luncheon buffet—he froze.

"Maxwell! Dear Maxwell!" His mother excitedly rose from her chair, then clung to the back, overcome with tears. Her hair was gray, and she carried more weight, but he'd recognize her anywhere.

"Oh cripes." He glanced at Lydia, who sat serenely sipping soup, ignoring the drama.

She could have *warned* him.

So, even the complacent Librarian could have her revenge. Fair enough. He'd fled and left her alone to find her own way back. Had that put her off him enough? She certainly didn't seem prepared to leap into his arms or bed.

Scarcely able to swallow past the lump in his throat, Max made his way around the table and awkwardly hugged his mother. They'd never really been close. He didn't remember if they'd ever hugged. She felt so damned small—

"Dear Max, how I've prayed!" She wept into his waistcoat. "I knew you'd come. I knew you'd save us."

"That was more than I knew," he grumbled, glancing to Lydia in hope of help.

Fat chance. She regarded him blandly, as if this had naught to do with her. Which it didn't, he supposed, except he hadn't expected her to drag his mother up here where he felt safe—

Damned woman. Even in her revenge, she was making life easier for him, in an evil surprise sort of way. He could talk with his mother here, without all her students around.

"Why don't you sit down to this nice luncheon? I'm fair starved." Max pulled the chair out and took his mother's arm to help her into it.

"I'm sorry." She dabbed at her eyes and clung to his arm. "I'm not usually such a watering pot. Your father would be terribly displeased." In a flutter of beads and bows, she finally released him and settled into the chair.

"You are perfectly entitled to weep whenever you choose," Lydia declared. "Finding a long lost son certainly justifies weeping. Men should learn that they'll drown in our tears if they cause them."

Taking a chair across from his mother, Max growled at this inanity but didn't otherwise reply. He had no notion of what to say but watched the footman serve his soup. He'd feed his stomach before the pot of disapproval got dumped on his head.

"Your father wanted you to be strong, like him, not weak like me," his mother said, almost apologetically, as she dabbed at her eyes. "I tried so very hard not to baby you, because I wanted you to be like him. And you are, and so much more! I'm so proud of your accomplishments. I hope you can excuse my weakness."

"Lady Agnes, there is nothing weak about you," Lydia admonished impatiently. "If anything, Mr. Ives has half his strength from *you*. You persevered in the face of all odds. . . Women have to work three times as hard as men to overcome the obstacles in our way."

And there it began. She made him sound like a cad and a bastard for abandoning his mother. He figured she was only half right. "You started a school," Max added gruffly. "That wasn't easy."

"Well, it was at first." His mother picked up her spoon, apparently distracted by the topic. "I simply wanted the daughters I never had, so I invited a few of the nieces. And Gertrude invited a few more. And then word went around that we needed teachers, and well, it all just grew."

"We would be lost without the School of Malcolms," Lydia said firmly. "So many of us must rely on ourselves these days. Good husbands are in short supply."

"Especially when we have gifts they don't understand." Lady Agnes cheered up a little more. "I know it must be hard for you, dear Lydia, living out here alone because you're attached to our books. But marriage will solve that."

"Marriage?" Max asked in surprise. The librarian was planning on marrying?

"*Marriage?*" Lydia repeated, with a little more shock.

So, she hadn't betrothed herself while he was sleeping. Max was even more surprised at his relief. He couldn't expect a beautiful, intelligent woman to stay single because he wished it so.

Now that he gave it half a thought, Lydia deserved companionship. She shouldn't have to be both librarian and steward for this great crumbling monstrosity. And he most definitely was not the man to keep her company. He selfishly needed her to stay single until he had his business in hand.

"Well, yes, of course, dear," Lady Agnes patted Lydia's hand. "I dreamed of this, but it's very clear now that I'm here. You two are perfect together. I knew it the moment I first met you. We'll have a grand wedding. I wonder if we could book the entire train to bring in guests?

We could decorate it in pastel bunting and bouquets and serve comfits and champagne. . ."

What?

Max stared at his mother as if she'd gone mad before his eyes. "Who two?" he asked, unintelligibly, apparently having swallowed his tongue.

But Lydia understood his garbled question. She looked equally panic stricken but replied a little more sensibly. "Weddings are lovely, my lady, but perhaps we could simply have a nice party? I'd love a party. We could invite people for Christmas, perhaps, when the hunting is good. We'll have pheasant pies."

Max did his best to add to the distraction. "A small reception—in a week or two would be convenient—if you want a gathering while I'm here. I need people to testify in court that I am who I am. It would be jolly fun to watch Uncle Dave's face if I flood the courtroom with people who remember me. A party would be a good way to thank them for coming."

His mother studied him quizzically. "Of course you are who you are. Who else would you be? Has your uncle lost his eyesight? Why would you need witnesses?"

Lydia gestured for the removal of soup bowls and the serving of the entrée—at lunch. The staff had outdone themselves for his mother. Max used the moment to breathe and organize his thoughts.

When the servants departed, he continued. "Uncle David believes I'm dead, Mother. He told the judge I am an impostor. The judge has frozen all our funds until I produce witnesses who can identify me. As soon as I do that, I can take back the estate and give it to a new trustee. You'll never have to worry about money again."

"Oh, that will be nice, dear." She blinked owlishly. "It seems a little foolish though. I'll just go to the judge, shall I? If a mother can't identify her own child—"

"You stand to benefit from identifying me," he explained patiently. "I need *objective* witnesses, ones who do not expect anything in return for their testimony."

"Oh well then, Gertrude and Lydia and Phoebe—"

Lydia reached over to pat his mother's hands. "We would all do anything to help you, my lady. We're not objective either. Max needs his former teachers, classmates, Ives' cousins, perhaps?" She raised an eyebrow at him.

He nodded, relieved that she understood. "I mean to write my old school and ask for directions. If mother could write to our relations, I might have time to meet them half way and at least obtain their written testimony."

"I don't suppose the judge would like identification from all those ladies you knew. . . ?" Lydia asked innocently.

Max shot her a glare. "No, I don't suppose he would. Male witnesses are generally preferred."

His mother appeared lost in her own world, peering inside her head and not paying attention to their byplay. Max tried not to imagine all the women he'd slept with nearly fifteen years ago parading into a court-room in their matronly circumspection, gloved hands crossed, lacy hats bobbing on pompadours, skirts trailing. . . Would they even recognize him? He didn't want to find out.

Lady Agnes let out a heartfelt sigh. "Well, I suppose we could arrange a hasty wedding party. People will understand when the circum-stances are explained. Lydia, what about your family? Could they arrive within a fortnight?"

Max wondered if he crossed his eyes and banged his head on the table a few times if she'd wake up. Instead, he slammed his lamb slice onto a piece of bread and stood. "I need to return to work. Lydia, if I might have some of your time this evening?"

Looking as confused as he felt, Lydia simply nodded.

Max told himself he wasn't fleeing when he left the dining parlor. He was simply taking the more practical path. No man wanted to know that his mother was quite, quite mad.

NOT ENTIRELY CERTAIN WHAT TO DO WITH HER GUEST, LYDIA LEFT LADY Agnes in the guest library with pens and paper, making lists for her imaginary wedding.

Lydia immersed herself in the immense correspondence and tasks that she'd taken on this past year, apparently in training to act in place of the librarian until one was found. Or *made*? Could she teach herself?

Just before dinner, she gathered all her willpower and entered the tower library with a list of words she'd compiled, in hopes of duplicating her success with Max's request. The books whispered and rustled at her entrance, but none sang out with the information she needed. Sitting at the desk at the foot of the stairs, she concentrated on each word individually, listening for the whispers to grow louder. They didn't.

How had she heard Max's needs but not her own? What would happen if a letter writer requested information, and she couldn't provide it? What was the purpose of a library one couldn't access? She didn't even know where to place the towers of unshelved volumes.

Perhaps she couldn't hear the books unless the person asking for information was with her. That was a truly appalling thought since Malcolms were now scattered around the world. They couldn't possibly travel all the way here with the simple questions that they expected their librarian to answer. And since Lydia was here and she couldn't answer her own questions—well, that theory didn't hold much water.

Picking up Mr. C's final journal, praying he provided information she hadn't yet found, Lydia had dinner sent to her study. She'd rather not face Max and his mother's strange fantasy. Perhaps if they weren't together, Lady Agnes's sanity might return.

Marriage! To Max! Inconceivable. Well, as a fantasy, it was rather entertaining. If she were to marry, she'd like a husband as large as Max. Single men as physically superb as he were hard to find. Ones of intelligence—even more difficult. And after his kisses—she was admittedly curious about bedplay. But certainly not to the extent that she'd marry a man who would leave her alone until he died in a foreign jungle, where she wouldn't even know he was gone until possibly years later.

Glad to have that matter straightened out, Lydia tried reading Mr. C's journal to see how he'd learned to be a librarian, but he seemed to find the task as natural as breathing and hadn't required lessons.

He offered no solution to Lydia's predicament. Worse, he made it clear that a librarian simply could not leave the library for any extended period of time. He'd given up the love of his life when she refused to stay in this cold and drafty place and had returned home to England. He'd loved his books more than her.

Lydia had long since grown accustomed to the notion of a lonely spinster's life, but she felt a little sorry for Mr. C. He could have married had he wanted.

Finally admitting the answer to her predicament wasn't in this journal, Lydia carried her pens and papers to the small guest parlor. Mr. Folkston had informed her that Lady Agnes had decided to retire after dinner, so Lydia and Max should be uninterrupted.

Max was already there, pacing the far end of the room as usual. He'd really believed she was like all the other silly girls who'd rushed at him. That hurt.

He stopped pacing when she entered and offered a grim smile. "How long has my mother been like this?"

That wasn't an easier topic. "Never. She and Lady Gertrude always sound a little dotty when they're together because they finish each other's sentences and thoughts and no one can quite follow. But not once has anyone hinted that they might be insane." Lydia took a seat at the table she'd been using to write his journal. The papers had been abandoned these last days.

"So perhaps my aunt keeps Mother balanced, and she slips off into fantasies when she's alone? Then I must pray nothing happens to Aunt Gertrude!" Max flung himself into an easy chair, sprawling his long legs in front of him. "I will need to hire a companion to look after them."

Lydia tapped her pen on the table as she thought about it, but shook her head. "No, they would not like that at all. And there really is no spare room in the school. You will have to rely on the teachers and the rest of us to look after them after you've traipsed off again."

He grimaced. "Which makes me feel an utter cad, but my staying here would solve nothing—especially if it inspires impossible fantasies. So let's not speak of it right now."

"Would you prefer to speak of why you fled when you saw me at your mother's house?" she asked bluntly. "You knew I expected to return here with you."

"Natural reflex." He rubbed his face. "It's embarrassing, admittedly. But you were there with them, and I relied on you to be sensible. Instead, you let the hordes descend."

"They did the same when I knocked," she said dryly. "They're bored little girls. I had meant to stop them, but I was too late."

He looked up with what appeared to be hope in his eyes. "Then maybe it's not me?"

"Oh, it's you, all right," Lydia was forced to admit. "They hid from me. You, they meant to swarm."

He nodded. "It's hopeless. I suppose I must thank you for bringing my mother here. I need to send letters to everyone I ever knew and pray at least one will stand up for me. I counted on Mother writing all our relations. They would respond to her far better than to me."

"She'll happily send wedding invitations." Relieved that he believed her, Lydia managed a smile. "It is an innovative means of obtaining a response."

Max gave a heartfelt sigh. "I am almost tempted. Marriage would solve many things, like what to do with my sons when they need a home. And you are the only female I've ever met who I can trust not to make demands or push me over a balcony or otherwise have dramatic fits when I cannot be what you wish me to be."

Lydia suspected, despite his confidence otherwise, that she'd frequently be tempted to push him off the tower. Max was too accustomed to doing things his own way. "Has someone pushed you over a balcony?" she asked with interest.

He shrugged. "They tried. I don't push easily. Suffice it to say that life is very messy when I venture near civilization. I am utterly petrified at the idea of any kind of party to gather the witnesses I need. I'd like this done in a quiet, discreet manner, no women allowed."

"A reception of some sort may be necessary," Lydia warned. "But for now, let's start with the classmates you remember and the name of your school. I can rough out a request, read it to you, and let you decide if it's sufficient. Except for the school, the addresses may be difficult."

"I've spent the day summoning names from memory. It is not a very long list, I fear. I wasn't precisely a sociable sort when the other students insisted on mocking me."

"And you insisted on retaliation." Lydia had learned a little of his nature. He might not strike first, but he wasn't meek.

Max nodded acknowledgment. "School wasn't for me. But a few fellows didn't feel inclined to test their strength on me or poke fun at my slowness. I saved them from a contretemps or two. We rubbed along all right."

He gave her the school and its direction, plus the name of several students from all those years ago. Then he stood up and began to pace again. "I'm not certain if my Ives cousins will side with my uncle or will stand up for me, and I have no idea where any of them are. I'll have to write Ashford and see if anyone can provide a list. Surely the marquess will have a secretary."

"Many of them are married to Malcolms," Lydia pointed out. "I'll have information in the library. They may not send journals promptly, but they send names of newborns. Your older cousins are mostly married and producing a new generation."

Max sent her a wry grin. "Do any have as many bastards as I do?"

"As I told you, it's not unknown. The marquess has several illegitimate half-brothers, and he has twin by-blows of his own. They've all done quite well for themselves. Your own grandfather had several, I believe, but they didn't marry Malcolms, so I don't have accurate records. You need to give me the names of your sons, their mothers, and where they reside so I may enter them into the genealogy. I hope you're planning on visiting your son in Edinburgh." Lydia tried to keep the disapproval from her voice. Children needed parents, but she understood why Max might be a bad one.

"I was hoping he might come here. I'd rather go nowhere near his mother." He ran his hand through his thick dark curls—Ives curls. "Do you think you might have these letters ready in the morning?"

"Easily," she assured him, admiring the way he strode about the room with the grace of a great cat. "As long as you don't want wedding invitations," she added with a smile.

He swung on his heel and marched toward her, fire in his eyes. "If I thought it would do bit of good, I'd marry you in a minute."

He lifted her from her chair and covered her mouth with his.

SIXTEEN

MAX HAD NEVER KNOWN A KISS AS SOUL-SEARING AS LYDIA'S. IT WAS AS IF she *knew* him in ways he did not know himself, and she was offering everything he'd ever craved in one magnificent package of serenity, beauty, and intelligence—a package he could not have, he tried to remind himself.

But she held him with such fierceness, kissed him with such passion, and returned his caresses with such boldness when he skimmed her curves, that he longed for what he couldn't have. . .

On the verge of pressing her against the wall and demanding what he desired most, Max stiffened and forced himself away. He *never* assaulted women the way they beleaguered him. What had come over him?

Wise woman that she was, Lydia quietly drew away and left the room before he committed another sin, an irrevocable, unforgivable one.

BRIGHT AND EARLY ON WEDNESDAY, MAX RAN DOWN THE TOWER STAIRS, determined to apologize for his depredations—while wishing he had the right to explore where that explosive kiss might have led. He absolutely wasn't suited for civilization if he started assaulting women.

Looking chipper and rosy-cheeked, his mother lurked in the breakfast room, dashing cold water on his lust. Before her rested stacks of unreadable papers she'd wrapped in various colored ribbons, apparently as a sorting system.

"Good morning, my love! You look so handsome this morning."

Only a mother could call his ratty attire and overlong hair handsome. Max kissed her cheek in appreciation.

"I have arranged the guest lists in order," she unfortunately continued. "You and dear Lydia need to decide how many guests you would like, but I explored the castle a little last night, and I'm quite sure it will hold everyone, if need be. We'll have to bring in a few servants—"

There was the dotty mother he knew and loved—instead of going to bed, she'd been traipsing through this gothic horror, inspecting *bedchambers*. She'd be installing her teachers and students next.

Not ready to deal with madness at this hour, he headed for the buffet. "And good morning to you. I am only grabbing a plate for now. I have to sign the letters Lydia has prepared, and then I must crawl under the tower again. Will you be returning to the city? I fear you'll miss the morning train unless you're already packed."

He had come down early in hopes of seeing her off. She didn't seem prepared to leave.

"Do you think I'd miss a moment of this time with you?" she asked, returning to her piles of paper. "If you cannot tolerate the city, then I must come to you. Dear Lydia will not tell me why you ran the other day and why you will not stay with us. Might you explain? Surely you can sit down with a cup of coffee for a few minutes."

Max grimaced and poured the coffee. She'd come all this way for him. He supposed he could mind his manners a while longer. "If you're truly prescient, then you'd know, wouldn't you?"

"Well, it obviously has to do with women. I've jotted a note asking your son to join us here, so you need not see his mother."

She may as well have been a fly on the wall and overheard his wishes. He'd forgotten that about her. Max tried not to shudder. A son did *not* want his mother to know everything he did.

"Richard will start the university in the fall," she continued. "He ought to at least meet his father before you go your separate ways. But no, I do not know why you cannot stay with us." She sounded just the tiniest bit disgruntled, rather like a child who has been denied a candy she already knew she could not have.

"Let us simply say that there is a reason I have sons and no wives and that it is best if I stay away from young ladies and leave it at that." Astounded that he'd managed that declaration so easily, Max rewarded himself with a stack of scrambled eggs and fried new potatoes.

Lydia's composure must be having an effect on him. Or having explained once, he felt more confident in speaking again—at least to a Malcolm who understood idiosyncrasies. His father's family would roll on the floor in hysteria.

"You would be faithful to Lydia," Lady Agnes asserted with certainty.

Max felt that blow to the gut. He didn't know that now, did he? The thought of hurting honest, plain-spoken Lydia with unfaithfulness. . . He simply couldn't consider it.

"Once you're married, you'll settle down," his mother continued, oblivious to his reaction despite her so-called prescience. "It's obvious Calder Castle needs your talents. I'm sure there are a great many projects in this country you can take on without traipsing all over the planet. Now have a look at these lists and tell me which guests you want and which you don't."

Max sighed and pushed the bundles away. "I cannot read those, Mother." Look at him, maturely confronting his flaws and presenting them as if they were nothing! He deserved an extra bit of toast for that admission.

"Of course you can read!" She glared at him. "We sent you to a very good school. You just never liked paperwork and preferred working with your hands."

No arguing that. "Did Lydia tell you if she'd like to see her family? Perhaps a small gathering to celebrate her new status as librarian?"

He assumed that was her new status. He hadn't even asked how her meeting had gone. More proof that he wasn't fit for civilized company.

"That's this stack." His mother patted one tied in pink ribbon. "Lydia's family is old and dates back to Wystan and Lady Ninian's medieval ancestors. She is destined to be librarian. Mine descends from a different branch. But it will be quite exciting for us all to come together."

Max thought this particular fantasy had to do with tying him to one place, and he understood his mother's need. She'd been living in fear these past years not just because his uncle was the devil, but because Max had abandoned her. So she was waving magic wands and grasping at straws. There wasn't a lot he could do to alleviate her fears. Life was uncertain.

"It would be good to meet Richard. Does this mean you are staying here?" he asked, adding jam to his toast. He hadn't seen either of his other two sons since their infancy.

She stuck out her bottom lip in a frown. "I suppose I must, if you will not go to the city. I daresay Azmin and Phoebe can help run the school for a few weeks. Their university classes won't start again until fall so they have a little spare time, although Azmin and Dare may wish to visit Norfolk before the nice weather ends, just to be certain his niece is completely cured. They will understand when they realize how important this is."

She studied her stack of lists. "Do you really mean you *can't* read these or that you *won't*?"

"I'm sure my teachers told you I can't read. Lydia says it's an Ives family trait that springs up from time to time. I'm not trying to be difficult, although that's what my teachers thought. It hasn't stopped me from learning. As you so wisely pointed out, I work well with my hands. I learn from listening." Max felt a little freer having said this.

Not wishing to disappoint his parents and hiding his failures had been one of the many reasons Max had left these shores. Now that he was a successful man—if a truly lousy son and father—he had the experience to admit to his imperfections. He helped himself to more toast.

"Well, I never. . ." His mother tapped her finger on her lists. "So you never wrote me because you couldn't!" She brightened perceptibly. "All the more reason you should stay home now." Then a cloud covered her expressive features again. "You have *more* sons besides Richard?"

Max almost chuckled. His mother's mind was a twisty place. "Three all together," he said before biting into his toast. It should be interesting to see how that went over.

"Three," she murmured. "I have three grandsons! I don't think I know anyone who has three. This is quite exciting. When might I meet them?"

Feeling almost giddy with relief that she wasn't beating him over the head with a platter, Max nodded at the door. "Besides Richard, one is upstairs. The other. . . well, you can add him and his mother to your guest list, but I'll not attend any party with women, and it would take them months to travel here, so Christmas it would have to be."

Finally glaring at him, she rose from her chair. "I think I'll find Lydia. She's much more reasonable. And I want to meet my grandson, *immediately.*"

Carrying her short self like the grand dame she should be, Lady Agnes stalked out, leaving Max to muse over the managing madness of women as he chewed his bacon.

LYDIA HAD BEEN EXPECTING MAX WHEN HIS MOTHER FLEW THROUGH HER office doorway instead, a vision of bouncing gray curls and bobbing earrings. Lydia touched the brooch she'd fixed to her new scarf in an attempt to look vaguely aristocratic—an armor she needed after last night.

Max's kiss. . . She'd spent the night dreaming of his male scent, hard body, questing lips, wandering hands. . . and where they might have led. She'd woke up practically feverish with need.

But he'd shoved her away as if she were the enemy. She was quite certain he had been the one to initiate that kiss. . . But she'd obviously been too bold, like the women he despised. She'd been in way over her head and had done things. . . Her cheeks heated as she remembered caressing muscled buttocks. What had she been thinking? She hadn't.

She had to treat him as nothing more than another guest or he'd flee into the night.

Lady Agnes blew all those concerns straight out of Lydia's mind.

"I would like to see my grandson, please. I understand why you had to keep Max's confidence, but now that he has revealed all, I won't wait another minute." She dropped a bundle of papers on the desk. "And here are the guest lists for both our families. Cross out those you don't wish invited. I suppose you must consult with Max over his list since he refuses to read it. And yes, I now know he can't read. Why on earth the boy—"

"He's not a boy, my lady. He's a grown man, a successful, wealthy one. The fact that he has done that with his disability shows what an amazing son you have." Lydia stood and pulled the bell. "I'll have one of the servants bring Bakari down when his lessons are done."

"Bakari!" Lady Agnes settled in a chair and held a hand to her plump bosom. "Oh, I had not thought. . . Max's children are foreign! Oh, my, this is rather exciting, isn't it?"

Lydia bit back a grin. One never quite knew what road the lady's mind would take. "Certainly interesting, one must admit. Is the other one Italian? Chinese? African? Do we dare ask? But for now, I must finish these letters so they can go into the village. Do you have enough to entertain yourself for a while?"

"Oh, yes, of course—the Malcolm Librarian is as busy as a duke. I shouldn't intrude—"

"I've not proved myself to be the librarian," Lydia said very, very gently.

"Well, of course you are! The testers will prove that when they arrive. I'll be in the guest parlor, writing all this news in my journal, if you'll have the boy sent to me. Thank you so much!" She rose, patted Lydia's cheek, and pattered out again.

Lydia gulped. The testers? Mr. C's journals had mentioned being tested. . .

She would fail. She'd never be more than an assistant. But until then, someone had to run the castle. She would have to keep up the pretense to hold off the trustees and Crawley until the real librarian was found.

Passing on the order about Bakari to the footman, Lydia was just adding the finishing flourish to Max's letters when he strolled in. She flushed and pretended to continue writing until she'd calmed herself.

He looked like a hero just stepped out of a novel, a white knight without his steed. His broad shoulders strained at his tweed jacket, and she wished he wore hunting breeches so she could see more of his sturdy legs than the loose trousers revealed. He exuded so much *confidence*. . .

She could use that confidence right now. Hoping she didn't look too dewy-eyed, she set down her pen and pushed the letters across the desk.

"I used our best stationery with the gold borders so it appears businesslike. I'm wondering if I should order mourning paper for my own correspondence, but I hate the extra expense. Shall I read these to you before you sign them?" She was dithering. She shut up.

Undisturbed by her chatter, Max scrawled his signature across the bottom as she explained what each letter was. "I'd rather you straighten out my mixed-up head," he said as he wrote. "I want to apologize for last night, but I'm truly not sorry. I treated you abominably, but dare I think you didn't completely dislike what we did?"

Well, that was frank. Terrified she'd say the wrong thing, Lydia waved the paper to dry the ink and cool her cheeks. She began folding the sheets and placing them in the matching envelopes she'd already addressed before speaking. "I'm not sure how to answer that," she admitted. "I'm not accustomed to speaking of such things."

She'd behaved like a wanton, and he'd run away. But he hadn't minded? It didn't sound as if he had.

"Give it up, Lydia." He pushed the rest of the signed letters across to her. "You've been reading our journals for years. I'm fairly certain our ancestors were more than blunt upon occasion. We're human. Humans lust. And yes, I know I shouldn't speak of such things with ladies, but I'm an uncivilized cad and my time here is likely to be short. Do you find me repulsive or attractive?"

She set her jaw and continued the task of stuffing envelopes. She pushed Mr. C's red sealing wax across the desk for Max to use. "You know perfectly well that you are attractive to women. I am no exception, other than that I do not fling myself at you." She didn't think she had, at least.

He pressed his signet ring into the wax he'd affixed to the envelopes. "You are a genteel woman of refinement, mature enough to resist your urges, I surmise. Whereas I'm a heathen inclined to indulge my urges whenever opportunity offers. I've been learning to resist, but I usually end up fleeing the premises. I've not had to do that here because you offer me no encouragement, making it easier to stand firm. Sometimes. Last night was not one of them."

Aware of the fantasy-wedding guest lists under her elbow, Lydia regarded him warily. "Where are you going with this?"

"I'm not sure." He reached for the bell pull when he finished sealing the envelopes. "I'm actually wondering if we should heed my mother's prescience or madness or whatever it is. Or at least talk about it."

Beryl arrived, bobbing a curtsy and stealing sly glances at Max. He stepped behind the open door to put a barrier between them and let Lydia hand over the envelopes. Beryl pouted and tried to catch a glimpse behind the door, but Lydia pointed her out. With a sigh, the maid sashayed off.

Max closed the door, and Lydia stirred nervously under the intensity of his stare.

"Heed her prescience?" she asked weakly.

He took a seat in the worn leather chair by the unlit fire and crossed his ankle over his knee, drawing her awareness. She was no lady for noticing his muscular thighs.

"If Mother really does see the future and sees us married, maybe we should consider it now and not later. Even I know prescience can be affected by time and circumstances."

Lydia had to drag her gaze back to Max's broad, honest face before she could register his meaning. Her mouth fell open but nothing emerged. Clutching her pen, she tried to formulate a reply, but he'd left her spinning. "Married?"

"I know it's sudden, but it does make a certain amount of sense," he said, with an uncomfortable shrug. "We're attracted to each other. We rub along reasonably well. You are a woman who can take care of herself, so you won't mind when I disappear for extended periods of time. Unfortunately, I fear the only thing I can bring to the partnership is my ability to repair what's broken, but given the size and age of this place, that's not an inconsiderable factor. And I can hope. . ." He finally looked uncomfortable. "I can hope that we'll develop a bond similar to other married couples that will make me less attractive to stray females?"

Despite a disconcerting lack of romance in this proposal, Lydia almost smiled. She shouldn't be disappointed that practical Max thought in terms of partnerships and *bonds* instead of love. It was easier for her to respond honestly if he was being practical. "I thought animal magnetism meant the bonded *female* did not stray, not the male. I'm fairly certain *I'm* unlikely to stray. You are the one who becomes unsuitably involved."

He scratched at his recently-shaven cheek. "Well, as we seem to have some kind of reverse polarity that I was hoping would reverse the bonding situation. Since I am violently attracted to you, perhaps bonding would make me less attracted to any other female?"

He was violently attracted to *her*? Lydia had to settle her nerves and fluttering butterflies all over again. The most handsome, attractive, intelligent, available male she'd ever met in her life—and he was attracted to a plain spinster like her? How could that be?

"I don't think reverse polarity is working yet," she said wryly, having observed Beryl's behavior. "And I can't imagine you'll spend much time repairing this place if you're away in jungles. And I suspect you're simply flattering me in hopes I might offer a place to send your sons when they're out of school."

He rolled his eyes heavenward, sat up properly, then leaned forward. "I am an *Ives*. You should know by now that I need only ask one of a dozen titled wealthy cousins to add a cuckoo to his nest, and he will simply throw them in with the rest of the crowd. That's what I'd originally intended to do with Bakari. As you have so kindly pointed out, we propagate. We provide for what we propagate. I would expect to do the same for any of my nephews or cousins if circumstances were different."

He slumped again, but his gaze remained fixed on her. "In the spirit of honesty, the faithfulness factor and roaming jungles are valid concerns."

Lydia swallowed hard under the intensity of his gaze. "I am only the librarian under false circumstances, in order to keep the castle operating. If someone who can actually hear the books arrives, I will have to turn over the task to them. They might want a different assistant, leaving me homeless. I am not necessarily the independent woman you require."

"You *are* the librarian," he insisted. "I saw you find those books I wanted. They were exactly what I needed to determine the problem."

Flattery, she thought. But she yearned for him to be right.

Max continued. "But should you go blind, deaf, and dumb tomorrow, I can still provide a home for you. You need only ask."

"You are serious?" she asked, finally realizing it. "You would marry me because your mother thinks it's destined?"

"I'll marry you because I want you in my bed," he admitted with a laugh, his brown eyes dancing. "All the rest is speculation and wishful thinking. Except for the part where I find you attractive, intelligent, and a good companion, that counts as much as lust, I suppose. But I do understand you hold faithfulness dear, and I've never been faithful to anyone for a day in my life."

"I. . . I don't know what to say." She pushed a stubborn curl behind her ear. "Of course, I'm interested, never think I'm not. You are a fascinating man. I'm just. . ."

"Cautious, unlike me, I understand. And while you have a sterling reputation, I do not, I understand that too. And someday, you might find a man willing to stay in one place. But I hope. . . I think. . . you understand me as well. That you know I'm sincere, and I would not ask you if I didn't think I could make you happy. Somewhat happy, maybe. I'll try to be what you need."

Did she need a husband? Did she want a man who would never be around when she needed him? Apparently, this wasn't about *need*. It was about desire. She'd never felt desire and probably would never find another man she desired more. A pit grew in her midsection. "I'll take time to think on it," she whispered.

"I'd love to give you all the time you require, but I fear my mother is a force of nature. Perhaps I should take residence under the tower until she gives up and goes home." His smile was rueful.

"We can hold a reception and invite her guests without a wedding," she reminded him. "There is no reason to make such a drastic decision in a few weeks."

"We just have to keep our hands off each other," he said cheerfully, standing up. "The tower it is, then."

He walked off, leaving Lydia disturbed in so many ways that she couldn't count them all.

SEVENTEEN

MAX WISHED FOR THE COMPANY OF SOME OF HIS SENSIBLE ENGINEERING friends so he could ask if he was losing his mind or if he was just desperate. *Marriage*? He was actually considering marriage? Why on earth would he do that? He was the most unsuitable person on the entire planet for committing to one woman and one place.

But he wanted Lydia, and he wasn't so mad as to expect he could have her without vows. And maybe, just a little, he'd like to know he had a home he could visit occasionally without being bombarded by tears and accusations. His few days here had been among the most restful of his peripatetic career, despite the tilting tower, which was an interesting engineering challenge and not emotional quicksand. Lydia appeared to accept him as he was, and he could avoid civilization all he liked merely by locking the tower door.

That didn't mean she wouldn't change once she wore his ring and babies arrived, he reminded himself. Nesting women were an unreasonable lot, as he well knew.

Brooding, he climbed up to his chamber to change into his grubby work clothes. Bakari met him with excitement.

"My grandmother is here?" the boy asked, nearly bouncing. "May I meet her? I've never had a grandmother. She says she wants to meet me. Is she nice?"

Well, hell, that was to be expected. He'd never accomplish anything at this rate. "You've always had a grandmother. You just haven't met her. She's nice, which is why she wants to meet you. Just remember grandmothers are women, and they weep over silly things and get funny notions in their heads. Be polite and respectful, and you'll be fine."

Bakari nodded uncertainly. "Will you take me to her?"

"Have you finished the reading I gave you?" Max asked, trying to play the part of stern father.

Bakari nodded. "Those were easy words. Mr. Lloyd says there is a library. May I look for other books?"

His six-year-old son could read, probably better than Max. Max tried not to be too grumpy about that. This responsibility business was hard. "We'll ask Miss Lydia, shall we? Let's go down and meet your grandmother."

One more encounter with his mother, and he really might go quite mad. Then he'd probably elope with Lydia to places unknown. Pondering whether madness was infectious, Max took his son's hand and traipsed back downstairs again.

Despite the summer sun outside, the castle was chilly. His mother was comfortably ensconced in a padded chair near a small fire, her feet up on an embroidered stool, her shawls wrapped around her. She almost looked frail and elderly, until she glanced up and her blue eyes sparked with excitement. "Oh, my, aren't you a handsome one? You have your father's curls!"

A knot of tension relaxed inside him as Max made the introductions. He hadn't thought his mother would be given to bigotry, but he didn't know her well.

"Did you know you have a big brother?" his mother asked as she wooed Bakari into her snare. "I am hoping he will visit us here in a day or two."

His son's eyes widened in wonder. Max winced.

"We don't know that Richard will come," he reminded her. "Why don't I ask Lydia if she has books Bakari might read while you two become acquainted?"

His mother waved regally. "There is an entire nursery full of books and things on the third floor. I'm surprised you do not keep him there. You do have a tutor for him, do you not?"

"This isn't a permanent situation, Mother. Bakari needs to be in school. I'd rather he was near me until then." And he wasn't about to move into the main portion of the house where chambermaids roamed.

Although given the condition of the tower's foundation, he should probably consider it.

"Well, you'll be working here for a while, won't you?" his mother demanded, sounding quite normal and not demented for a change. "I'll just take Bakari up to the nursery and let him explore."

The boy looked at him eagerly. His son had to be bored out of his over-active mind. Max gave in. "Fine then, although perhaps you should ask Miss Lydia first."

Watching his mother and his son walk away, hand in hand, as he must once have at that age, Max suffered a prescient vision of his own. There walked the family he never thought to have—and might have with Lydia, if she didn't kill him first.

Of course, if he didn't fix the tower, there would be no library and Lydia would despise him.

HEARING A CARRIAGE ON THE DRIVE, LYDIA ALMOST JUMPED UP WITH expectation, thinking they might have visitors from the city. But then she remembered it was too early, and she pressed her lips together in a grimace. Only one local man would arrive with carriage and team.

She would like to refuse him, but she wasn't comfortable with Mr. Cadwallader's level of rudeness. Besides, she liked knowing what the enemy was plotting.

Zack eventually arrived bearing a card on a salver. "Lord Crowley to see you, miss."

"Take him to the formal drawing room. Offer tea. I'll be with him when I have time." That seemed officious enough. And the two-story great hall was uncomfortably chilly and gloomy.

Of course, putting off the inevitable left her squirming in her chair. She thought she'd made herself clear the last time he was here, and again, at the solicitor's office. The library would never be for sale. Why would anyone else want this rambling old fortress?

After she decided he'd cooled his heels enough, Lydia did her best to don her Malcolm Librarian/duchess persona. She checked her hairpins, straightened her scarf, raised her chin high, and marched off to the medieval hall that served as the castle's main drawing room.

Crowley had abandoned his tea and was prowling the ancient armament adorning the walls. He glanced up at Lydia's entrance, then returned to studying a broadsword.

"These need oiling," he complained. "They'll rust."

"And good morning to you, my lord." She imagined herself as a stout gray-haired duchess filled with consequence. "I know you don't understand, but I am a busy woman. I don't have time for social calls."

He scowled. "Women haven't the mind for business. That's why it takes you so much time to complete it. You should marry and have babies and let men who understand finance handle money. I made a perfectly good offer for this property. Even your solicitors agreed it was fair. You cannot maintain a property this size on your own, Miss Wystan. How do I convince you to let me take it off your hands?"

"I have been maintaining this property for years, my lord." She quelled her righteous ire at his insult. "You surely didn't think Mr. Cadwallader had time? It is quite impossible to sell—"

The floor rumbled. A loud ominous crack shuddered the rafters. Plaster dribbled from the overhead beams. Or perhaps it was just dust.

Trying not to panic, Lydia nodded curtly at her visitor. "I'm sorry, my lord. The answer is no, now and forever. Good day."

She departed sedately, as if rumbling floors were perfectly normal. She didn't run until she was in the corridor leading to the tower. A few more ominous rumbles followed. A crack zigzagged down the wall by the garden door.

Where was Max? Bakari? The servants? She ran outside, expecting the tower to tilt and collapse at any moment.

No one was in the yard. Did no one hear the crack but her? Had anxiety driven her mad?

She circled the outside of the tower until she reached the open door into the ancient byre.

Muddy and rumpled, Max leaned on a filthy shovel as if he hadn't a care in the world, talking with the stable lad.

"What did you do?" she cried as she approached. "I thought the roof was caving in."

Max straightened and the boy ran off, apparently on some errand. "Sorry. I hadn't realized it would affect the hall."

Lydia stopped to catch her breath and force her heart not to leap from her chest. "What did you *do?*" she repeated.

"Knocked a hole in the wall into the inner tower. Your plumbing isn't just medieval, I think it's prehistoric."

"Prehistoric?" She could scarcely breathe for imagining the walls tumbling around her.

"I suppose the Romans aren't pre-history. What are they called?" He pointed at an outcropping in the tower wall. "The original garderobes aren't connected to a moat or stream but to a complex system of pipes and vaults that empty out in a drain field down the hill, providing natural fertilizer for the crops that must have once grown there. But as best as I am able to tell, that system was built with the original inner tower or *before* it. I'm not a historian, but my guess would be it was originally Roman."

"*Not* prehistoric, but Dark Ages, certainly," she murmured, trying to puzzle it out to prevent quivering in terror. "I know the Romans fortified this area back in the first and second centuries. We're on one of the highest hills, so it's possible there was a fortification here, but it should have been little more than a mud hut. Until now, the tower hasn't tilted or shook. You aren't working with Baron Crowley so I will be forced to sell, are you?"

"Why would I do that?" he narrowed his eyes at her change of topic. "Who is Crowley and why does he want you to sell your library?"

"He's a neighbor. I think he owns mines and wants the land. The walls aren't coming down? We're safe?"

"Mines?" He frowned up at the sky as if looking for answers there, nodded, then studied the tower. "New mines might explain why the old system is failing. I'll need to order a few loads of brick. Will the trust be able to pay for them? My liquid funds are mostly frozen. I can pay for my minor expenses but repairs of this size require a large outlay."

She ought to shake him. She really should. Her *life*, was under that roof, and he talked about *bricks*?

"What on earth will you do with bricks? Look at this place." Lydia gestured at the towering stone walls in exasperation. "Every inch is stone."

"Except for the wood bits," he replied with a grin that proved he really did not understand her panic. "Bricks are faster, cheaper, and it's easier to find workmen who know how to build with them. They will be underground, so no one will notice."

"*What* will be underground?" She clasped her elbows, trying not to tremble. The man was impossible! He stood there in all his Ives strength and glory, as solid as a mountain, fully confident he could produce miracles—literally out of clay—not giving one thought to what would happen should he be wrong.

"Your improved sewage system. It won't be an easy task, mind you. It won't be cheap either. But if you want to keep your tower and use your plumbing, it has to be done."

Stricken, she could only stare. No plumbing?

"You *can* afford it, can't you?" he asked again. "I come free but labor doesn't."

"How much?" she asked worriedly. "So far, I've only been given a budget for regular maintenance, and that's been neglected for a year. The roof is starting to leak. . ."

Is this what Crowley meant when he said women had no head for business? Should she have been planning for major repairs?

Max watched her sympathetically. "These old places need a lot of cash. I can do this cheaply as any man in the kingdom, but I'm not a magician."

"*All* the plumbing?" she asked in desperation. "Perhaps if we just closed the tower bath. . ."

He shook his head. "If it was the well, yes, but that's elsewhere. The sewage all goes through one ancient tunnel, and it's in a state of collapse. Mr. Crowley's mines might be responsible, but those vaults are old enough to be Roman."

The library might sit on a nearly two-thousand-year-old foundation, right. Her knees quaked, and she thought she ought to sit down. But

Max looked like Atlas, admiring the world he was about to take on. The dratted man enjoyed this!

"Should I be thinking about moving the books to the main portion of the house?" she asked, trying not to sound weak and terrified.

He looked startled. "What? No, of course not. The Romans built to last. You couldn't find a stronger foundation anywhere. It was the tinkering with the plumbing and possibly Crowley's miners using dynamite that interfered with the original workmanship. You only need worry about raising the funds to pay for the repairs."

She swayed, possibly with relief—or terror. "If you could provide an estimate?"

Crowley's carriage raced down the winding drive in the distance. He'd been right. She didn't know how to run a business.

She must learn.

"I'll see what I can do once I know the price of supplies." Max watched her with what might almost be admiration. "Most women would have fallen into my arms, weeping, after I gave them bad news."

Lydia smiled weakly. "Most women have more gowns than I do. Falling into filthy arms is not a direction I can afford."

Max laughed, flashing white teeth.

She could have a man like that for husband? What was she waiting for? A god?

To maintain her equilibrium, she added, "If we married, would that make you responsible for repairs?"

And then she strolled away as if her knees weren't weak as water and her spine a column of jelly.

MAX SHRUGGED INTO HIS DINNER COAT LATER THAT EVENING, STILL pondering Lydia's question. He didn't much fret over the part about being responsible for this money pit. He was fairly certain the library's trust would pay for that, and the vast array of wealthy Malcolms would donate to the cause. If he had his hands on his own funds, he could donate as well.

The part tripping him was the "If we married. . ."

Was she really considering marrying a roaming heathen like him? Madness definitely must be infectious.

Nervous energy had him jerking at his cravat and attempting to look the part of gentleman. Bakari watched him with interest. Lloyd finally gave in and took the tie from Max's hands, swiftly wrapping it into a neat knot.

"Are we expecting the queen?" Lloyd asked with pointed sarcasm. "For Miss Lydia will not notice if you wore frogs at your throat."

"I'm pretty sure she'd notice frogs." Max stepped away from the mirror. "But knots, probably not, you're right." He just felt as if he were strangling. He couldn't say that aloud.

He should have taken the coward's way out and eaten in his room with Bakari and Lloyd. He'd be far more comfortable there. But he couldn't leave Lydia to his mother. And he needed to know if Lydia had made any decisions about his rather badly done proposal.

He'd proposed. He'd actually proposed to a woman. He wasn't quite over the shock. Did other men feel this unmitigated terror at a lifetime commitment?

Should he go into the city and buy a ring and try properly on bended knee?

How badly did he want Lydia to say yes?

As he took the tower steps down, Max attempted to analyze all possible answers to that daunting question. By the time he reached the dining room, he'd decided all the advantages were his in this match. He was pretty damned certain he was hoping for a *yes*.

He just wasn't expecting one. After a lifetime of humiliation, he supposed he could withstand one more rejection. He was made of sturdy stuff these days.

He had a niggling notion that now that he knew what he wanted, he wouldn't walk away without trying again. And again. That's when he knew he was doomed.

He tugged at his cravat once more before he entered. He'd let his dotty *mother* send him down this impossible path. That proved he needed to clear his head and escape.

He entered to discover Lydia and his mother already at the table. Well, he was late, as usual. That was to be expected.

What wasn't to be expected was a guest—a male one who looked a great deal like his own image in a mirror, only a lot skinnier and younger.

"Richard?" he asked, not because he didn't know the answer but just to confirm he could still speak.

The lad was studying Max equally avidly. He nodded and with a great deal of effort replied, "Do I call you Father or Mr. Ives?"

EIGHTEEN

Watching Max pacing the length of the small parlor later that evening, Lydia wondered if one might harness his energy and put it to good use. He could probably illuminate the entire castle.

They'd let Richard choose a room for himself, and he'd instinctively taken one in the section of the house designed for male guests. It was a very small section, proving this had always been a Malcolm stronghold.

"His mother was twenty when we met," Max was trying to explain. "Married to a man who wasn't interested in women, if you know what I mean."

Lydia had read a great deal of personal information these past years. She also had some memory of a gentleman in her family's village for which such a thing was said. She didn't completely comprehend, but she nodded so as not to interrupt Max's thoughts.

He ran his hand through already rumpled curls. "I didn't understand at the time. I only learned it later when she told me she was carrying my child. I thought she was experienced and understood these matters. I was eighteen and knew nothing at all. I thought her husband would kill me. Instead, a child gave his marriage legitimacy. He was willing to support Richard if I set aside funds for his future."

"But you left the instant Richard was born, so you'd not be tempted again?" Lydia wasn't entirely sure how to handle this conversation, except as commentary for his journal. Was he saying he wouldn't produce any more illegitimate children, that he had more experience now? Except he had two more *mistakes* to his name.

"The marriage wouldn't look legitimate if Susan continued to fall into my bed," he said dryly. "Any time we saw each other. . . Edinburgh is much smaller than you realize, and I hadn't learned how to say *no* to a beautiful woman. And this wretched magnetism assured that she wasn't the only one latching on to me. I was too green to finesse the ugly scenes. I had to leave. I'm not sure Richard understands that, and there is no way I can explain it to him."

"He'll believe whatever his mother told him anyway. It's interesting that once her husband died, she told her son the truth. There doesn't seem to be any resentment that I can see. He is a very fine, level-headed lad." Lydia jotted notes, but she was more fascinated by the man than her work.

"Susan and her husband were both blond and small. Richard is dark and tall, like an Ives." Max shrugged. "I'm sure he had questions. He might never have asked them if Susan hadn't gone to my mother and demanded support after her husband died."

Lydia smiled at that. "Your mother would not have taken that news lightly. Did you hear the thunder on the other side of the world?"

"When the letters caught up with me, they filled a mail bag," he admitted with a laugh. "I'm rather amazed that she has not removed my head for not telling her about the others."

"She has been living on the dream of one son who never comes home. To have three grandsons she might coddle. . . She will collect them all, one way or another. It's an interesting way for her to visit the world through their eyes."

"You are not any more upset than my mother." He stopped in front of the table where she took notes of this conversation.

"Had I been married to you, I would have cut your throat," she said wryly. "I'm a vicar's daughter. I believe in vows and faithfulness and all that. Have you ever heard the Malcolm marriage vow? *I vow to love, honor, and take thee in equality for so long as we both shall live. . .* ? Equality means the wife doesn't have to put up with a straying husband."

But he would stray once he left here, she knew. It was inevitable. She had to think straight and not let his masculine proximity undermine her resolve.

Max placed his hands on the desk and leaned forward until their noses nearly touched, and her pulse escalated. His was a rather large and manly nose.

"*Equality* is a concept I understand better than *love* and *honor*. My father may have been a brilliant investor and my mother a dotty socialite, but he listened to her and used what he learned from her to make us all richer. That's what a partnership is about—respecting and understanding each other's differences. That only happens if both partners are equal."

Considering she fraudulently held her position, Lydia didn't feel very equal. And Max was the educated grandson of an *earl*, while her education and origins were much humbler.

"I have no problem with equality," he continued, dismissing her fear as if he truly believed they were matched. "If only I could control the behavior of others. . ."

"And control your *own* behavior," Lydia reminded him forcefully, leaning forward until their noses did touch. "It takes *two* to make a child."

He tilted his head and kissed her.

She could no more resist his kiss than he apparently could resist the women who fell into his bed. She caught his rough cheeks between her hands and kissed him back.

Shoving aside all her neatly stacked papers, Max sat on the table. Accepting her invitation, he threaded his fingers through her hair and plunged his tongue inside her mouth.

He'd taught her this heated exchange last night. Hot lava flowed through her blood. Unbalanced, Lydia grasped his shoulders—his muscled, steady shoulders that held her as if she were a wisp of nothing.

Max swung his legs over to her side of the table and yanked her fully against him, until she inhaled earth and shaving soap and masculine musk and nearly swooned in his arms. She ran her hands under his coat and pushed up his waistcoat so she could feel the ripple of muscle in the same way he touched her. She gasped when he reached her breast, but her corset was impervious. She wanted out of it, right now.

"I have this overpowering urge to make a child with you," he whispered against her mouth. "A daughter this time, one like you, with sunset hair and a laughing smile and caring nature. Marry me, Lydia. I will do everything in my power to be faithful."

He might believe that now. . .

But what she didn't know wouldn't kill her. Instead, she had every certainty that she might die if she never knew what it was like to share this man's bed.

"You will make your mother a very happy woman," she whispered, refusing to give him power over her. She had to go into this the same way he did—logical, practical, *lustful*, but not in the least bit romantic. She would *not* swoon at his feet like the others.

Max carried his kisses down her throat. "I am likely to make you a very unhappy woman. You stand forewarned."

Fear churned in her stomach. His honesty in this allowed her to be very clear that this was not a true marriage, in any sense of the word she knew. But she'd been destined to lead a lonely life anyway. Why not enjoy this brief affair while it lasted?

"I am likely to haunt you around the world to force you to accept your responsibilities," she warned, in all fairness.

Carrying his kisses as far as they could go, he began untangling the ribbons and buttons she hid behind. "If haunting is the price I must pay, it's worth it. Believe me when I say I have never felt like this, I have never attempted to seduce a woman, and I most certainly never ever proposed marriage. *You* are driving me mad, not my mother. Say yes, Lydia, and do us both a favor."

She wanted to say *Prove lovemaking is worth marriage,* but that was no different than falling into his bed like every other woman. Did she have the strength to resist. . . ?

He lifted her to the table and ran his hand under her skirt. Heat flooded her senses when he found the flesh at the top of her garter and beneath the lace edge of her drawers. He untied the ribbons and pulled down her stocking so his bare hand stroked bare skin while he kissed her.

Lydia nearly slid off.

"Say yes, Lydia. Say yes and make us both miserable." His big, callused hand slid up her thigh as far as her drawers would allow.

"Yes, please," she murmured, not entirely certain which question she answered, his proposal of misery or his seduction.

"For this one night, I will make you the happiest of women," he crowed.

Before she had any idea what he was about, he lifted her and carried her out of the parlor, straight to the guest bedchamber she had taken for her own. Carried. *Her.* As if she were no more than a child. For that alone, she'd forgive him almost anything. Breathless, she clung to his neck and tried to protest, but he simply kissed her senseless.

Max laid her against the turned-down covers, continuing with kisses in places no man should touch. He was so *close*. . . She inhaled him with the air she breathed, felt his weight more strongly than the bed beneath her.

Only when he stepped back to shed his coat did Lydia dare exhale, and then the vision of raw Max emerging from his civilized clothing swept her breath away again. He cast his waistcoat to join his coat. In shirt sleeves, his cravat untied to reveal the brown bare throat beneath, the linen barely concealing his muscled torso, Max was the image of every Greek god she'd ever imagined.

"What are you doing?" she whispered, insensibly, because she could *see* what he was doing.

"I have found inexperienced ladies are too slow to figure out a man's fastenings." He tugged his shirt from the band of his trousers. "And I want your hands on me sooner rather than later."

"*My* hands. . . ?" But now that he said it, that was precisely what she wanted—her hands on him and vice versa. How very odd. She'd never noticed a craving to touch bare flesh before.

He kneeled over her, his bare torso above her, his knees pressing down the mattress on either side. With deft expertise, he began unfastening her bodice. "All ladies should wear their buttons in front. As a husband, am I allowed to decree that?"

Shattered by a vast expanse of bronzed male chest and. . . broad brown nipples, Lydia could only respond in kind. "I have no maid to help me dress. Do husbands do that?"

He untied the ribbons of her corset cover and unknotted her front-tying corset. "This husband would dispense with whalebone entirely, if given a choice. The other pretty lacy things can be enticing. And perhaps gowns I can tug off your shoulders need not fasten in front." He leaned over and ran kisses over the naked flesh he'd exposed.

Her plain linen shift still covered her breasts, but she could feel the heat of his mouth clear to her soul. And other more physical places. In fact, places she had never thought about began to ache and pulse. If he only came home once a year to do this. . .

His tongue sampled the tip of her breast, wetting the thin cloth. Lydia surrendered any pretense of thought and simply fought swooning from sensation. She ran her hands over his chest, touched his nipples as he did hers, and longed for his lips again. To that end, she slid her hands around his neck and tugged his mouth back to hers.

He obliged, plunging his tongue between her teeth with a demand that echoed lower cravings. Lydia pushed aside her vague knowledge of what happened between a man and a woman and surrendered to desire.

Somehow, his rough hands—those hands that worked so well on worldly problems—removed her bodice, tugging it from her shoulders and arms, allowing her corset to fall open. Her breasts spilled wantonly into those large palms. She shuddered with need as he played her like a fine instrument, dispensing with her final frail garment.

Rolling over, Max placed her astride of him. Lydia gasped and tried to hide her nakedness with her arm. He laughed and pushed her skirt and petticoat past her hips. "You are Juno, goddess of marriage and childbirth, queen of all. Do not conceal your beauty, my goddess. Cast your spell on me."

He half sat to suckle at her now bare breasts. Lydia clung to his hard shoulders, aware of strong thighs beneath her bottom, and of a pressure. . .

Goddess of childbirth. . . He wanted babies. And babies came from that place that ached with need.

He had her skirts off and her under him again, with only her drawers as protection.

• • •

MAX THOROUGHLY ENJOYED LYDIA'S STARTLED, EXCITED RESPONSES. HE didn't feel in the least pressured into this act. He was the one eagerly tearing off her clothes, not the other way around. Admittedly, he'd done his fair share of clothes-tearing in the past, but only out of jaded experience, because it had been expected. He'd never enjoyed this heightened degree of lust for one woman, a woman who evidently enjoyed what he was doing and did her inexpert best to offer him the same pleasures. Lydia filled his vision, his thoughts, and his hands. His desire to claim her extinguished all other considerations. He rubbed his erection against her drawers, increasing the pressure, and her feminine moan was sweet music to his ears.

She wasn't delicate, so he didn't need to feel like a rutting bull on top of her. Still, once he'd wrestled her down to her drawers, he slid to one side so his weight wasn't too suffocating. Her sighs as he lapped at her extended—rosy pink—nipples engorged him to the extent that he had to undo his trousers. He retained enough sense to know he should go slow with a virgin, but he could smell her desire, feel her moisture as he rubbed between her thighs. Everything male in him reacted when her hips rose into his questing hands. He slid a finger inside to calm her while he continued their head-spinning kisses.

She went still at the invasion, but he'd learned a thing or three about the female body over the years. He tickled the nub of her sex, inserted another finger, and she was writhing with willingness in seconds. With gratitude that this desirable woman wanted this as much as he did, Max slid down her drawers.

She dug her fingers into his shoulders and kissed him fiercely. He gloried in her physical response. His Juno was no shrinking violet, but a woman with needs as strong as his own. Reassured, he shoved off his trousers. He wasn't wearing drawers.

Kissing, stroking, he parted her beautiful thighs, answering another of his questions—her moist hair was a darker red in this place untouched by sunshine.

"I vow to take thee in love, honor, and equality." He murmured the wedding vows as he positioned himself.

"Love?" she murmured weakly, before crying out as he pushed his cock into her narrow passage.

He'd said *love*. He'd never said that before. It was probably just his lust speaking.

Beyond words now, Max drank of Lydia's strawberry-scented lips, stroked her incredible breasts, and ripped past the barrier of her maidenhood. She was his now, now and forever.

The realization momentarily scared him, but his animal body didn't care. He drove deeper.

She bit his shoulder as he drove her to the heights of ecstasy, moaning and writhing. She was already on the brink of release. He need only. . . touch her. Her climax fed his, and he lost his mind to bliss.

Later, when he regained consciousness, Max held her shuddering and weeping into his shoulder and contemplated the enormity of this commitment.

He would not see Burma anytime soon. He had to fix a tower, win back his father's estate, and if he planted a child in these next few weeks, he'd have to linger to see it born. After that. . .

Lydia might be glad to see the back of him.

NINETEEN

LYDIA WOKE WITH THE DAWN, AS ALWAYS. A MAN'S NAKED BODY LAY sprawled half on top of her, his weight crushing her into the mattress.

Max. She rather enjoyed the intimacy of male flesh on hers.

Will she, nil she, she was married. Well, she hadn't repeated the vows, but she'd behaved as if she had, and now a child might come of it. So, yes, she was very married in her own mind. She'd chosen this uncivilized heathen as her mate for life. . .

Because his mother had said they were fated. That part didn't make a great deal of sense, but the physical part. . . Yes, that made good sense. She'd never felt better. Well, she was sore, but she was curious and interested in exploring more. Her breasts seemed to swell with the need to be touched. She thought the manly part stiffening against her thigh might indicate Max was interested as well.

The tower rumbled as if it had just awakened too.

Max grumbled into her shoulder, kissed her cheek, and pried himself out of the pillow. "Thunder?"

Lydia gestured at the window. "No clouds. The tower."

"Cripes." He nibbled her shoulder and caressed her hair over her breast. "You are my sunshine, but I fear the tower is my mistress for now. I'm ordering the bricks. We'll figure out how to pay for them later."

"Such a romantic," she whispered, daring to caress his broad chest. How extremely odd that she felt comfortable doing this, as if he'd always been in her bed. Is that what his mother had seen? That their souls were somehow connected? Or their bodies, anyway.

"I've never had to romance a woman, just swive them." He leered down at her, rolling over her so his swelling sword pushed at the sore place between her legs. "And as much as I would like to repeat last night, I will respect your ravaged virtue. Will you allow me to come to your bed again tonight?"

"Could I stop you?" she asked with interest, lifting her hips to indicate a little soreness might be healed easily.

"No," he answered succinctly, accepting her invitation.

Lydia closed her eyes and succumbed to the bliss of his powerful thrusts. He was a big man and filled her in ways she had never dreamed. She bit back her screams as he plunged deeper than he had the night before, igniting an explosion that rattled her more thoroughly than the trembling tower.

His muscled arms strained on either side of her head as he spilled deep inside her, shuddering with the power of his release. They both muffled their cries. They would need to move to the tower tonight, and send Lloyd and Bakari elsewhere. She wanted the freedom to explore this new adventure without condemnation from anyone overhearing them.

"Magical," he grunted, collapsing on top of her. "I should have sought a Malcolm sooner. I will never want another woman again."

"That doesn't necessarily mean other women won't want *you*," she warned. But his words warmed her as much as his body did, even if she knew this wasn't a promise, just a wish.

The shuddering tower shook them awake again. This time, Max sprang out of bed, yanking on his trousers and shirt and hastily buttoning. "I'd better shore up that wall until the bricks arrive. I'd hoped to explore the underground foundation more."

"Do I need to find out if it was built on the bones of saints or dragons?" Lydia asked sleepily, admiring muscled buttocks and lamenting when he covered them. She had never known she was a wanton.

"I doubt you'll find thousand-year-old journals to tell you. But you might want to peek at the oldest books, just in case." He leaned over and pressed a kiss to her forehead. "I love you. I need to practice saying that."

"You need to practice *feeling* that," she said dryly, pulling the covers over her breasts. "I am told that lust and love are not the same."

"That is why I love you," he crowed. "You are a sensible woman."

He dashed out. She could hear him running up the stairs to his room. Lydia would like to hear him explain his state of undress to Lloyd.

She'd like to explain to herself why she had just agreed to share her life with a man who would forget her as soon as he sailed away.

She supposed, in a way, it made sense. While all was confusion and travail, she could pretend she was the Malcolm Librarian, and Max could pretend he was the marrying kind. For this moment in time, they could support each other's fantasies. She would treasure this bliss she had never expected to know when the time came to part.

She bathed in the guest bath, wondering if she was eroding the foundation as she did so. She dressed in her plainest gown, prepared to tackle her chores and not reveal her new status as fallen woman. Besides the chafing between her legs, she didn't feel fallen. She felt as if she glowed inside and the whole world would notice.

Richard was at the breakfast table alone when Lydia entered. That shook her a little. She'd have to learn to live with Max's *sons*. Plural. She'd never even had a brother.

"Good morning, sir. Shall I call you Master Richard or just Richard?" she asked as she filled her plate.

"My mother just calls me Dick," he said, somewhat diffidently. "But I prefer Richard. Lady Agnes says you are to be my stepmother."

Lydia refrained from rolling her eyes and declaring the lady an interfering witch. Everyone who knew Lady Agnes knew that anyway. "We will see about that, but if you prefer Richard, then Richard it shall be. Where is Lady Agnes this morning?"

"Writing letters. She writes lots of letters. She brought her own paper with her. It has gold cherubs in the corner. She used to send me letters when I was at school." Richard dug into his stacked plate of oatcakes and sausages.

"That was kind of her. I believe knowing she has a bright grandson like you has made her very happy." While Max had made her very unhappy. Lydia didn't see the need to mention that.

She carried her plate to the seat across from him. She had some understanding of why Mr. C had preferred eating in his tower. One never knew who would be at the table, and conversing with strangers was difficult. But this was Max's *son*. She was Max's wife, almost. She needed to remember how one behaved around family. It had been years since she'd seen hers.

The boy shrugged and lapsed into silence after his brief burst of speech.

"Have you met Bakari yet?" she asked, not knowing what webs Lady Agnes had been weaving.

Richard nodded. "He's not British."

"Your father is British. Bakari's mother is Egyptian, which is a nationality even older than ours. So Bakari is the best of two fascinating countries. Admittedly, that might make it difficult for him in school since some people are not as worldly as your father." Lydia tried to sound as if she were worldly too, but mostly, she read a lot.

Richard frowned a little as if he were considering this. "He's small. He'll be bullied."

"I'm afraid so. I am hoping we may find him a tutor until he's a little stronger. He must be very excited to have a big brother." My word, the responsibilities for this family kept growing. Would she be able to manage?

Especially if she got booted from the castle.

The boy nodded uncertainly. "I suppose. I wanted brothers, but he's pretty young. Are you really marrying my father?"

Lady Agnes shouldn't be raising the hopes of young boys on the basis of *prescience*. But after last night. . . she and Max were for all intents and purposes, married.

"It does appear so," Lydia admitted, not feeling as if the possibility were real quite yet. She'd only *met* the man. But she'd known him for years through his correspondence. She knew how Max's mind worked, even if she often disapproved of its workings. But now she had a tiny glimpse of why he was the way he was. "Will that matter to you since you've just met him?"

Richard shook his head. "I'm going to university. I don't need parents."

Lydia wanted to laugh at that. "You sound like your father. Whether you need us or not, we still walk this world and would appreciate being acknowledged upon occasion. Although I understand why you would consider me insignificant. Still, everyone needs a home. This one will always be open to you. I shall try to be helpful and not too parental."

He finished chewing his toast, then pushed aside his plate, obviously eager to be off. "Do you think I might see what my father is working on?"

"You have full run of the place, just as he has. But you might want to listen to his cautions. Some of the walls appear to be in a precarious state."

Richard flashed a slight grin just like his father's. "I believe I noticed. Thank you, ma'am." He ran off.

Well, this past week had certainly been eventful. Now, if only she could learn how to make the books speak to her. . . She'd ask for information on marriage.

UNDER THE TOWER, MAX HAMMERED A BOARD INTO PLACE TO ACT AS temporary brace. He'd just asked Lydia to marry him, and his mother was already notifying half the kingdom. He whacked the board again. His meddling mother might have been another reason he'd run away from home. He couldn't run now.

Wiping his sweaty brow, Max watched his sons—his *sons*—hauling in more lumber. Richard was doing all the lifting, but Bakari ran after him as fast as he could go, steering the ends so they didn't hit the walls.

He should have Lydia look up *fatherhood* in the journals, but he feared that would be a year's worth of reading. Hands-on practice would have to do. "Don't walk where I've marked," he warned. "There's an old tunnel under this dirt."

They carefully stacked the boards where he indicated, avoiding the rope he'd hung to block off the crumbling part of the floor.

"How will we bring bricks down here?" Richard asked.

"Excellent question. We'll need men and wheelbarrows. If we had time, I'd construct a track similar to ones used in coal mines. But we have more people than time, so wheelbarrows it is. You've done a good job, thanks. Did Lloyd promise you a riding lesson?"

Bakari nodded eagerly. Richard shrugged. He seemed more interested in the construction than horses, Max thought. Both were important lessons. He dusted himself off and set down his tools. "Let's go up and see how those old animals are faring. Once we know how well you ride, we'll look into fancier livestock."

Bakari peered worriedly through the doorway into the black interior beneath the library proper. "I think a dragon sleeps in there, and we are waking him."

Interesting insight. Remembering the ghost walking through that wall and Lydia's question about saints and dragons, he wondered what fed their fantasies. "I hope not, but I suppose dragons guard hoards, and Miss Lydia has a hoard of books."

"May I see them?" Bakari asked.

"You'll have to ask Miss Lydia. These are very special books and not everyone can read them. That is why she's the librarian, and we're not." Max hoped she learned to read them, anyway. He hated to see her fretting over her inability to find what she sought. He knew what it was like not to have access to vital information because his eyes and brain didn't communicate.

Once he was outside in the fresh air and sunlight, Max enjoyed a few hours of testing the mares on country lanes with his sons. Bakari wasn't big enough to manage mule or mare, but he bravely attempted it for a while, then settled for riding in front of Max so they could explore. Richard decided they needed a map to know their boundaries, and Max concurred. If this was to be his home now, he needed to know his parameters.

By Friday, Max had had more time to think about staying in one place with wife and children. It still terrified the stuffing out of him, but it probably wasn't any worse than being fifteen and sailing away with strangers to foreign lands. He simply had more sense now and knew enough to fear.

Thinking about Lydia in his bed smothered common sense *and* fear. These last nights had been a revelation he savored—and wanted to repeat. In many different ways. Just imagining all the ways he could take Lydia. . . would cripple him.

When his work was done for the day, he led his troop back to the house to wash and change for dinner. His mother had rearranged his accommodations again, sending the boys to the main block and ordering Max to the guest room, where he belonged.

"Lydia needs her privacy," Lady Agnes said sternly. "And she needs access to her library at all hours. You will simply have to learn to live with servants the way civilized people do."

Lydia was nowhere to be seen to protest this commandment.

Since he'd be sleeping with Lydia, Max didn't object, too much. Entering the guest chamber to change out of his filth, he found the cheerful, round-faced chambermaid theoretically tidying the bed. Instead of quietly departing, she immediately sat down and bounced on the mattress. "The sheets are clean, sir. Would you care to test them?"

"No," he replied curtly, stepping back into the hall.

She pouted and swayed toward him, tapping him on his filthy waist-coat. "I could help you bathe."

Well, so much for hoping that bonding with Lydia would end this magnetism. What did he have to do to build a bond with Lydia that marked him off-limits?

And was he fooling himself to think it might happen?

Perhaps he could persuade Lydia to hire only male servants. Or aging crones.

Rather than deal with the seductive chambermaid, Max stalked off in search of Lydia, hoping she might find insight to his predicament in the library. Maybe if he joined her in the stacks as he had last time. . .

He followed her voice to the guest parlor—where she entertained a gaggle of females. Max froze in the corridor to study the scene.

Lydia was wearing colors! And a dress so fashionable she outshone the other ladies. Light blue-and-white striped underskirts covered all but the toes of pretty, blue shoes. A dark blue silky tunic thing clung to her lovely bosom and curves. Shiny braid and bows adorned the long bodice lapping over the skirt, and Max wondered how in hell he'd get her out of it.

She sat there, sipping tea as if she were the queen in the company of her ladies-in-waiting, very much in command of her own household. Max didn't even bother identifying her guests. In his muddy, reeking clothes, he backed away. Even so, one of the younger women glanced up eagerly and seemed ready to rise.

The patter of small boots warned the chambermaid was on his heels. Cursing, he darted into the guest bath and locked the door. If he ever needed proof that civilization was not for him, it rattled at the latch now.

TWENTY

LADY AGNES'S ANNOUNCEMENT OF A WEDDING MAX HADN'T PUBLICLY mentioned brought half of Edinburgh's Malcolms to the castle door. Suffering a rush of embarrassing congratulations, Lydia was distracted by an odd commotion in the corridor. Lady Dare's photography student must have heard also, for she studied the doorway with avid interest. The only unmarried woman in the group noticing. . .

Max.

"If you'll excuse me for a moment," Lydia murmured, rising.

The ladies had brought all her boxes of new clothes with them, and she'd tried on this one they'd called a visiting gown. The light fabric felt heavenly, and the bows and ribbons made her feel feminine, but for practical purposes, it was a nuisance. The long train required lifting and maneuvering and ladylike steps so she didn't show her ankles while doing so.

Lydia knew perfectly well that her guests were dying of curiosity but were too polite to follow her. They were Malcolms, after all. Lady Agnes had apparently sent invitations to all her local family to help plan her son's nuptials. While Lydia delighted in the company, she was terrified at how quickly the reality of a ceremony was coming together.

She was similarly terrified that perceptive Malcolms would discern her inadequacy as a librarian if she gave them too much of her time. Would they demand she be tested?

She rustled down the corridor to where Beryl waited between the guest bath and bedroom. The maid looked a little bewildered.

"Are you lost?" Lydia asked, equally confused. "Doesn't Mrs. Folkston need you to help set up the guest chambers in the main house?"

Beryl blushed and curtsied. "I finished moving your clothes to the tower and put fresh linens on Mr. Ives' bed and carried up his laundry. I'll be on my way now."

"Thank you, Beryl. With all these guests, we'll have to hire more help, I know." Lydia watched the maid rush away.

Lloyd should have been tending Max's laundry and chamber.

Lydia tapped tentatively on the bathing room door. "Max? She's gone."

He stuck out his dusty head and leaned against the jamb in all his filth. "The guest room won't work," he said angrily.

"I can't send Lloyd to move your clothes back upstairs," she whispered. "You'll have to do it. Your mother is interfering again."

His expression didn't soften. "Fine. I'll do it, but I'm not coming down until all the women are gone."

"You're being ridiculous. Phoebe and Azmin won't attack you. Their husbands are about somewhere. Find them once you're decent or your mother will put together a wedding involving fireworks, the queen, and an army of pipers." She abandoned him to return to her guests.

Max would abandon *her* soon enough, Lydia knew. She had to learn to keep their lives separate. And if his mother meant to move in while planning a circus, then he could very well play the part of son or host or whatever he was.

After everyone departed to their rooms to dress for dinner, with still no sign of Max, Lydia took the inside library stairs to her room—Mr. C's room, Max's room, her room. . . a blamed hotel suite. Had Max run away again? Terrified she—or the maids or her company—had driven him off, she stifled panic with anger. Her head was about to explode with all the tasks she must accomplish. Entertaining his family—*his* family, mind you —shouldn't have to be her duty.

As she climbed the spiral stairs, the stacks whistled, whispered, and beckoned, taunting her, like bullies. She grabbed a volume sticking out from a shelf and stalked up in a fine snit.

She slammed into the suite's parlor to find Max on the floor, sketching on a news sheet with black ink over the dense print, as if he were Bakari drawing the universe. He wore a clean shirt but most definitely wasn't dressed for dinner. He'd left the shirt open at the throat, wore no coat or waistcoat, and his hair still hung in damp ringlets on his brow. She flung the book down at him. "I am not dressing for dinner with *your* relations if you're not."

She stalked back through the study—*her* study—now littered with Bakari's drawings and Max's scribbling. The globe had been relegated to the floor and the desk had become a playground of books stacked presumably to replicate the supports of the cellar. *This* was what it would be like to be married.

She swung on her heel and strode back to the parlor, where Max sat, rumpling his hair, holding the book she'd thrown, and looking puzzled. "I am to expect that you take over my house, my rooms, my person, unload all your family and problems, while you do nothing but play in mud because you're *afraid* of the maids?"

He shoved up from the floor holding the book and looking as grim as she felt. "I am *afraid* of hurting you, shaming my family, and causing your friends to look at me in disgust and at you with pity. I am not suited for. . ." He gestured helplessly at the fussy parlor with its floral draperies and velvet couch.

Lydia almost softened at the thought of this big, confident man not wanting to hurt impervious her. Unfortunately, Max continued speaking.

"I can carve my way through a jungle with a machete, but I cannot carve my way through your maidservants and friends without harm. I cannot sit at your dinner table and converse about the latest news in the paper or novels or any of those other things civilized people do. I came to this place because I thought *I wouldn't have to.*"

"Fine, then don't." Lydia snatched the book from his hand and swept out again. She'd known all this. It was her own fault for not understanding that it meant she'd have to do everything herself, as always.

She hated being rushed into things because she never had time to think them through. Upheaval and chaos were always the result.

She would change out of this foolish gown and back into her old wool, forget their guests, and go down and work on correspondence as she was meant to do. Or read every book in the damned library so she knew where to find what without the books talking to her. Or—

Max caught up with her in a few strides. He grabbed the trailing bow down her back and halted her in her tracks. "How the hell did you get into this thing? I thought you were the queen of France or princess of Scotland, and all I could think of was how I could pry it off you."

Lydia didn't know whether to laugh or weep. Max thought of a gown's *construction*, and not it's fashionableness or how well it looked on her. Well, he had said she looked like a queen, but that was simply because she had dressed fancy for a change.

He truly wasn't accustomed to civilization.

"Self-buttoning on the bodice, ties everywhere else," she said in resignation. She had never been the kind of person who could stay mad. She was much too reasonable—and too busy. "I am supposed to try on the dinner gown. It is the whole purpose of the ladies arriving with the boxes. I believe your mother has given them to believe that the gowns are my trousseau and that we are making a formal announcement tonight. What did you mean, you don't want to hurt me? You're already hurting me by hiding up here."

"It's better than finding me in the arms of your dratted maid, or the schoolgirl I saw in the parlor, or any other female who might catch sight of me. I know you don't believe me, but I have looked down the barrel of shotguns when women thought I was cheating on them or men thought I was after their wives. But what am I supposed to do when females develop the vapors in front of me? Let them fall on the floor? And if one grabs my cravat and kisses me? Fling her against the wall? I may not like civilization, but I'm not completely uncivilized."

He had all her buttons unfastened by the time he finished his rant. Lydia shrugged out of the fitted tunic as she hurried through the bathing room and maid's chamber to the bedroom. To her relief, someone had carried up all her boxes. She tried to imagine how she would feel if she found Max in another woman's arms, but she was not an imaginative sort, and their liaison was too new for her to say she trusted him.

"A *gentleman* might not throw a strumpet against the wall, but *I'm* not averse to doing so," she decided. "I do have some advantage over other women in that I am large and strong and don't need a shotgun to remove unwanted pests."

She untied ribbons and bows and pushed off the train, then the skirt and pannier bustle.

Max caught her waist and lifted her from the circle of fabric and wire. His hot hand scorched even through her exceedingly fine new elastic corset. "And you may stamp rats with those dainty boots and throw wolves over your pretty shoulder, but you should not have to do so for *me.*"

"Then learn to do it yourself," she huffed.

His masculine proximity was too tempting, and she refused to fall at his feet like a schoolgirl. Escaping his embrace, she threw open box lids until she found what she sought. "You are asking me to go downstairs and entertain your sons, your mother, and all her guests, and their husbands. I do not know these people well, Maxwell. I am from England. They are not my family. They are *yours.* And you need their help if you are to prove that you are not dead."

He yanked open the wardrobe door and removed a dinner coat. "Fine. I will embarrass the lot of you to prove I'm me. How many maids are serving?"

"Mrs. Folkston brought in her grand-niece, that is all. Mr. Folkston and Zach will do most of the serving. You will be fine. Lady Dare brought one of her photography students. They do wedding portraits. They are expecting you to make an announcement tonight. Since— among other things—Azmin captures malevolent spirits with her photographs, I suppose she is verifying that you won't beat me when everyone has gone home."

"Do you expect me to make an announcement?" he asked, rummaging for clothing from the stack he'd carried up.

"Your mother will if you don't." Lydia shook out the gold silk skirt with the dashing ruffled cream-and-russet underskirt. She had never worn impractical colors like these, but her heart sang at just the lovely lightness of the fabric. She concentrated on sliding into the trailing underskirt without wrinkling or tearing anything rather than look at Max dressing behind her.

They were sharing a bedchamber. She should be embarrassed, but they'd shared a great deal more than a room these last nights.

"What was the book you carried up here?" was his surprising reply.

"Book?" She spun around, vaguely remembering carrying a book. She was always carrying books. Distracted by the sight of Max in starched white linen, fastening his cravat at his throat, she almost forgot the question. Narrow-hipped, broad-shouldered, dark curls rakishly tumbling over his brow, Max reminded her quite forcefully why they were even having this conversation.

Fighting a surge of lust, she pounced on the book. Opening the pages, she frowned. "A journal from one of your ancestors. He was an Ives, although on the wrong side of the blanket. I wonder if my growing up in England is causing problems with this more Gaelic library. . . Perhaps I should have gone to the Wystan library in Northumberland."

He tapped the pages impatiently. "Why *this* book?"

"Because it wasn't in place." She scanned the pages swiftly, flipping through until one leaped out at her. "The journal writer tells us his home included an ancient watchtower and Malcolm journals, apparently very old ones that his mother had collected. But she kept them in a proper library because the tower was crumbling. He tore down the tower and added windows where the doorways once were." She showed him the sketch.

He studied it, then handed it back. "Very pretty. But your tower is in solid shape. There's no need to remove it, unless you need windows in your study or more in the guest room."

She felt a flutter of relief at that assessment. "His wife was a librarian, and he was an engineer of sorts, mostly mining, though. There is reference to a keystone that saved some structure. I don't know why his journal is in this library and not wherever his is."

He looked at the date of it. "This journal is well over a hundred years old. If his descendants did not keep up the property, the books may have been unsafe. Or they may have overwhelmed a normal library and been moved here."

"He was an Ives. *You* are likely related to his descendants," she said dryly. "That is probably why the book caught my eye."

"Caught your eye, did it?" he asked, raising a knowing dark eyebrow. "Out of the thousands of volumes in there, the one about my engineering ancestor and his librarian wife simply leaped out at you?"

"Singular, but not useful." With disappointment, she set the volume down and returned to dressing.

"You don't analyze, do you?" Max buttoned his waistcoat. "You take everything at face value, not taking time to wonder *why* one book would catch your eye. You're waiting for magic to happen. But that's not how it works."

Lydia hoped the corset she was wearing was tight enough for the new bodice and began struggling into the narrow sleeves. "How am I supposed to *analyze* an enormous library of whispering books?"

"I don't know. I can't read, remember? That's your talent. I never saw anyone read and comprehend a book as swiftly as you just did." He helped her with the stiff bodice, then shrugged into his tailored coat. It was country wear and not a fancy tailed coat, but the black emphasized his weathered bronzed complexion.

"Then I'll just read the entire library. Although what good that will do if I can't read Gaelic, I can't say." In a huff, she started pulling the pins from her hair so she might brush it into some semblance of order.

"How many languages does the library contain?" Max took the brush from her and gently pulled at the tangles. "I love your hair. It's like holding sunshine."

She wanted to melt at his romantic flattery, but she was too agitated. Her entire life, her home, depended on understanding a library that wouldn't speak to her. "I don't know. Mr. C could read Gaelic, Latin, Greek, and some Italian and French. I know Latin and Greek and can figure out many phrases in Italian and French, but I've not run across them often in the books I've seen. Gaelic is a problem. And if that is the basis of this library, then I don't belong here. I will be found out any day and cast from the castle."

Max grabbed a handful of hair and tugged her around to face him. He was large enough to almost make her feel small. Almost. He touched his nose to hers. "You *belong here*. Hire a steward. Live in the stacks. Figure it out. But do not leave, not ever. Understood?"

Never leave? While he traipsed the world with women falling at his feet.

She crushed his cravat in her fist, stood on her toes, and nipped his nosy nose.

TWENTY-ONE

MAX THREADED LYDIA'S HAND THROUGH THE CROOK OF HIS ARM AS THEY strolled toward the enormous drawing room in what once had been the great hall. He'd like to appreciate the gas-lit chandelier and sconces and the pegged oak floors littered with carpets from Persia and Turkey, but the people swiveling to watch their entrance had him fighting the urge to bolt.

He'd attended occasions like this as an eighteen-year-old. They had turned out very badly. Of course, back then, he hadn't known not to study the bon-bon box of female confections. He ignored them now, instead, attempting to recognize the gentlemen guests from Lydia's descriptions.

His mother rushed to greet them. "You look so much like your father that I have to hug you!"

Max was fairly certain his father had never turned up with bite marks on his nose. He shot Lydia a look as he hugged his mother. Lydia demurely smiled as if they hadn't just been shouting at each other. The bruised memory distracted him from the gathering crowd.

"Come along, Maxwell, let me introduce you." His mother tugged his arm.

Despite the argument, he preferred Lydia's no-nonsense company.

Actually, he was trying to picture his betrothed flinging lusty ladies against the armament-covered walls, but he hoped he could defend himself well enough that she needn't do so.

"I think Lydia can manage, Mother. Why don't you take a seat by the fire and sip your ratafia?" He supposed that was mean, but he had to start asserting himself with females sometime.

"It's only proper I act as hostess, my lady," Lydia said in a pacifying tone. "Is my new gown too violent a color?"

"Oh, no," Lady Agnes declared, easily distracted. "With your hair, it's absolutely ravishing. Perhaps you should do color instead of white for your wedding gown."

"Ivory, perhaps," Lydia suggested. "Would you ask Lady Dare about color while I introduce Max to the gentlemen? She's an artist with an eye for these things."

Interesting. Distraction worked, at least with his mother. He needed to learn Lydia's technique for isolating herself, because he had a feeling she did that regularly. Nose biting might not be the preferred method.

"Can the gentlemen escape to another room?" Max murmured as she led him toward the table where decanters and glasses waited. "There is a pretty young thing sailing in from starboard."

Lydia's bow lips didn't curve, but he caught mischief in the blue of her eyes as she slanted him a look. "A mere child. Surely you can handle her?"

"Miss Wystan, thank you so much for allowing me to see your magnificent home. I'm over the moon delighted to be photographing your wedding." Fair-haired, blue-eyed, obviously one of his mother's students, the *child* looked at Max as if he were ice cream and chocolate all wrapped in one—evidently anticipating an introduction.

He was pretty damned certain distraction did not work on the dessert-deprived.

"That's good to know, Miss Laurel. I believe Lady Agnes could use more ratafia, if you would be so kind?" Lydia sailed onward, forcing Max with her, leaving the student gaping.

"Deftly done, my dear," Max said in approval, registering direct command as another defense. "You have a managing way about you. It won't stop her, though."

"Lady Phoebe and Lady Dare aren't following us. Apparently it is only the single ladies in this company that you must avoid." Lydia hesitated, then added honestly, "And possibly your mother. Don't mistake me—she's a wonderful woman. . ."

"But a meddling witch," Max cheerfully agreed. "A harmless one I needn't fling against walls."

Lydia halted before a professorial sort in tweeds and a sturdy gentleman with oil staining his fingernails. "Lord Dare, Mr. Blair, Maxwell Ives. I think everyone can sort out who is whom. I need to speak with the ladies." She strolled off, abandoning Max to strangers.

The professorial one stuck out his hand. "I'm *Doctor* Dare, actually. The viscountcy is recent and unexpected so forget the title. Apparently, my wife has volunteered to take your wedding portraits. Unless you have need of a physician, I am relatively useless. If you require help with engineering problems, as the ladies seem to think, Blair here is your man."

Both gentlemen had the dark-haired good looks of an Ives. Max had a vague recollection of an Alexander Dare in one of his sojourns to his southern cousins' homes. But Blair was a stranger.

Relaxing his guard in male company, Max shook the physician viscount's hand. "Should you happen to remember me as a recalcitrant, sulking youngster, you might identify me to a judge. Otherwise, your presence makes the ladies happy and that counts."

Dare tilted his head to study Max but didn't light up with recognition. "All Ives look alike to me," he admitted.

Gut twisting, fearing his strong family features would be a problem, Max turned to the stranger—his cousin Phoebe's husband, if he did not mistake. "Blair, good to meet you. Lydia is learning your typewriter invention. But I'm thinking I need an archeologist to work out this plumbing problem."

"I'm more mechanical than structural, but I'd love a tour of that tower foundation, if we have time tomorrow," Blair responded. "Hugh Morgan and I are removing some of the medieval tenements in Old Town and learning how to develop adequate plumbing is essential. The doctor and I were just discussing the disease factor of these primitive edifices."

The round-faced, smiling maid arrived bearing a tray of nicely browned tartlets. "A nibble until the meal is served, gentlemen?"

Max turned his back on her to top off his glass at the liquor table.

"Mr. Ives, sir, tartlet?" she insisted, following him.

He swung back to his companions who stood tart-less, watching in bemusement. Grimacing, Max snatched the tray from the maid and passed it to them.

"Oh, sir, you needn't do that! Please, let me, you'll ruin your coat. . ." She began dabbing at an imaginary spot on his lapel with a napkin.

"For heaven's sake, leave the gentleman alone." The young photography student approached, grabbed the napkin, and pointed back to the ladies. "Ladies should be served first."

Max sighed. He knew he should express gratitude for the rescue, but he also knew it wasn't rescue. Without a word, he strode away from the quarreling women and back to Lydia. He took a seat beside her and threw back a swig of good Scots malt.

She glanced from him to her male guests. He assumed he noted the quarreling young women because her lips tightened.

"Not the stage for wall-flinging," he murmured. "If I leave the room, they'll most likely go back to normal."

"You are not leaving the room," she said grimly. "Your mother planned this dinner for you."

"Did I tell you how regal you look in all that finery?" Max asked in amusement. "I know where I can buy a jeweled scepter and a tiara, although I suppose you would prefer a necklace. Diamonds? Amethysts?"

Her lips turned up, as he'd hoped. "A mace," she said defiantly.

He grinned in appreciation. Dinner was finally called, and he breathed easier as they departed for the eccentric dining room with the round table. The student was placed on the furthest side from him, behind a silver epergne some ambitious soul had polished for the occasion. Normally, he'd wish the centerpiece to the devil. For tonight, it meant he could concentrate on Lydia and his cousin Phoebe on either side of him. He rather enjoyed a table with no head or foot so there was no precedence he had to memorize.

Relaxing a little, he followed the conversation as it bounced from

Phoebe's animal shelter to Dare's new medical project to Blair's latest invention. Lady Dare, in her colorful sari, spoke of the latest efforts in color photography. Perhaps he'd been attending the wrong sorts of society functions. He warily watched a new young maid delivering trays from the kitchen, but she merely darted nervous glances and ran off like a frightened hare.

Over the epergne, the pretty student attempted to attract his attention by offering food commentary so obviously directed at him that it was painful. His mother had a word with her, and she was reduced to wide-eyed, longing looks that Max easily ignored.

He had actually reached the point of enjoying the lamb medallions enough to compare them to one of the few fine dinners he remembered in rural regions when a footman entered with a card in hand instead of food.

The servant uncertainly presented it between Lydia and Max. "The gentleman asks to see Mr. Ives."

"At this hour? In the rain? Do we ask him to join us?" Lydia let Max take the card, realized her mistake, and leaned over to read it. "David Franklin?"

Conversation halted. Max debated telling the footman to heave his uncle back into the rain. But this was Lydia's home, and he respected her hospitality. One glance at her worried expression warned that heaving would not be the best path to her bed.

It certainly hadn't taken long for news of his whereabouts to spread.

"Now I know how men were tamed," he muttered, pushing back his chair. "Offered war or women, we'll take the easy route every time."

Phoebe looked at him strangely, but Lydia chuckled.

"Gentlemen, if you'd like to stand witness that I did not murder my uncle—"

Apparently having been informed of the legal battle over Max's non-death, they pushed back their chairs before he could complete the sentence. His mother looked as if she'd like to join them, but Lady Dare placed a gold-bangled hand over her arm and whispered something pacifying. The women all stayed put.

"Pistols or swords?" Max murmured as they traipsed down a

corridor lit only by oil lamps. Apparently the gas lighting was just for show in the grand hall.

"One assumes your uncle is not young?" Blair asked.

"He was younger than my father by some years, late fifties now, I'd wager, but hale and hearty. I doubt I'll give him an apoplexy if I wave a pistol under his nose."

"I'm surprised he came alone," the inventor said.

Knowing the Ives family a little better, the good doctor refrained from commenting.

"It's a tactic," Max acknowledged. "He's come here to show his true colors and browbeat me. He'll not expect me to have support."

At age eighteen, larger than most full-grown men, Max had scorned the need for anyone's aid. He'd learned a little strategy since then.

He strolled into the paneled medieval hall as if he'd lived here all his life. He didn't particularly feel like a king or even a lord. But he had to admit the wealthy surroundings gave him an advantage over the rain-soaked gentleman warming himself at the dying fire. The chandelier's lighting had been turned off, and the wall sconces lowered to burn dimly.

His uncle noted Max's companions with surprise. He recovered quickly. "Can't face me alone, can you? Any impostor who would cheat an old lady is a coward."

Oh well, so much for any hope of a peace treaty. Max crossed the Turkish rug to confront his step-uncle. Once, he'd thought Franklin a formidable man of admirable intelligence. Today, he saw a graying, rain-soaked bully clinging to his power.

"I believe it is yourself you think I'm cheating, since my mother has little left to lose." Max countered the twisted accusation with truth as he never would have known to do in his youth. He proceeded as if they hadn't just clashed swords. "Good evening, Uncle David. We're in the midst of my engagement dinner. Had we known you were interested, we might have sent an invitation. You will excuse my friends for believing a visit at this hour might be an emergency. Surely you haven't reached bankruptcy in less than a week?"

The fire gleamed on his uncle's fading blond hair but concealed his eyes. His anger was only reflected in his choice of words. "It's true then?

You think you can marry into Lady Agnes's insane family and steal a dead man's estate? It won't work, you know. I have witnesses to prove you're not my nephew. Perhaps I should introduce them to your fiancée so you don't cheat her as well."

Max's companions poured themselves whisky and leaned against the mantel, silently providing encouragement with their presence but leaving the floor to Max. He appreciated their confidence in his ability to defend himself.

"If you came here to insult me, then I must apologize for my youthful mistake in believing you as brilliant as my father." Just to give his fists occupation, Max poured a tumbler of whisky and didn't offer his uncle any. "In which case, I made a grave error, leaving you terribly overwhelmed by the difficulty of managing so large an estate. Does that mean Cousin George isn't any help either?"

His uncle scowled. "Everyone knows Maxwell Ives has been dead for years. The poor sod couldn't even read much less perpetrate a fraud of this immensity. You will never prove your case."

At the mantel, the viscount-physician raised a wry eyebrow. "Is there no memory from your childhood you can drop on him so he gives up this folly, and we can all go back to our dinner? I've been told there is champagne chilling in anticipation of your announcement."

Max shrugged. "My only memories of my uncle are of a stuffy office and books of numbers and discussions of cents and per-cents well above my head." Max hesitated, recalling those days. "*Well* above my head, since I was most likely a very young schoolboy. Once my father realized what a disappointment I was, he left me in school or with my cousins. Since I left these shores at fifteen, there aren't many memories to recall."

"See?" His uncle turned to the viscount. "He has nothing. The messages purportedly from my nephew were written by men of letters, not the lazy dolt who could barely write his name. The recommendations in those posts are from that Glaswegian spider who's been weaving webs around every decent investment in the city. Once he has his hands on the estate, Hugh Morgan will own us all."

"Ah, forgive me again, sir," Max said, biting back a grin as his uncle revealed his hand. "I failed to introduce you to my guests, Lord Dare and Mr. Andrew Blair. I believe you'll know Blair as partner to the spider who will indeed be managing my investments once the court returns them."

It was difficult to tell in the dim light, but Max thought his uncle turned an unhealthy purple.

"You will *not* usurp all my decades of hard work. You may resemble an Ives, but so do dozens of others I can present. Without proof, you are nothing. I will offer Lady Agnes a decent residence on the side of town not riddled with pestilence, and I will see that she has an adequate allowance so she may have the parties I remember she enjoys. She'll see the error of her ways and drop your support. If you have half a brain, you will accept the substantial sum I'm offering you to take the next ship out. Leave before I humiliate the ladies by having you flung from the courtroom as the fraud you are."

"Had you offered my mother that ten years ago, I might have taken you up on it," Max acknowledged. "I have no use for you or civilization or juggling pounds and cents. I left in the first place so as not to humiliate my family. Instead of being grateful, you tried to rob my mother of her family home, you deprived her of income, and forced me to find Morgan to handle my affairs. And now you insult my intelligence. I'll see you in court, sir, and you'd best pray the judge is lenient for I'll not be."

"That school will fall down on your mother's head!" His uncle raged. "I am merely attempting to remove her to somewhere safe."

"There's a major civic development project scheduled for the property across from the school," Blair offered. "A fortune can be made if those old tenements are torn down and replaced with modern buildings to house lawmakers and the like."

Max sighed and studied his uncle with despair. "You have spent too much time with your accounting books, Uncle. You've forgotten that the point of money is not to watch it grow but to make people safe. Just as fair warning, my fiancée is the Malcolm librarian. She holds the family genealogy, and we have corresponded for years. Neither she nor anyone else who really knows me doubts my identity. It is your problem that you never took the time to learn who I am. Do you need a room for the night? I can ask Miss Wystan if she has a bed for you."

"I'm staying with Crowley. He has a thing or two to say about Miss Wystan. Do not think you'll be living here in comfort once the judge throws out your case. You'll be fortunate you're not both cooling your heels in prison for the next decade." Slapping his wet hat back on his head, he stalked out of the hall.

Max fought a frisson of fear. Could Lydia's neighbor prove the land wasn't hers? Or was this an ugly reference to testing Lydia's talent? How would his uncle know about that?

If Max had brought disaster down on the *library*, he had even more reason to marry and win his estate back. He'd need the wherewithal to fight her enemies.

TWENTY-TWO

Two weeks later

"I do wish I could be on the champagne train with our guests." Lady Agnes sighed while sorting through a basket of delicate lace. "It will be such a lovely party! But I love helping you with the gown and flowers and menu. I need to be two people."

Lydia winced as the seamstress stuck a pin into her hip instead of a seam. "I hope you did not provide too much champagne. The men drank it with whisky at the engagement dinner and became much too boisterous."

She feared the encounter with Max's uncle had been the reason for the hilarity, not the formal announcement of betrothal. But Max had brushed off whatever had happened.

"Max said his funds are limited until the court frees them, so it was only one case. And that nice Miss Trivedi helped us find pink ribbons for a fraction of the cost. I know how to be frugal!" Triumphantly, she found the lace she wanted and pulled it from the basket.

Max had spent these last weeks practically living under the tower, except when he was down in the village ordering bricks or bringing laborers up the mountain. She knew he was sending telegrams to his friend in the city as well—avoiding asking her to do any more correspondence.

That was worrisome, but she had her own hands full with the wedding, staffing the castle, looking for a steward, and desperately attempting to answer letters without the use of the journals. She didn't know how to approach him with her insecurities.

She feared that if the court didn't accept the few witnesses who had responded to Max's pleas, he would have wasted all his available funds on his mother's dream of a magnificent wedding. Lady Agnes's notion of frugality didn't precisely correspond with Lydia's.

Or maybe she was just excessively nervous.

"Have the trustees given you full possession of the trust yet?" Agnes asked, working out a tangle in a ribbon. "You wouldn't have to fret so much about money then, would you?"

"They said I must be tested?" Lydia hadn't had much time for studying all the documents, but those words had stayed in her head. They'd keep her awake nights if it weren't for Max exhausting her.

"Tested?" The older lady frowned, stuffed the ribbon back in her basket, and shook her gray curls. "Foolish men. *Tested*." She humpfed.

That did nothing to reassure Lydia, so she chose to block it from her mind, for now.

For fittings, they used one of the smaller rooms on the upper floor of the castle that may have once housed a seamstress, judging by the mirrors and wire dress form. Lydia was learning more about the sprawling fortress than she had ever known while working for Mr. C.

Max had expanded her world considerably.

She admired the full length of her wedding gown in the cheval glass. She'd insisted that it be plain, without an excess of frills. Lady Agnes wanted a train of lace flounces. The result was an elegant ivory silk that clung to her full figure in front and a detachable train covered in blond lace in back. She hoped she didn't have to walk down many steps.

"I really must ask Mrs. Folkston if all the guest rooms are ready," Lydia fretted. "They haven't been opened as long as I have been here, and that's been years."

"Don't fash yourself, as I've heard people say." Lady Agnes opened what appeared to be a jewelry box. "Your servants know what to do. I've asked one of my teachers to join us. She'll make a good steward so you needn't worry over household details. You have quite enough to do."

Lydia felt her ample stomach sink to her feet. "A female steward will never do," she murmured. "Really, my lady, you must quit interfering, or you'll drive Max away again."

His mother held up a string of pearls and eyed it critically. "She's a Malcolm, dear. She'll be fine. Do you think you should wear pearls to match the ivory or would you prefer a contrast? Your eyes are such a deep blue that I don't know if sapphires will do them justice."

"I'll have hydrangeas for my bouquet, so blue will do." Lydia fidgeted, needing to escape this suffocating room. She could practically hear the correspondence on her desk screaming to be answered. And she wanted to remind Max to crawl out of the tunnel he'd discovered before the wedding party arrived.

As far as she was concerned, this wedding wasn't even real. It was a show Lady Agnes was staging to convince everyone that Max was her son.

Given what she and Max had been doing every night these past weeks, formal vows merely proved any child she might bear was legitimate. She'd not realized how much she'd longed for a child of her own to love, until she started counting days while fretting that Max would feel trapped into staying.

She hadn't realized a great many things, and now she was making a lifetime commitment to a man she scarcely knew, in front of people who might declare her a fraud, while a court might declare her new husband officially dead. She might as well stand on the edge of a cliff and wait for a strong wind.

"The tower is trembling again, dear," Lady Agnes said, sifting through her box for sapphires. "I do hope Max knows what he's doing."

"OH, CRIPES," MAX SWORE AS HE SLID DOWNWARD IN A RUSH OF DIRT AND stone through a hole in the collapsing floor.

His sons shouted in terror. With the forethought of experience, Max had already established a framework for such incidences. He caught one of the braces and let the stones rush on without him. Straining his arms to lift himself up, he swung his legs back to more stable ground before anything else could give way.

He was already covered in filth from head to toe anyway. He peered down into the black stream far below, assessing the walls that could be seen in the dim light. "We may need to consider Portland cement, iron pipes, and a pumping station if the rocks are this unstable."

"It must almost be time for the dinner guests," Richard said, a little nervously. "Perhaps we should stop now and clean up?"

Max grimaced. He'd far rather explore what was down below. But he understood his son's concern.

"First, we put up boards blocking this passage and add warning signs. Some of our guests have inquiring minds." He crossed two big timbers over the hole, then two more to block entrance to this part of the corridor. "Do we have anything to create a Keep-Out sign?"

Bakari produced a charcoal pencil from his pocket. "Will this work?"

Richard propped a thin board between the timbers and wrote letters on it. For good measure, he drew a skull and crossbones. "That's for people who can't read," he said in satisfaction. "That's why tavern signs have drawings on them."

"He knows history," Max muttered, gesturing for them to head out. He didn't know whether Richard realized his father couldn't read, but it didn't seem to matter to the boys. They just wanted to dig in dirt and drive nails for fun.

Soaked in smelly slime, Max emerged from the cellar just as the first guests arrived—his wedding party arriving early for tonight's dinner.

Thrilled at the sight of fancy thoroughbreds, the boys ran for the stable. Max scowled and aimed for the garden door before someone took him for the night soil man—except his clothes reeked more of oil than sewage. Interesting.

He had this next week to present witnesses in court that he was the same ignorant boy his relations had known nearly twenty years ago. After his uncle's insults, Max thought maybe he should greet his guests in all his filth and prove he hadn't learned a thing. Irritated at his own thoughts, he took the path behind the kitchen hedges and pushed at the garden door.

It didn't open. For the first time in the weeks he'd been living here, someone had bolted the damned tower door.

Now what did he do? Stalk through the front door with the guests? Go through the kitchen in all his stinking dirt and traipse through the entire house? There was only one corridor to his tower chamber and that was at the front.

Had he been in any of the primitive outposts where he was most comfortable, he would have found a bathhouse or a lake or a pump and just sluiced himself off. No one would have cared that he was wet and dirty. Here, men were supposed to be immaculate and smell of expensive shaving soaps.

He didn't want to bring shame on Lydia. . . Except, he realized, Lydia would simply look at him, laugh, and point at the bathing room.

This was about *him*. *He* was the one harboring a childish memory of being laughed at, taunted, and made to feel like an ass.

He'd faced lions, savages, and floods since then. He could handle a few pampered dandies, especially if he thought of Lydia's castle as his home. In his own home, he could do as he damned well pleased. If his guests were offended, they could leave. Max stopped and savored the sweet taste of power.

If this was his home and the choice was his, he'd rinse off before dripping through the kitchens. Max strode off to the stable and lowered himself into a horse trough. He should install pumps once he had the tower repaired. Maybe an outdoor shower for the stable lads and gardeners, after Lydia hired them again. The cistern held plenty and refilled easily.

Richard and Bakari ran out and laughed at him as he dunked his head to scrub his hair and came up sputtering. Several of the new arrivals glanced his way out of curiosity, but they had no reason to recognize an uncouth field hand bathing in his clothes. Max was grinning by the time he ordered the boys to fetch him a cloak to cover himself.

He dried off as best as he could with a horse blanket. Clothes dripping, he wrapped in a cloak and stomped in through the kitchen door. The servants froze at his entrance.

"You'll have to mop up after me, I fear. It was either this or offend our guests." Without further apology, Max traipsed across the stone floor and up the servants' stairs. One of the young maids, naturally, followed at his heels with a mop. But apparently his stench put off any amorous inclinations. Huh, lesson number three—stink put women off.

Guests were already in the billiard room. The ancient table sagged. The room was lined with books and reading chairs instead of hunting trophies, but it was the closest imitation of a male refuge the castle possessed. The men glanced up as Max passed wrapped in a cloak and leaving a trail of slime, but they returned to their game, as if weird apparitions were normal. Ives then, and Max snorted in relief.

Ladies gathered in the great hall, sipping tea and delicately dining on cakes. They stared as he dripped down the carpeted corridor, rightfully so, of course. But they didn't follow.

He was pondering muck and oil as a natural deterrent by the time he reached the tower, unmolested. Lloyd popped out of the guest room where Max still kept most of his wardrobe. He figured Lloyd and probably Marta had to know he was sleeping with Lydia, but for his mother's sake, he kept up the pretense of occupying the lower chamber.

"I've taken the liberty of running a hot bath," Lloyd said stiffly. "Your attire is in the bathing room with your shaving gear. Do you need any further assistance?"

That was the man's way of saying *You're late, you stink, and you need a shave.* Max appreciated his reticence. "I'll be fixed up in a trice. Is Miss Lydia waiting on me?"

"Her mother and sister have arrived and are with her now. If you have no further need of me, I must see to Masters Richard and Bakari." He bowed and hurried off, no doubt relieved Max didn't need assistance as most gentlemen would.

Lydia's family had arrived. This wedding really was happening.

It had seemed a fine idea a few weeks ago, before he knew all the insecurities lurking behind Lydia's serenity. She presented a fine façade of strength and confidence that had everyone believing her foundation was sound, when it was as unstable as the tower she lived in.

He lacked experience in shoring up the foundations of ladies. . . Well, the emotional kind anyway. He was pretty good at corsets. Refusing to look backward, Max sank into the tub and scrubbed, creating an oily sheen in the water. Tomorrow, he would be a married man. Within the week, he hoped to be a wealthy one again. Planning any more future than that risked insanity.

"HERE, WEAR THIS TO DINNER. IT MAKES ME FEEL LIKE A PRINCESS." LYDIA adjusted the lace mantle over her mother's rounded shoulders.

She'd hastily cleared away evidence of Max's occupancy before bringing her family up, but they seemed too distracted by the lovely suite to notice small details, like the building blocks in the study.

"In that gown, you almost look like a lady," her sister Sara said admiringly, with a touch of jealousy. "Being a librarian must be most lucrative."

Lydia shook out the midnight blue skirt adorned with pale gold ruffles that she'd been told complemented her hair. "I have been saving my earnings for years. Open the wardrobe, and you'll see what I've been wearing. But Mr. Ives is from a wealthy, noble family. I thought I should attempt to appear like a lady for his guests. Why don't you borrow that shawl on the shelf? It's a good color with your hair."

Her mother and sister had darker red hair than Lydia. She was trying to learn about colors. The green shawl should work for both of them.

"Please do not take this wrong, dear," her mother said hesitantly. "But why would a wealthy gentleman settle for a vicar's plain daughter? Is there something you'd like to tell us?"

Her family had been with her only a few hours, and already they were eroding what little confidence she possessed. They meant well. Lydia knew they did. But they made her feel like an ugly stepchild. Perhaps they just raised the memories of her youth as a plain, overlarge misfit.

She did her best not to doubt herself—and Max. He'd not been particularly attentive these past weeks, but he'd been working hard, and so had she. Planning a wedding and learning to run an estate while desperately attempting to find the journals she needed consumed every minute of the day.

At night—that was a different story. Max certainly seemed to find her attractive in bed. That ought to be enough.

"You'll have to meet Mr. Ives, Mama. You'll understand. He's not at all like the shallow gentlemen you're thinking about," she said, if only to bolster her confidence.

Sara admired the shawl in the mirror, then wandered through the adjoining rooms to study the office where Max had substituted wooden blocks for books in his effort to produce a copy of the tower supports. "Papa would have loved this office."

Lydia had left all the trust documents Keya had sent on the desk. She'd studied them in hopes of learning more about testing her as librarian. She could find no mention of who did the testing or how, but there was certainly mention of it, proving the solicitors had done their homework.

Finding nothing reassuring, she'd tried to make heads or tails of the estate's maps and boundaries. She'd hoped Max might look at them, but of course, he really couldn't.

Praying she wasn't in over her head, Lydia twisted the sapphire ring Max had given her. He and his mother had chosen it from the jewelry box. He'd promised her any ring she liked once he'd won his case, but she liked this one because it was a family heirloom, and Max had picked it out. It made her almost feel as if this wedding were real.

Well, the ceremony would be real enough. The marriage itself. . . Again, she hid her doubts. "I wish Papa could have lived to see my study," she called to her sister, while she pinned her cameo brooch to the mantel around her mother's shoulders.

Both her mother and sister were considerably shorter than herself, so she could not loan them any of her other finery. They'd grown stouter than Lydia remembered as well. She gestured for her mother to precede her from the bedchamber. They had to descend and meet the guests at some point.

"Papa always loved you better," Sara claimed, lifting her skirt and petticoat so they didn't knock over the blocks covering half the floor. "He used to let you sit with him for hours."

"That was because you attended school, and I didn't," Lydia reminded her. "He called you his pretty butterfly."

"He loved all three of you equally," Mrs. Wystan said firmly. "I'm sorry Elizabeth couldn't attend, but she couldn't leave Scottie with his broken leg. She said she's sorry to miss this, but she thought it best if she stay home with all the children."

Elizabeth was their prettiest sister. She'd had a lovely wedding. Lydia had helped make her gown and find the flowers for the church and planned the reception. She would have loved seeing her again—and maybe showing off just a little. She wouldn't reveal her disappointment. "The children must come first, of course. Perhaps once everything is settled, I'll be able to visit. I'd love to see my nieces and nephews."

"You'll have time?" her mother asked warily.

She hadn't been able to get away while Mr. C had been ill. Now that she was performing both his duties and hers, Lydia didn't have an answer, so she pretended not to hear. She'd been having a nightmare lately that she left the castle and the door locked behind her, refusing to let her back in.

"It's hard to imagine you're in charge of all this," Sara said in awe as they descended the main stairs. "Will you show us your library? I'd love to see journals on rearing children who imagine ghosts and goblins."

Lydia had dreaded the moment when a guest asked her to find a specific book. She put it off now. "Perhaps there will be time later. You haven't talked young Geordie out of monsters under the bed yet?"

"Not monsters. He's quite convinced he's talking to Papa's ghost. And there is a spirit in the cemetery of a young girl he likes to play with. *Play with*, mind you. He'll be labeled strange if he does not give it up." Sara didn't hurry down the stairs but stopped at each bend to admire the scenery from the windows and to examine the open cubicles.

Their mother hadn't encouraged any of them to develop their various Malcolm abilities for fear their father's parishioners would call them witches.

Perhaps that fear held her back? Lydia cast a longing look at the wall concealing her secret library, but she couldn't leave Max fending off relatives on his own.

Feeling like Boudicca off to do battle, she led her troops onward and prayed she was doing the right thing with this wedding.

TWENTY-THREE

Garbed in one of the new suits he'd ordered so he didn't shame Lydia, hoping he could pay for them soon, Max lingered at the entrance of the great hall, studying the occupants. He recognized his aunt and few others. A new female he didn't know—surely she wasn't part of the wedding party?—glanced up. He avoided looking directly at her.

Not seeing Lydia, Max steeled himself for the moment of truth. By the windows waited a tall group of males who could only be family. If he couldn't convince them of his identity, his goose was cooked. He stalked past the females as if they weren't there.

His tension eased as he thought he recognized the men his mother had chosen to stand up with him tomorrow. They watched him expectantly, testing. One was obviously a tall, dark Ives. The shorter twins were several years older and auburn, like their mother.

He acknowledged a fourth, slender, blond man and his higher title first. "Rainford. How's the duke faring? Did he prevail and you're a physician these days?"

The marquess grimaced. "Don't ask. That's a topic for a night of drinking, not a wedding." He glanced at his companions waiting for Max to identify them.

Max shook his head at the lot of them. "It may be over twenty years, but you really don't think I'd forget the clowns who nearly drowned me, did you? And for honesty's sake, if I were a real fraud, I could easily have had someone research everyone my mother invited. It's not as if any of you are monks."

"We taught you to swim while drowning you, didn't we?" Rainford asked.

"There are easier ways of learning," Max replied dryly.

The others remained silent, waiting, simply because they were obstinate that way.

With a sigh of exasperation, he nodded at the dark-haired earl who stood taller than he. "Ives, your proboscis is still larger than mine." He turned to the auburn twins. "Bran, Brendan, I can still tell the two of you apart because Bran squints."

"It's him," Bran said in disgust. "I was hoping for an imposter we could pound into pulp and dump down an oubliette."

"This is a *Malcolm* fortress. You don't really believe the women had an oubliette, do you?" Max asked, fighting a grin of extreme relief. "I'm hoping to uncover a hypocaust and prove the Romans were here first."

"How did you persuade the women to even allow us on the premises?" Bran asked, still the mouthpiece for the twins. "Will they allow us to explore?"

Max shrugged. "I didn't know it was sacred ground. I've roamed everywhere. It's all about books and not very interesting, except for the tower."

The questions started to fly. Max could almost shut his eyes and pretend he was twelve and summering in Surrey with his cousins again. But he couldn't tear his gaze from the entrance. The image of Lydia kept him company all day as he dug and hauled and calculated. Lydia, laughing. Lydia, with fire in her eyes. Lydia, naked in his bed. He was obsessed by a woman in the same way he'd once been obsessed by engineering designs. Lydia wasn't a bridge or railroad, but she was the gateway to his uncertain future just as physical structures once had been.

She rewarded his anticipation in spectacular fashion. Wearing a dark blue gown to match her eyes and emphasize her curves, her long elegant throat enhanced by a circle of sapphires from the family jewels, and her sun-goddess hair adorned with glittering pins, Lydia drew every eye in the room.

"My word, Maxwellian," Gerard, the Earl of Ives and Wystan murmured, using an old sobriquet. "She's a veritable Valkyrie. You have met your match."

The men with him murmured their appreciation. With eyes only for Lydia, Max didn't listen or notice the approach of danger until she was upon him.

Richard's mother grasped his cravat, stood on her toes, and kissed his jaw. "Our son didn't mention that you'd grown into such a handsome man, Maxwell," she purred.

Fascinated by Lydia and not the pouter pigeon clutching his chest, Max watched his intended's expression with trepidation twisting his gut. From experience, he knew most women would be furious at seeing him mauled by a voluptuous beauty. Others might turn cold and walk away. Lydia, his contrary Lydia, grinned broadly at his predicament and steered her companions toward the other ladies, confident he could deal with his own problems.

From the color of their hair, Max gathered the women with Lydia were her family. Their first sight of him was of a diamond-bedecked lady pawing him. Far from being humiliated, Lydia *laughed*. At him, of course.

He loved that woman. He loved her with all his heart and soul and not just the part of him that had noticed her first. He'd fight tooth and nail to make her feel as he did right now, like he would explode with happiness and anticipation.

To that purpose, he had to learn to deal with his magnetic disability. He glanced down at the woman who had carried his first-born son. "Susan, you look charming this evening. Why don't you introduce yourself to the earl and marquess while I speak to my bride?"

He hadn't seen Susan in sixteen years, but he still recognized her fluttery lashes and pout. They no longer made his heart pound. He left her without a qualm to cross the room to his betrothed.

LYDIA WAS A LITTLE SHAKY AS SHE INTRODUCED HER FAMILY TO LADY AGNES and her cadre. She'd been terrified of meeting Max's friends, of being asked to find books she couldn't, of introducing her critical family to the more eccentric, aristocratic Malcolms. The books had been calling seductively to her all day, promising escape. What if they finally wished to speak to her?

But she couldn't abandon their guests, even when she entered her own drawing room to see a gorgeous lady in Max's arms. The sight had shaken all her other fears away.

But then Max had beamed at her as if she were the sun and moon and stars, and her world had righted again. A man who could do that could surely tilt the tower back in place.

She knew the instant Max came up behind her. She stepped back to be closer. He placed a large, reassuring hand on her shoulder and whispered in her ear. "What the devil is Richard's mother doing here?"

She almost laughed again. Nervous laughter, perhaps, but Max did have a way of keeping her feet on the ground. "Invited herself, I understand," she murmured, "to see that Richard isn't being locked in a dungeon."

In a louder voice, she said, "Mother, Sara, this is Maxwell Ives, my betrothed. Max, Mrs. Lovell Wystan and Mrs. Ralph Brown, my mother and sister."

Seeing Max through her family's eyes, Lydia could understand why they might doubt he was interested in dowdy, plain her. Dressed in a tailored black dinner suit with crisp starched linen, glittering studs in his cuffs, a fresh cravat over his elegantly embroidered silver waistcoat, Max gave every appearance of wealth and aristocracy. They'd never seen him in a three-day-old beard, reeking of excrement, and coated in filth.

By the time pleasantries were exchanged, dinner was ready. Max caught Lydia's elbow and held her back while his mother happily arranged the guests in order of precedence.

"My cousins recognize me," he said in relief. "Have you been introduced to Rainford and Ives yet?"

"When they arrived," she whispered back. "You have an interesting family. They didn't ask about the library but wondered if they could visit the roof."

Max snorted inelegantly. "Give them an inch of permission, and they'll take a mile. You'll find them in your library soon enough. I just wanted to thank you for not making a scene over Susan. She's always been forward."

Daringly, Lydia stood on her toes and kissed his freshly-shaved cheek. "I have high expectation that your tastes in women have improved greatly since you were eighteen. I'm sure she was just admiring your fine tailoring." She smoothed his lapels.

She needed Max's assurance to survive her wedding dinner. She was dining with an earl and a marquess! The men who would be standing up for Max were even more intimidating than Max with their suave good looks and elegant London attire.

"Who's the brown wren on the other side of the epergne?" Max whispered, leading her into the dining room. He maneuvered into the chair beside Lydia, discarding his mother's carefully arranged place cards.

"Belle Malcolm. She has been teaching at the school but her experience is with running a large estate. Your mother brought her here to be our steward. I'm sure there's a story there, but I haven't had time to learn it. If she bothers you, we will send her back with your mother."

The new steward mostly kept her gaze on her plate, Lydia noticed. That wasn't the best test—especially with the epergne hiding Max—but perhaps Miss Malcolm was not a woman who liked men.

Susan was happily entertaining Max's bachelor cousins. Richard's mother was still in her thirties and beautiful. Lydia was grateful Max didn't seem interested in her sophisticated looks and flirtation.

"The moment I saw you laughing at my predicament with Susan, Cupid's arrow struck. I swear it did," Max told her, as if saying the day had been warm. He cut off a particularly succulent bite of his roast and placed it on her plate. "I've never loved anyone before. I thought I did a time or two, but that was infatuation and lust."

Lydia felt a warm tingle in her midsection that she blamed on Max's proximity. She associated the seductive rumble of his voice with his hands kneading her breasts, and it caused terrifying flutters in the vicinity of her heart. "Gratitude," she murmured. "You're just grateful I didn't murder you."

He chuckled. "That, too. I am most exceedingly grateful for your patience and understanding. But that's part of the whole. I love your beauty. I love the way you respond in bed—those are more parts of the whole. But what I feel is *more,* as if a silver chain binds our hearts."

The tingle in her middle became a raging wildfire. She had never thought of herself as particularly lovable. She might, on occasion, be indispensable. Mostly, she thought of herself as practical, a convenience. She loved her family in a compartmentalized way, because they were family. How did she, in her narrow, confining realm, love an expansive man like Max, one who seemed to encompass the entire world?

Before she could formulate any sensible reply, the marquess of Rainford stood up and raised his glass in toast. The other gentlemen took turns doing the same. With a little coaching from his mother, even Richard stood to say a few words at his first adult dinner.

By the time they finished their toasts and plates of Marta's delicacies, Lydia was feeling a little lightheaded, even though she'd imbibed only watered wine.

"I think this is where I'm supposed to lead the ladies away so you may carouse with your friends," she whispered to Max. "Do not leave me alone too long or I may run and hide."

He patted her hand. "I make no promises. They have hard heads and years of joshing me to catch up on."

"Oh dear, no." Lydia set down her napkin. "I cannot do it all alone. I love the company, but I am not a night owl, and I am out of energy. Are couples supposed to walk to the altar exhausted?"

"Probably prevents one or both from running," he said with a laugh. "They're too hungover to think and too fatigued to fight their families. Shall I announce the gentlemen are leaving when you do?"

The warmth in her midsection spread at his understanding. "I don't suppose telling them there are reports of a ghost of a Roman soldier guarding his hoard of silver would distract them?"

"It would," he crowed. "But do you really want drunken guests on the ramparts at this hour? You're the librarian. You're allowed to be elusive and eccentric. Flee. Leave the others to do as they please."

"You won't mind?" she asked a little too eagerly. She might not believe herself the Malcolm Librarian, but she would love to pretend for one evening.

"If you will trust me to handle Susan and the wren, I will trust you not to find some excuse in your books to call off the wedding." He leaned over and kissed her nose.

The library was definitely calling to her, and hope pattered in her heart. "My turn to be grateful for your understanding," she whispered back, before standing and making her announcement that it was time for the ladies to withdraw.

The guests stood. One of the auburn twins protested and suggested the men join the ladies.

"That's Bran," Max murmured. "He doesn't know when to keep his mouth shut. And he's angling for Susan's attention."

Lydia nodded understanding and addressed the protester. "And deny the ladies a chance to gossip about you? Shame on you, Mr. Pascoe. Enjoy your brandies and reunion. We'll see you in a little while."

Since there was no small withdrawing parlor in the main block, Lydia led the way back to the great hall where tea trays had been laid out and the sconces turned up. As if she were accustomed to being the lady of the house and doing as she pleased, she saw her guests settled, then excused herself for business.

Her own inhibited family murmured objections, but Max's Malcolm relations quite took it in stride and waved her off. She should probably worry about what mischief they were up to, but she heeded the call of the books.

Maybe, finally, they would open to her?

Eagerly, she slipped through the concealed door in her office and lit an oil lamp.

An ominous wind whistled up the stairs as it never had before. Pages rustled. Books shifted uneasily. She climbed upward, hoping to see a misplaced volume or two push out at her.

Nothing. They told her nothing.

She sat at the top of the stairs, with the wind tossing her hair, and cried.

If anything, the books were telling her she would lose them all.

TWENTY-FOUR

MAX DID HIS BEST TO ABSTAIN FROM DRINKING MORE THAN A SIP FOR EACH toast, but even his head for liquor was feeling it as Gerard lifted his glass once more.

"To your magnificent bride." Taller and more elegantly lean than Max, the Earl of Ives and Wystan swung his glass as if he hadn't downed half a bottle. "If time weren't so limited, I'd pursue her myself. She is a goddess."

Max grinned and drank to that. "You'll have to find your own librarian. My goddess is attached to the castle."

Max felt that like a hook in his soul. If he didn't fix the tower, if anything happened to the library. . . Lydia would be more than devastated. He couldn't begin to imagine how they would go on in such a case.

He loved her. He'd promised to give her a home. But if he couldn't give her the home she needed—

She'd never said she loved him.

"Tell us the tale of the Roman soldier," Bran insisted, munching from the fruit tray the staff had delivered.

The Roman soldier? Ah, the distraction Lydia had concocted and he'd offered. He might not read tales, but he'd learned to tell them over long, lonely nights over campfires. "I'm not a historian," he warned. "The more scholarly among you will have to fill in the blanks."

"In other words, we should make it up ourselves," Gerard said with a laugh. "The Romans conquered our blue-faced ancestors back in the first century, when dirt walls made adequate defenses."

"The savages probably considered any walls as corrals to pen in iron-wearing eccentrics," the solemn marquess added without inflection to indicate humor or cynicism. "Maybe our pagan ancestors built the tower to keep an eye on the soldiers."

Max grinned. His family was inclined to view the world through broader perspectives. "I've found evidence of a primitive watchtower, although from what I've uncovered so far, our more civilized ancestors built on the foundation of an old Roman site. The Romans liked their creature comforts. The original foundation shows a sophisticated construction more suited to Romans than to Picts or Britons. My theory is that a number of those soldiers married our blue-faced ancestors and remained behind to fend off other invaders."

"They remained behind with a hoard of silver?" the marquess asked. Normally a serious fellow, he was just drunk enough to play along.

"Silver was mined around here." Gerard waved his long fingers vaguely. "But these days, oil is the new gold. Everyone is hunting it before the Americans corner the market."

"I thought it was coal they mined here." Max wondered if the earl was concocting a tale of his own. Oil? Oil could be had in *Scotland*? His mind drifted back to his tumble earlier—the hole had smelled oily.

"The coal mines have exhausted the easy, lucrative seams. Since everyone wants oil now, deeper coal production is becoming economically unfeasible. Your Romans wouldn't have known what to do with oil though." Gerard sipped his brandy.

"Well, they would have burned coal to heat their baths, so they may have mined these hills. But whoever built the vault beneath the ancient part of the tower wasn't a poor soldier," Max said, leading them on. "The original tower was built of impenetrable stone, not wood and wattle. It may initially have had wooden stairs, but at some point, they were replaced with iron. There's an immense cistern, an impregnable well, and a sophisticated drainage system that fertilized and watered the fields."

"Iron lodestone in these hills too." Gerard added. "So you think your sophisticated Roman architect—not a soldier from the sound of it—mined silver in his sewage field?"

"Or coal to heat his bath," Bran added helpfully. "To attract nubile blue-faced maidens. Shouldn't we visit the maidens instead of talking about them?"

"Even I'm not drunk enough for blue faces," Max said facetiously. "But if you're wishing to leave to see Susan, she's Richard's mother." He'd sent his son away once the hard drinking had started. "She's looking for another rich husband. Except for the new steward, my mother conveniently did not invite any of her nubile maidens to this dinner." For which he was most grateful.

"Will the maidens be here tomorrow?" Bran asked. "I'm only asking for Brendan. He needs to marry wealth."

His silent twin punched him.

"I'm fairly certain none of Mother's students or teachers are wealthy. Malcolms tend to marry money and spread the wealth around." Max rose, happy to direct his companions to the hall, hoping Lydia would be there.

"Then why the devil did our forefathers and fathers keep marrying them?" Bran complained.

Max pounded his smaller cousin on the back, nearly toppling him. "You'll find out once you meet the right one. Start earning your own way, my boy. Marrying for riches is outmoded."

They entered the great hall to find his mother and the married ladies in a huddle, bent over books and writing material, no doubt plotting Max's future. Lydia wasn't with them. Neither was the brown wren. Susan, however, looked up eagerly.

Max was pretty certain he felt the tower tremble in warning. He fled in search of Lydia.

THE MOMENT MAX STEPPED THROUGH THE DOOR AT THE TOP OF THE STAIRS, the wind died and the books settled. Lovely, Lydia thought. *She* was the cause of the disturbance. If the people who tested librarians saw the ominous wind, they'd heave her out on her head.

Max sat on the narrow step above her. "That gown isn't really suited for these treads, is it?"

Lydia knew her smile was watery as she wiped her eyes with the back of her hand. "I really wasn't meant for finery. It's nice to play dress up, but I'm still a steward, if only of the library. I'm not sure what I will do with myself if I hire your mother's steward."

"Is that what you're crying about?" he asked in concern. "We don't have to hire her. Your butler seems quite capable."

"The Folkstons are good with the household accounts, but there is apparently far more to the estate than even I know. Have you looked at the maps on the desk?" Lydia untangled her lovely silk from the iron treads and took Max's hand to stand.

Her heart and soul ached, but she couldn't disappoint Max with her lack of confidence. Any woman in the universe would be thrilled to have him for husband and not need more. She, unfortunately, wanted what she'd never had—belief that she was good enough for a man like Max and for a library that needed magic.

"I've glanced at the maps. It appears the estate includes the entire hill the castle overlooks, which makes sense for a fortress. What is inexplicable is why they would build the entrance road on the most precarious side of what is otherwise a gradually sloping hill." He lifted her up and straightened the long train of her gown so she wouldn't trip.

"That's not inexplicable to hermits," she said, some of her humor returning with Max's presence. "Mr. C liked keeping out strangers. But the map is covered in little numbers and circles. I don't know what they mean, so I wasn't sure what it's saying."

"Survey language, how many degrees latitude and so forth to mark your boundaries more clearly than *the old oak by the broken fence*," Max explained.

Lydia lifted her petticoat and skirt to climb the last stairs to the suite. "Is it possible there might once have been a town on the sloping side? Like Edinburgh—the castle guarded the highest point and the town formed in its shadow?"

"We can speculate all we like, but short of digging up a mountain, I guess we'll never know. You need a book from the ancestors who built this place," Max said.

And just like that, Lydia heard the call. She froze and glanced down all the dark stairs. Why did the damned library only answer Max's questions?

Grimacing, knowing this was her duty, she bundled up her skirts and petticoat and descended the stairs over Max's protests. The book hummed and sang and by the time she reached the last landing, she practically heard a chorus of demand.

But only one book pushed from the shelf—an ancient tome of faded, cracked leather. Even without opening it, she knew it was in Latin, in washed-out, crabby script. To prevent tripping on her long skirt, she placed the book in the apron she made by holding up her gown, and returned upstairs, where Max watched with interest.

His fascination enhanced the fluttery feeling in her midsection, even though she wasn't thinking about coupling.

"Bedtime reading?" he suggested, taking the book and opening the door.

"Not tonight. My Latin is too rusty. I feel as if I could sleep for a week." She loved the easy familiarity of talking with Max, his acceptance of her need for a book, and having his strong hand at her back. He made her feel feminine and delicate, even when she knew she was not.

"Will you tell me now why you were weeping?" He set aside the book once they entered their small parlor and reached to unfasten her heavy necklace.

"Because the books are angry with me." She didn't have any other way of explaining it.

"I don't know how that's possible. Is there anything I can do?" He added the necklace to the table with the book.

Lydia rubbed her nape and stretched her neck. "I think it's because I can't hear them."

"Frustrated books! Only fair, given how many times they've frustrated me." He massaged her aching muscles. "Does this mean you're not angry with me? I tried not to linger too long, but you were gone by the time the others were prepared to leave the table." He began working the fastening of her gown.

Max's insecurity with women's emotions rendered him human and increased the fiery fluttering she didn't know how to identify. So Lydia swung around and kissed him, thrilling in the power to do so anytime she wished. "Not you at all. You are my rock. But I am terrified I'll lose you once it's discovered I'm no librarian. If I have to leave this tower, will you sail to Burma?"

Max responded with alacrity, covering her with kisses. "It's you I want, not a stack of stones. If you don't have a library, maybe you can go with me to Burma."

The notion excited and horrified her equally. "I don't know who I'd be without books," she protested.

He pushed her toward the bedchamber. "There is a whole universe out there you haven't set eyes on."

"There's a whole universe in *here* that you haven't seen," she retorted, although she still felt weepy that she might never see it all either.

While she stepped out of her gown and petticoats, Max crossed the room, yanked back the draperies, and opened the door on the tiny balcony. "The castle's tower is inside an even greater edifice. Come look."

Lydia grabbed a robe against the cool night air and joined him. Darkness spread across the hillside, obscuring the trees in the distance.

Max gestured at the sky. "The stars are different everywhere. You could travel the world and never see this exact piece of sky. Or that field or those trees. You can allow yourself to be confined by these walls or you can go outside and find rooms full of flowers and people and animals you've never met. That world is every bit yours as this tower."

Admiring the beautiful star-studded sky, Lydia leaned into him, enjoying Max's hard arm circling beneath her breasts. "And it's nice to occasionally explore that outside tower, even as it's amusing to learn the various neglected rooms in the main part of the castle. But like visiting foreign lands, I'm just *visiting* those places. Home is my library."

He hugged her tighter. "For me, the world is my home. But the best room in my home is wherever you are. So if you need this library to be home, I will find a way to save it. Once I do, they can't send you away."

"That's quite preposterous, and you know it." But she kissed him again. "I love that you say these things though."

"Tomorrow, you will be mine and will read Latin to me," he whispered into her hair. "Tonight, we will pretend this room is the only world we know."

Could she make Max her whole world? Lydia feared she couldn't, but for tonight, she accepted his offer.

TWENTY-FIVE

"My word, all of Edinburgh must have been invited," Max's bride-to-be marveled, watching the latest arrivals from the parlor window of their tower suite.

"And half the empire," he added, draping his wedding clothes over his arm and kissing Lydia's rosy cheek. His goddess looked even more delicious when the sun rose and highlighted her glorious hair. He battled the need to kiss her all over one more time. . . "I invited my old school-mates, remember. And I daresay my mother extended an invitation to every Malcolm or Ives in existence."

"Well, she only had two weeks to prepare, so maybe not quite all," Lydia said in amusement. "This lot is too early to have arrived by the Edinburgh train. Perhaps the one from Glasgow?"

"Possibly. Or they rode up yesterday and stayed the night in the village. I need to sneak down to the guest room and pretend I slept there before Lloyd shows up." He leaned over her shoulder to admire the procession of carts and horses on the rough drive. "They won't all want to stay the night, will they?"

"If they mean to attend the reception, they might. The ceremony was scheduled late to allow time for the city guests to arrive. Do you recognize those two officious gentlemen wearing suits?"

Max muttered an obscenity as he located the pair.

Lydia glanced at him in curiosity. "Not invited guests?"

He groaned. "My step-uncle and his son. Mother may have invited them, if only to rub their noses in fate. And they probably came from the baron's place. Isn't that his carriage following?"

"Crowley has people with him. I don't recognize them," Lydia whispered. "Surely the trustees wouldn't send someone to test me today, of all days?"

"They're probably old friends of Mother's," he said reassuringly. "I'll clear the rest of the evidence of my existence from the suite. You can invite your family and your nosy Malcolm friends up, and you can hide until this afternoon. The bride needn't play hostess. Mother will be in her element, greeting guests."

Max wouldn't have her fretting on their wedding day. Basking in Lydia's grateful smile, he gathered up his possessions, then slipped down the hidden stairs to the guest room. He didn't have to put on starched linen and tails just yet.

While his Ives cousins slept off last night's excesses, Max went in search of his sons. He found them in the breakfast room—alone. Even the ladies hadn't come down yet.

"We have a responsibility to entertain our guests," he informed them, slapping together toast and ham and anything else that would go on toast.

His sons looked interested, if rightfully wary.

"Mr. Lloyd said we were to stay out of the way until the wedding," Richard said. "But I'm old enough to help."

"Excellent. We need to keep the ladies and the gentlemen apart, just the way we did last night." Max thought that would work out as nicely for him as it did for Lydia, if the new arrivals meant her harm. "The ladies will want to gossip and the men will want to *do* things, like hunt or explore or play cards." Max was making this up on the fly. It wasn't as if he had much experience at civilized entertainments. He just knew his gender.

"We can take them to the library to read," Bakari suggested.

The boys had never seen the journal library, only the reference one in the guest wing and the one passing itself off as a billiard room. "You may ask if they'd like to see the *guest* libraries if you wish. We do not want them expecting to see Miss Lydia's private one."

"But most of them will want to drink and play games, won't they?" Richard said.

"And eat," Max agreed. "I believe the ladies have already ordered *al fresco* dining for early guests. Laddie will direct the gentlemen to the outdoor buffet. Mrs. Folkston will lead the lady newcomers inside to refresh themselves. That's where you come in."

Praying to all the omnipotent spirits who had kept him alive this long, Max ate his breakfast and outlined his hasty plan to separate out his uncle and the baron and anyone who might cause Lydia grief. Giving the boys free rein to enlist any of the current guests who might drag themselves out of bed early, he left them bolting down food and making impossible plans.

He'd far rather be digging a sewer than playing host to financiers and aristocrats. He figured he'd make a royal ass of himself before the day grew warm. But Lydia didn't mind if he was an uncivil ass, he reminded himself. And if she didn't, no one else mattered.

He wasn't a man who wasted time on fear, but he was having a hard time convincing himself that conversing with stuffed shirts was necessary. Yanking on a ratty country tweed coat over an old waistcoat and leather breeches, Max set out to act as host for the wedding breakfast and bodyguard for his bride. If he meant to steer this lot to the courtroom to identify him, he needed to play nice.

"Schoolmates," he muttered as he left by the garden door. "Courts. Judges. No murdering of uncles," he reminded himself as he walked toward the gathering guests.

"Or barons," he added, noting the man Lydia had identified as Lord Crowley studying the sloping field at the back of the castle. Max headed for the stable, where a number of gentlemen were admiring each other's horseflesh.

Out of pure spite, Max stood there, waiting for his elegantly attired guests to either recognize him or mistake him for a servant.

A less stylish gentleman standing to one side studied Max surreptitiously. Max returned the favor. There was something familiar about the slouching shoulders and skinny frame—

When the visitor pulled out thick spectacles, Max grinned. "Percy! I didn't think you'd come."

His old classmate pushed his wide-framed spectacles up his nose just as he used to twenty years before. Stepping up now that he was recognized, he held out his hand. "You haven't shrunk and you still dress like a coachman, Dwarf."

The mention of the ridiculous nickname swiveled a few heads in their direction.

"You came in on the Glasgow train?" Max asked. "Have you breakfasted? Or are you just waiting on those other well-fed idiots to finish bragging about their steeds?"

More of the braggarts pivoted to study him.

"A bite wouldn't be amiss," Percy admitted. "I was trying to determine if any of the braggarts might be you."

Max chortled and held out his hand to another almost-familiar stranger who dared approach. "And I suppose you're all here to see how I managed to persuade any woman to marry me?"

"We're more interested in how you managed not to get yourself killed." One of the horsemen joined in. "I can still take you in the ring if you're as obnoxious as I remember."

"*Dingo!* Did no one ever teach you not to antagonize your host? And I thought I was uncivilized!" Max shook hands all around, desperately attempting to place faces with names while retorting to insults. Dingo wasn't the man's name, of course, but as schoolboys, they'd lived by irrational sobriquets.

"I'm more interested in the castle than why you're alive or need us," Percy said diffidently. "My students will want to hear all about it. That tower is a perfect example of medieval architecture at its best, even if it has been mutilated for modern use."

Opportunity knocked. Vowing to make Percy godfather to his next-born, Max swung his arm to indicate everyone join him on the gravel drive back to the untended lawns. A few gardeners had arrived these past weeks to clip and mend, but it was much too late to return the landscaping to any former glory.

Max pretended he didn't see his uncle and cousin conversing with more officious gentlemen on the far end of the buffet. He helped himself to ale and regaled his guests with castle history and lies while they worked their way through the generous repast the kitchen had provided.

Decked out in newly acquired suits, his sons worked the crowd, directing the gentlemen to the stable, to a tour of the "Roman cellar," to the guest door and library. Mrs. Folkston—also garbed in new finery—discreetly guided female guests to the main entrance and accommodations.

A man nearly as broad and dark as Max stepped up to introduce himself. "I'm Simon Blair, Drew's cousin. My wife and your bride are acquainted. I've built mines. How filthy will I get if I poke around a bit below the tower? Olivia won't appreciate mud."

"Maxwell Ives, pleasure, sir. I've heard about you. The front section of the tower should be safe, but once you wander deeper, I make no promises. Maybe after the ceremony? I'd love to have an expert opinion."

Blair slapped him on the back and moved on, bringing Max face-to-face with his uncle.

Max waited to see if his uncle might acknowledge that Max really was his nephew. From the look on his uncle's face, Max assumed hell would have ski slopes and ice-skating rinks before that happened.

Refusing to allow ugliness to mar his wedding day, Max regaled the rest of his audience with the growing fiction of a wealthy Roman engineer building the first tower with plumbing and baths and the proceeds of a silver mine.

By this time, the Pascoe twins had wandered out, thwarted in their efforts to woo nubile young ladies. They contributed their version complete with Roman ghost and buried treasure.

Even the baron listened—which nicely kept him from bothering Lydia. A keg of ale was emptied and a second arrived. The tour through the cellar gained more interest as more guests trickled in and heard exaggerated tales of silver mines. People would believe any story told by a person of authority, poor fools.

Apparently satisfied with his perusal of Lydia's grounds, Lord Crowley took advantage of a pause in the storytelling to introduce himself.

"Henry, Baron Crawley, your bride's neighbor." He held out his plump hand.

Instead of shaking it, Max shoved a mug of ale in it. "I don't believe Lydia invited you."

"I had guests who were invited," the baron said offhandedly. "And visitors from Miss Wystan's trustees wished to have a word. Perhaps now is the time?" He gestured at the two suited strangers who'd arrived with him. "They've obtained the test the Librarian must pass before she can claim her full status."

LYDIA SOOTHED HERSELF WITH TEA AND TOAST AND THE JOURNAL THAT HAD called to her last night. She knew any moment her mother and sister would knock at her door, and the rest of the wedding party would follow. But for right now, for these few moments, she happily translated Latin and inscribed what she learned. This was her true calling.

The journal writer was a woman, naturally. As best as Lydia could tell, the book was written before the outer walls of the tower were completed. She read with fascination about life in the inner tower before it became a library. The woman was too busy to write as much as Lydia would have liked to read. But she spoke of the kitchen housed outside the old walls in a stone outbuilding that had been there as long as anyone remembered. The remains of the Roman encampment? She mentioned the cistern and the well and her gratitude that her husband's family had such amenities.

She also mentioned a bathhouse, an armory, and a dungeon, which might also have been built from Roman ruins. So this had not necessarily been a Malcolm stronghold from the beginning.

Of course, it hadn't. Malcolms married warriors and lords in those evil days when women who knew how to read and write or lived alone were called witches. Or they became nuns, which probably wasn't a good option for half-pagan descendants of Druids.

Dungeon? The tower had a dungeon? Did Max need to know that? How did one fit a dungeon in with a cistern and well?

She had just begun reading about a village of craftsmen growing up outside the tower walls when the inevitable knock sounded on her door. With a sigh, she set aside the journal.

Her mother and sister strode in bemoaning Lydia's shabby gown and braid. Behind them followed the ladies Lydia had only recently come to know—Lady Phoebe, Lady Dare, and Olivia Blair, who lived half way to Glasgow and had children to mind, so didn't visit often. She must have been on the early train.

The ladies descended on Lydia in exclamations of joy and admiration, steering her toward the bedchamber as if they'd lived here all their lives. Lydia began to feel a trifle better about her wedding day.

"We left our men outside with Max," Phoebe said. "He has his sons leading tours beneath the tower. They'll be digging up the Roman bath if we don't start this ceremony soon!"

Lydia could only imagine. . . She almost laughed at the vision of Max and his best men walking up the aisle in mud-encased shoes or worse. "Surely the marquess and the earl aren't out there, are they?"

"The marquess?" her mother asked in astonishment, stepping away from Lydia's elaborately gowned entourage. "Surely a proper lord would not dig under the tower?"

"The earl is an Ives. I don't know about the marquess, but Ives curiosity is greater than common sense." Lydia hugged her mother. "Do not fear. We will all be as grand as you wish for a few hours."

"Your hair, we must start with your hair!" Olivia cried happily. "I have brought an assortment of pins and combs and ribbons you can pick through as you like. I know you disdain ornament, but today, you must shine."

"I was very shiny last night," Lydia informed her. "Lady Agnes emptied her jewel box over my head."

"I wish I'd had my camera here." Lady Dare was setting up said camera. "In the future, we'll all have glamorous portraits of our wedding days to hang on the wall. Real people, real memories, not artificial backgrounds and fake poses for a painter."

"Posing for a camera is equally artificial," Olivia pointed out.

They quarreled amiably as they brushed and pulled and tugged at Lydia's hair. If she believed the ladies, her hair wasn't as vulgar as she thought. They exclaimed over the color and the fineness and the frizzy curl as if it were a stack of gold instead of a haystack. Of course, Max claimed to like it, too, but he'd say anything to persuade her into bed.

She'd drifted off into a vision of their honeymoon night when another knock resounded on the outer door.

"That must be our tea." Uninterested in hair or clothes, Lady Phoebe was rummaging through books on the bedchamber shelves. "I'll fetch it."

When she returned, she was grim and pale and holding a letter instead of a tea tray. "The trustees have sent the committee to test your librarian skills. Why would they do that on your wedding day?"

Lydia was in too much shock to even consider an answer.

TWENTY-SIX

TORN BETWEEN THE ASSORTED VEXATIONS THREATENING THEIR WEDDING DAY, Max gave up blocking his uncle and ran after the two officious suits knocking at the front door. He'd find a dungeon cell and lock them in it. Why, by all that was holy, would the trustees send a committee to a *wedding*? On a Sunday. Without any warning.

The message Max inferred from this attack, especially delivered by Crowley, was sinister. The solicitors meant to prevent Lydia—and possibly Max—from taking over the property they wanted to sell. It was a modern version of storming the castle.

He dashed up the front stairs and into the great hall only to see the two strangers escorted out the other side. With his mind on the goal, he didn't even notice the room full of women—until Susan intercepted him.

Panicked, he glanced around. Ladies everywhere, watching, easing closer. In a fit of frustration, Max grabbed a claymore off the wall, holding it like a shield in front of him. "Out of my way, Susan. Don't come between me and my bride."

Susan looked startled. Others tittered. No one stopped him as he rushed through the immense hall into the corridor beyond, just in time to see the footman steering the interfering bastards toward the guest library.

Pointing the sword in his hand, Max shouted, "Zach, stop right there! They are uninvited intruders. They might mean harm to Miss Lydia. Throw them out or lock them up!"

Both men turned and blanched at the sight of Max in his tweeds and leather breeches, wielding a sword almost as large as they were. They weren't hefty invaders but paunchy, bespectacled, office sorts, the kind of civilized gentlemen who wielded paperwork like weapons. Max avoided the sort on principle. He wasn't sorry to terrify them.

He could hear the ladies rustling into the corridor and knew they listened and watched and could suffocate him in silks and coos at any moment. A chill crept up his spine. His only allies were outside. He didn't have time to sort this lot out, although he heard his mother speaking impatiently.

Trapped between women in silk finery and document-wielding businessmen, forced into the same uncomfortable position that had sent him fleeing as a lad, Max stood his ground. Even if no one else understood, he was confident that Lydia knew why he might lose his temper and behave uncivilly to women and bespectacled solicitors.

Max pointed the claymore at the cowering gentlemen. The footman watched Max nervously, as if he might go off his head. Maybe he would.

Amazingly, the ladies stayed behind him. He didn't have time to ponder that curiosity. "Either you leave, sirs, or I'll have Zach lock you in the wine cellar until Miss Wystan has time to ask the reason for your presence. And that will be sometime tomorrow, at best."

"We haven't come all this way to be put off," the older, balding one protested. "It is Miss Wystan's duty to subject to our testing. The position of executor may be appointed, but the library itself must be maintained by a true librarian." He sniffed in disdain at Max's sword.

Max remembered those days of being looked down upon by these sorts. He'd learned a few things since and grinned wickedly. "And it is my duty to protect Miss Wystan with my life. Would you prefer that I send Zach for pistols? Or should I just behead you here? The wine cellar is quite comfortable, I'm told, better than the dungeon. We have one of those too."

Well, it could have been a dungeon. There weren't any cells anymore. Max had no problem stretching the truth.

The dreaded rustling of petticoats approached, but it was his mother's voice he heard. "Don't worry, Maxwell, we'll manage from here. I don't believe anyone notified me of the testing committee's arrival, so I'm quite certain they must be impostors. Come along, ladies, let's lock them up until we have time to question them."

The two strangers went wide-eyed and cringed backward. At a bunch of women?

Max swung around to face a sea of crinoline, silk, and. . . *swords*. The ladies had all followed his example and armed themselves from the great hall's arsenal. Even Richard's mother held a dagger. Some of them looked almost formidable, as if they knew how to use their rapiers. The broadswords—not so much.

"Father!" Richard shouted from the garden door behind the terrified solicitors. "Father, come quickly. Someone has fallen into the tunnel!"

"Hell and damnation!" Max shoved past his cowering captives, leaving them to the bloodthirsty women.

LYDIA PULLED ON ONE OF HER OLD GOWNS, QUICKER TO DON THAN FRILLS and trains, and hurried downstairs to greet the testing committee. The great hall was filled with chattering guests—*wielding swords*. She saw no sign of the strangers sent by the trustees.

Rushing along behind her, her bridesmaids halted to observe the spectacle.

"Why is everyone armed?" Phoebe asked in puzzlement. "Should I have worn my *sgian dubh*?"

"I don't like the idea of weaponry near my library," Lydia said uneasily. "I intended to ask Max about removing some of the collection elsewhere. It's a trifle. . ."

"Medieval?" Azmin, Lady Dare, suggested with amusement.

Lady Agnes emerged from the grumbling crowd, holding a hand to her ample chest and breathing hard. "There seems to be an emergency," she announced.

Seeing no sign of solicitors, Lydia immediately went into panic mode. "Max? Max is all right? And the boys?" Had Max's fear of women *fighting* over him come true and he'd fled? The ladies certainly seemed to be bristling with hostility, but that could just be the swords scaring her.

"Someone has fallen down a well. Max and half the wedding party are out there playing in dirt." Gesturing at the door, Lady Agnes appeared more put out than afraid.

"All the *male* half of the wedding party," the female steward-to-be said from behind her. "I think the men have a secret means of communicating. I just saw the earl and marquess rushing out through the front entrance a moment ago in dishabille. I hope those aren't the only shirts they brought with them if there's to be a fight." Those were more words than Miss Malcolm had said all last evening.

"Have Lloyd prepare some of Max's shirts. Ask their valets what they need," Lydia told her. "What happened to the testing committee? Didn't a deputation arrive?"

"We've taken care of them for you." Towering over her sister, Lady Gertrude, the other half of the School of Malcolms, spoke with dour authority. "You needn't concern yourself."

That sounded ominous, but Max in danger was more important. "I'd best see what is happening outside then." She lifted her old skirt and started for the garden door.

"You can't do that, dear!" Lady Agnes cried. "Max shouldn't see his bride before the wedding."

Lydia heard the snickers behind her. She didn't redden. They were married ladies, after all, and her friends. She liked having friends she could trust. "There won't be any wedding if Max falls down a hole. It's dangerous under the tower."

While Lady Agnes practiced fainting, Lydia strode out, followed by half her entourage and a number of guests she didn't recognize. The new steward hesitated over Lady Agnes, but then hurried to join Lydia, as a good steward should.

Outside, men in both suit coats and shirtsleeves were hauling Max's stack of lumber through the garden byre doorway. She found Bakari lingering nervously at the back of the crowd. "What is happening?"

He grasped her hand anxiously. "A big hole opened in the bottom of the tunnel yesterday. We blocked it and put up warning signs that even someone who cannot read would understand. But someone must have taken the signs down. Father said he does not know what is down there but it is unstable. Is that the right word?"

Bakari had a large vocabulary for a six-year-old, but he was still a child. Lydia crouched down to hug him. "*Unstable* means the tunnel is crumbling. Your father knows that. He will be careful. Tunnels aren't deep. The person may have hurt their leg and simply can't climb out."

Richard appeared behind Bakari and shook his head, where Bakari couldn't see him, indicating her assumption was wrong. Lydia felt her stomach tighten and was grateful she'd eaten little. She pushed Bakari into Olivia's hands. The lady knew what to do with children.

"Perhaps I had better see what is happening for myself," Lydia said with what she hoped sounded like confidence. "Perhaps the men might like refreshment? Richard, would you be in charge of that?"

Letting a few of her entourage protectively shuttle off Max's sons, she made her way through the crowd of male strangers. They glanced at her with curiosity, rightfully so, she supposed. Olivia had fixed Lydia's fiery hair in elaborate curls and entwined them with ribbons and sparkly pins so she appeared like a queen from the neck up. From the neck down, her frayed black gown wasn't suitable even for a servant. But it suited for pushing into the dirty dark byre.

She gestured for the other ladies to remain behind. "It's full of cobwebs. Wait here, please."

Inside, she let her eyes adjust to the gloom. Stacks of lumber and bricks filled one corner of this front chamber. Men hauled down a few more timbers and added them to the pile, tipping their caps to her and hurrying back out.

She recognized Laddie and one of the stableboys emerging from the tower cellar's interior. "What is happening? Is Max all right? Is anyone hurt?"

"The man Mr. Ives calls Cuz is down the tunnel," Laddie answered, respectfully pulling on his cap brim. Laddie wasn't a talkative sort on the best of days.

"Mr. Ives is climbing down to pull him out," the other, older man with him said. "But it's a right crumbly tunnel, iffen you ask me. And deep. Anyone fool enough to get himself in there ought to be left to get himself out."

Cuz. His cousin? Max's cousin had fallen into. . . what? A sewer? A cistern?

Lydia was trying not to panic when a suited gentleman blocked the outside light and started shouting, "Where's my son? What happened to my son?" Entering, he startled at seeing Lydia—or any woman at all, presumably.

"Mr. Franklin?" She'd never been introduced to Max's uncle, but she was good at putting two and two together.

"Where's George? They told me George was hurt. Where is he? If that devil has harmed him, I swear, I'll—" His face was nearly gray with fear, which didn't go well with his fading blond hair.

"Max is apparently trying to save a fool who bypassed warning signs," Lydia said, interrupting the tirade. Since he hadn't bothered asking who she was, she saw no reason to explain. "I can't say if the fool is your son. Unless you have knowledge of sewers and cisterns and the like, I'd advise you to stay out of the way of those who do."

"Who the devil are you to talk to me like—"

The tall marquess dipped his platinum-blond head as he entered from the low interior door. He looked dusty and unhappy but spoke with respect. "Miss Wystan, good. The idiot is likely to suffocate if we don't find some way of hauling him out. Max is going down with some equipment. He says to ask you if there is anything in the library about an oubliette?"

As if just noticing George's father, the marquess nodded politely. "Excuse me for interrupting. You were saying?" His cold tone indicated he didn't actually wish to hear Franklin finish his tirade.

Apparently recognizing the striking marquess, Max's uncle wisely shut up.

"An oubliette?" Lydia shuddered. How would she ever find a book on an oubliette? "That's a medieval torture device, isn't it? Why would the library have such a thing?"

"Because the original tower was a fortress designed to protect its inhabitants from enemies. It was not a particularly civilized period. If you have any books at all on the construction of the foundation, those would be useful as well." The marquess looked at her expectantly.

He didn't know she couldn't find anything.

"I thought I gave Max everything we had. I'll bring down those books," she suggested. "I don't remember any mention of an. . . oubliette."

"Max seems to think there may be a trap, at least. His cousin was apparently searching for imaginary silver and has fallen deeper than the drainage tunnel into a part Max has not explored. It's apparently very tight." He didn't look at George's father.

"Is Max. . . is Max in any danger?" Lydia asked, trying to keep her voice from shaking.

The marquess looked sympathetic. "The tunnel is not in good shape, but he's knowledgeable. He has Simon Blair with him. They both know mining. They're working at shoring up the sides. They were hoping a device might already be installed for pulling the prisoners out—or at least for lowering food to them. But they didn't wish to dig through rubble to find out."

"And if there is no device?" Lydia whispered, unable to imagine the dark grim place they worked in.

"Max plans to dig him out," the marquess said. "But the walls in that section appear to be undermined from below. I'll tell him you're looking up the dungeon, and he'll stick to propping up the walls a little longer. His cousin's likely to suffocate if left in there too long."

Max's uncle moaned in despair.

TWENTY-SEVEN

MORE PEBBLES RAINED DOWN FROM THE DRAINAGE TUNNEL. MAX WISHED for a hat. Why the devil was there a *void* beneath the damned sewer?

From the ragged opening in the ceiling, Simon lowered a brighter lantern so he could have a look at where Max was digging.

The light illuminated a narrow shaft with dirt and pebble walls and the remains of what might have been wooden supports. Wood that old could not support the stone sewer forever. The rubble indicated that what once might have been a mine shaft had been filled to provide a foundation for the more solidly-built sewer above.

Maybe this was where Cadwallader's ghost had descended—a tunnel to the spirit world. Or a graveyard.

"Someone created this channel for a reason," Max called to the men above.

Having disappeared into a void beneath the pebbles that Max couldn't access, his cousin was ominously silent now that his cries had been answered. Max didn't trust George, but he didn't think a senseless bookkeeper like his cousin could build a trap in Max's own damned cellar. George had just been his usual doltish self, assumed the warning sign meant Max was hiding something, and had gone where he didn't belong.

"We're looking for any signs of iron," Simon called down. "They may have had chains to lower a cage. Have you found Mr. Franklin yet?"

"There appears to be a fresh pile of rubble over in the far corner. I want to prop up the walls before I risk going over there. The soil is slick with oil and water, and there's likely subsidence that's causing the dirt to give way." Max had never mined shale, but Gerard had been right. This smelled like oil. "I figure George slid into that corner and the ground gave out beneath him."

Or a rusted metal grate covering an oubliette had fallen through, which was why he needed Lydia's knowledge. Before he'd gone silent, George's screams had indicated he was trapped and suffocating. That didn't sound as if he'd fallen into a mine.

Like any bloodthirsty adolescent, Max had listened to the teacher's description of medieval torture devices. He didn't think even mad Englishmen would dig storage holes beneath sewers. This had the design of a trap—an ancient one.

"You don't want to fall in on top of him," Simon agreed. "I have someone tying a rope ladder in case we can't stabilize the walls, but he has to be conscious to climb up it."

One way or another, Max would have to lower the ladder into that black hole before the ceiling caved. His only hope was that Lydia could find another way out. Rebuilding a medieval shaft would take too long.

LYDIA RACED THROUGH THE YARD, BACK TO THE GARDEN DOOR, FORGETTING there were dozens of aristocrats waiting inside for reassurances she didn't have to offer. Poised and confident in their perfume, pearls, and silk, the women crowded around her the moment she entered. Their elegance reminded her of all she was not and never would be.

Not only was she not a beautiful lady, she wasn't even the one thing they thought her—a librarian.

Her ineptitude might be the death of Max. With heart breaking, Lydia brushed past, shaking her head at the questions she heard but couldn't answer. She slammed into her office, locked the door, and escaped into the silence of the waiting library.

It *waited* for her. She could tell. To her, the library was a sentient being, disapproving, calculating, more judgmental than her family had ever been. It would spit her out or swallow her whole if she failed.

She'd asked it how to be a librarian and it hadn't replied. She'd asked for information on the tower for Max, and it had given her everything *he* expected.

"*Max* needs this," she shouted at the waiting emptiness of towering books. "Max needs to know if there is an oubliette!"

Thundering silence.

Failure was not an option. Weeping would not help. She had to *force* the books to give up their information.

"I need to know about the dungeon!" she cried. "Max's life depends on it. *My* life depends on it. *The future of this library might depend on it!*"

As she shouted, her fear blew a hole in the wall of composure she'd projected her entire life. She didn't radiate just helpless frustration but *fury*. Rage at all the times in her life when she'd been lost and helpless and had no means of dealing with the world except with fake calm and wishful thinking. Those wouldn't help Max now. She needed the *library*.

The tower trembled. Or perhaps she did.

Her sisters were the foolish creatures who railed and swooned and panicked if things didn't go their way. Lydia had never been like that, especially after her father had fallen off the roof. She'd known someone had to be the strong one, the cautious one. As the eldest, she had always been the epitome of moderation, the solid foundation others counted on. She might weep in private at her inability to control anything, but she never displayed how she felt.

Until now. With her placidity in shreds, Lydia shook her fist and railed at the silent books. She wept and poured out her heart and soul in tears and terror. In a rage, she yanked out volume after volume, starting with the bottom shelf, demanding that the books respond. The journal yesterday had made no mention of an oubliette, but the books surrounding that journal must be from the same time period. . .

"I need you!" she cried as the books remained silent. "I need your help! Please, please don't let him die because of my incompetence. I know you have the answers. Please!"

Feeling as if she'd taken a knife and ripped herself open, she dropped to her knees and hugged the strewn books to her breast. "Speak to me," she commanded. "I'll do whatever it takes, be whatever I must be, but speak."

Oubliette, a breeze whispered.

Lydia glanced frantically at the mess she'd made. How would she see a book pushing out at her now that they were on the floor?

Oubliette, the breeze repeated.

What had she said to gain this response? That she would be whatever the library wanted her to be? Did it want her to be the librarian? Max had said she didn't analyze, and she didn't. She'd always accepted whatever life threw at her. . .

She wasn't accepting the library's silence. She was demanding its help. She believed wholeheartedly that she was worthy of the library and its vast store of knowledge and had commanded her troops to obey. Or begged, perhaps, but she'd opened herself to the terrifying realization that she could do what Mr. C had done, if only she knew how.

Gathering this tiny bit of confidence, she demanded, "I need the journal on the oubliette, and I need it *now.*" She was the Librarian. She must act like it. She must *believe* it, as she pretended to do in the solicitors' office. She held out her palm.

And there the book was, opening to crabbed Latin script it might take days to parse and translate.

And she knew what it said. Opening her mind, Lydia *heard* the voice in her head. It spoke more clearly than it ever had before.

Clinging to the precious volume, trembling with fear at this invasion of her mind, she obeyed what the voice told her. She determined north from south and made her way past the stacks to the wall opposite her office.

I prayed future generations would never need to know this door. The woman's voice was low, almost an angry Latin chant, but Lydia heard and understood. *The fulcrums are concealed beneath the lions.*

Lydia faltered when she found the brass ornaments on the back wall. She'd known they were there. She'd polished them a time or two. Was her desperation simply feeding her mind? Had she gone insane?

The voice quieted.

Lydia started to panic again, pushing and pulling at the ornaments, looking for the hinge. "I can do this," she repeated over and over. "I can do this. I can hear you. Speak again, please. I love him. I love him so very much, and I've never told him so. If you ever loved anyone, please speak to me."

As if she'd never grown silent, the voice began again, still in Latin, still clear to Lydia. *Twist the second one and push to the left at the same time.*

A narrow door slid to one side, leaving a pitch dark opening she had to crouch to look into.

"Max," she called hesitantly. "Max, can you hear me?"

She couldn't even hear her own voice in the void. She spoke louder, with more confidence. "Max, I have the book. It told me to open this door. Are you there?"

A shout of fury and a rumble of rock nearly brought her to her knees. "Max!" she screamed.

"Lydia?" His voice was distant but clear. "I'm good. The ground slipped under me. Where are you?"

Relief flooded through her and tears rolled down her cheeks. "I'm in the library. There's another concealed door in the back, a very small one."

The voice in her head grew louder, more urgent. Words rushed through her so quickly, they emerged from her lips without registering in her head. She feared she spoke Latin. Max didn't know Latin. She struggled to regain control of her vocal chords, but she was shouting now.

Max called to her in bewilderment.

It didn't matter. She scrambled down the crude iron ladder built into the wall below her, a ladder her head said was there.

A rush and tumble of stone rang loudly from the far side of the cramped passage. Max shouted orders. Men yelled back. Her pulse escalated as she made her way across rocks. She'd brought no lantern. The voice in her head wanted a candle. She didn't have one of those either.

"Max," she cried in her own voice.

"Speak English," he cried desperately. "Or Gaelic or French or anything but Latin!"

An Anglo-Saxon obscenity escaped her lips. She covered her mouth in shock. She thought she heard Max's wry chuckle.

But the book was in Latin, and it was Latin that continued to emerge, faster than Lydia could translate. She could only duck her head under the low ceiling and follow her feet. Her feet seemed to understand the instructions better than her head.

"She's saying something about a trap door to a mine shaft," a weak male voice said from nearby.

"By all the fates, I thought you were dead, George." Max sounded relieved. "Is she telling us how to break out of this hole?"

"Why won't she speak English?" the querulous voice asked.

"Because the journal is in Latin," Max responded sensibly. "If you can translate, we may both escape alive."

"You're sitting on my head, just like you used to do," George complained.

"Only after you kicked me," Max retorted.

"You were bigger than me. Still are. You'll break my neck."

The voice in Lydia's head shouted with irritation in a language that sounded more Gaelic than Latin. Max retorted in a similar language, which seemed to pacify the lady's anger.

"She's insulting the entire male gender," Max said with a laugh.

How could he laugh? How could he accept that she was speaking in tongues? Because he was a Malcolm. He'd lived with insanity most of his life. Lydia reached the solid barrier of another wall and began feeling the rocks, speaking rapidly in a dead language from her books.

"Your Latin lady says there's a trap door, that her sons built it. Something about not approving their. . ." The weak voice hesitated over the translation. "I think that meant bastard. They didn't approve of this hole."

"By George, he knows Latin." Max sounded closer. "Lydia, do you have anything to hammer with? Another rock maybe? Let us know where you are. It's a pretty damned tight fit in here. We're likely to tumble out as soon as you find the door, so be careful."

She could hear other men shouting louder now. But the walls were thick and solid. She cried more Latin as her hands pried at the stone. She pounded with her keys so they could hear her.

"I think I've got you," Max called. "You're near the floor. Stand back and let me kick."

"She's saying there's a latch on the outside," the feeble male voice complained. "Quit being a bully and listen."

A latch. What kind of latch would last centuries? Leather, perhaps. Iron. Lydia ran her hands along the walls until the voice in her head sighed in relief and directed her to a niche in the stone. Finding a lever, she cautiously pulled. "I think I have it. It's pretty rusted. Do I have time to go back and look for oil?"

"She's speaking English again," the stranger cried.

And so she was. The medieval lady had departed. She was on her own.

"No time," Max said tersely. "The rock fill has loosened. If we can't leave this way, we have to climb out of this hole. That means more people above us in the tunnel with ropes and ladders."

Risking more lives or crushing Max and his cousin or. . . Lydia twisted and yanked at the decaying lever. She heard Max kicking from his side.

Metal grated. Stone moved. Lydia hastily stepped back, trying to keep her footing, having no idea of the precariousness of the stones she'd crossed on.

Max's excited shout rang out as his boot pushed free.

"I think the lady said the trap door was mostly for feeding the prisoners," Lydia said tentatively. "It may not be large enough."

"I'll damned well make it large enough. I have a wedding to attend." Max drew his boot in again and pounded at another stone.

An ominous cracking warned the wall wasn't happy.

"Run, Lydia. This is likely to all come down. Light a lamp on the other side so we can find you."

"I can't leave you, Max. I haven't even told you I love you," she cried. "Can I pull the stones from this side?"

"If you love me, then for the sake of any child of mine, get the hell back to the library!" Another stone flew out of the wall.

"That's disgusting, Max." The weak voice was growing stronger and another thud hit the wall.

Lydia clasped the fabric over her abdomen. A new sensation took root, one that wasn't lust or fear but. . . life? Throwing a despairing glance to the crumbling wall, she followed Max's wise advice and protected the innocent. She hurried across the narrow passage and climbed up the metal rungs to the library.

Lloyd and Marta were waiting for her. With cries of distress, they helped her out.

Once back on her feet, Lydia hugged the loyal servants. "Fetch Max's mother and aunt. Tell them Max is coming in through the library and may need help. They'll know what to do."

She didn't know where she found the assurance to say that. Even an hour ago she might have doubted the giddy old ladies of doing anything except wringing hands.

But she knew better now. They held the wisdom of their Malcolm ancestors—just as Lydia did. And Max, if only he accepted it. Ancient knowledge flowed through them in the same way they inherited blue eyes or black hair.

Now that she was safe, the servants rushed to do her bidding. The clatter of falling stone echoed across the empty shaft. Inside the inner tower, Lydia couldn't hear what was happening in the yard. She lit a lamp and held it up in the doorway for Max to use as guide.

"I see the light," the weak voice cried.

"About time," Max answered with a distinct tone of sarcasm.

Lydia screamed as a crash and tumble of stone sent the two men sliding from their prison into the shaft.

TWENTY-EIGHT

BRUISED AND SHAKEN FROM THE FALL, MAX REVELED IN THE BEAUTY OF Lydia's screams, knowing they meant that someone cared.

He grabbed his cousin before the dolt toppled, then shouted at the light ahead. "We're fine, my love. You're brilliant. We may need a helping hand to haul the idiot up. He seems to have injured himself."

His betrothed didn't disapprove of his thick-headedness. She'd said she *loved* him. He could topple mountains with that knowledge.

Max had never really understood what love was. He still didn't. He just knew Lydia filled him with joy.

Since his prim Lydia was uncharacteristically shouting some of the Latin lady's obscenities, he thought maybe he'd unleashed the passion she'd only shown him in bed. He could live with that. She had every right to be furious with him for ruining their wedding day.

She left the light and disappeared from view.

For a moment, a gray shimmering phantasm hovered between him and the library. Max froze. Was that the old librarian?

I told you, she's more valuable than she understands, the ghost whispered. *Be good to her.*

The shimmering image evaporated, exposing the iron rail in the wall. Relieved that he didn't have to battle a ghost, Max caught a rung, but

George was clinging to him like a limpet, one arm dangling uselessly at his side. Sore all over, Max couldn't see a good way of hauling him out without help. Ghosts were bloody well useless.

Richard appeared in the entry above. "Father! They're forming a party to dig you out."

"I sent the ladies to inform them otherwise," Lydia said in her normal pragmatic voice, returning to hold up the lantern. "Richard was at the door, and I thought him trustworthy enough to introduce to the library."

The library, of course. She couldn't haul in just anyone. "Excellent thinking, my love. Rich, I think if you can grasp George's coat just at the shoulder—watch his arm—we can guide him up. How steady are you on your feet, Cuz?"

"Steadier than when you're sitting on my head, *Cuz*," George grumbled.

"Your head needs sitting on if you thought we were hiding silver in a dungeon," Max said with scorn. "I only dirtied your shirt last time. Test me again, and I'll break both arms."

Between them, they hauled George into the library stacks. The chamber was lit only by the lantern Lydia held.

George glanced around at the shelves and the stairs spiraling out of sight to the invisible ceiling above and shuddered. "No wonder Crowley wants this place demolished. It has to be the lout's idea of hell."

And then he passed out.

Once they'd found Dr. Dare to set George's broken bones, and Max took himself off to bathe, Lydia allowed her family and friends to sweep her back to her suite. She was too shaken to argue.

She was an entirely different woman from the one who had left these chambers a few hours ago. Or perhaps not entirely—she had just discovered parts of herself that she hadn't known existed. She was quite reasonably rattled.

"You saved the day, O Great Librarian," Phoebe crowed. "Really, I think we should garb you in royal robes and hand you a broadsword to greet the testers. Did the Vikings have witches? I think you're a direct descendant."

Lydia's mother muttered about witches but Lydia focused on *testers*. "The trustees actually sent the testing committee *today*, why?"

"We'll ask later," Olivia said briskly. "Let me fix those pins in your hair again so we can attach the veil. The preacher has arrived. The chapel will be filling."

Could she repeat what she'd just done? Could she summon any book she needed—or a *spirit*? She desperately needed to read books on librarians. . .

Longing to rush back to the journals to see if she might research what she prayed was her new position, Lydia impatiently allowed herself to be pushed and pulled and pinned and dressed in her finery.

It was extremely fine finery, she had to admit, fingering the satin and lace and admiring the result in the mirror. Her new corset cinched in her waist and raised her breasts, and the delicate, fluttery lace disguised her size—as long as no one stood close to her besides Max. She almost grinned at that.

Max loved her. Max still wanted to marry her even after she'd turned into some kind of medieval harridan. Max wanted to have *children* with her. And he would protect them just as he'd protected his dolt of a cousin, because that's who Max was—a defender. A knight of her own.

She could easily forget about medieval harridans, testers, crumbling tunnels, and lawsuits as long as she thought about Max.

"Photograph!" Azmin demanded when the last frill and furbelow was in place.

"With my ladies-in-waiting, please." Lydia gestured for her gorgeously garbed friends to surround her. They'd all dressed as they'd pleased and made a colorful peacock display to offset Lydia's plain vanilla attire. Her only color was her lovely sapphire necklace and blue hydrangea bouquet.

Azmin glittered with gold jewelry and wore a gauzy sari in iridescent blue, green, and gold. Phoebe had attempted fashion in a raspberry-and-cream striped gown with a dark blue bodice to stay with the wedding's blue theme. Olivia looked her usual lovely blond self in a sedate gown of soft blue silk that disguised the signs that she was increasing.

Lydia's mother and sister fought back tears of joy. Azmin joined the group, then squeezed the bulb to flash her camera light and capture the moment.

"These are dry plates," Azmin said, as if that meant anything to anyone. She pulled a plate from the camera, popped it into a wooden box, and produced another from her bag. "Let me take one more of just the bride, in case the chemicals weren't laid correctly. I do wish they'd hurry and develop the color solution. This would be so gorgeous! I'll have to touch up the final with paint."

After the portrait was done, Lydia's mother and sister hurried downstairs to warn everyone the bridal party was on its way. Her ladies lifted her train so Lydia could navigate the stone stairs. At the bottom, the servants respectfully lined the corridor, holding a flowered arch for Lydia to walk under. Tears welled as she smiled and thanked each individual.

This was her day. If she never knew another happy moment, Lydia would remember this one forever. For the first time in her life, people noticed *her*, instead of the other way around. She didn't particularly like attention, but for this one moment, she felt lovely and important. She lifted her chin in pride and let all her other problems subside. Today, she married Max, a man who loved her just as she was.

With the servants trailing behind her like an honor guard, Lydia walked through the towering, paneled great hall, down the art-studded long corridor on the far side, and into the chapel where her guests waited. Lady Agatha had insisted on potted rowans at the altar.

Admiring the trees, Lydia didn't worry so much about heads turning to watch her. She wanted to acknowledge each and every guest, but her gaze fixed on the amazing man in elegant tailed coat and slightly crooked cravat waiting at the altar, dwarfing his tailored, aristocratic grooms. Max's gaze fastened on her as if she were the only person in existence, and excitement danced in his eyes.

Her heart nearly pounded through her chest, and her smile brightened.

HIS BRIDE'S SMILE ILLUMINATED THE CHAPEL BETTER THAN LIGHT THROUGH the stained glass. Max basked in the glory of her happiness. He hadn't protected Lydia from aggravation, but she still smiled at him as if he had saved the day. How could he not love a woman that understanding?

For Lydia, he would climb a mountain or swim an ocean. Surely he could manage a few minutes in front of the kind of gathering that had once made him quake in terror.

Tenser than he'd been while buried in an oubliette, Max had waited until the last minute to walk out in front of dozens of guests, half of them female. He deliberately gazed over the heads of the audience, watching the entrance, hoping his disinterest would fend off any magnetic reactions. If any female looked his way, he didn't notice. *He didn't notice.* Usually, he knew instantly when the magnetism kicked in. Did this mean his magnetic field didn't work in a church?

Or because he *loved* Lydia? And she loved him. Did that mean they were bonded? He didn't think he'd ever known love before. Disapproval, yes. Disappointment. Resignation. But unconditional love? Never. Women liked to show him off. His mother was *proud* of him occasionally. But that wasn't quite the same thing as what he felt in Lydia. The connection between them was strong and true. He prayed that meant she'd never have to worry about his faithfulness.

Once his lace-bedecked bride entered the chapel, she didn't hesitate. With her glorious red-gold hair shimmering in the stained-glass light, Lydia strode down the aisle, her joyful smile solely for him. Max thought he might burst his buttons with love and pride. She was the most gorgeous creature he'd ever laid eyes on. The quality of her soul shone from her eyes. The beauty of her character danced on her lips. And if he looked any lower, to that splendidly revealed bosom, he'd cripple himself. He contented himself with imagining removing all that lace.

He held out his callused hand, the one he'd spent soap and time scrubbing as clean as a civilized gentleman's, even though he wore gloves now. She clasped his palm eagerly.

Around them, the women had arranged potted trees. Max knew this symbolized the Malcolm Druidic heritage, so the eccentricity barely registered. He simply prayed nothing stopped this ceremony. He'd never meant to be anchored to one woman or one place, but this felt right. He could relax here, as he had never been able to elsewhere.

All he had to do was conquer all the challenges waiting for him. Building bridges was easier.

The preacher spoke the Malcolm vows of love and equality, and Max repeated them without hesitation. He had wanted to order a fancy wedding ring for his bride, but Lydia had wanted them to both wear rings to signify their commitment. So they had chosen plain bands from the village silversmith. Jewelry got tangled in equipment and Max never wore it, but he felt this as a piece of Lydia's heart and wore it proudly. When he finally kissed his bride, the genteel crowd erupted in cheers, egged on by his incorrigible schoolmates and groomsmen—who tossed flour as well as rice. The mice would have a field day.

"We have a dungeon I can throw the barbarians down," he murmured against Lydia's lips. "You have only to say the word."

"They have been celebrating your daring rescue while we dressed. I suspect by evening they will all be drunk enough to pour themselves into the cellar. Why waste your energy when it's better spent on me?" she suggested, before turning back to the cheering audience and lifting her bouquet in acknowledgment.

Chuckling, Max led his lovely librarian down the aisle and through the flowered and beribboned arch held by the servants, back to the great hall where a repast had been laid out for the guests.

With not enough tables to serve a crowd this size, a buffet had been set up. Most of the guests circled it while the wedding party ate at the head of the room, under the arch the servants planted in buckets of soil.

While Lydia and her ladies fussed with veils and lace and whispered excitedly to each other, Max lifted a glass in toast to the men who had answered his call even after twenty years of absence. "I am far beyond honored that you gentlemen have taken time from your busy lives to aid a prodigal in his time of need. I hope to toast you soon at your own happy nuptials. Who is next? Rainford?"

The blond marquess grimaced. "The duke has arranged an assortment of exceptionally suitable maidens for my perusal. An heir is essential, so I suppose I'm next." He glanced at the dark and dashing earl at his side. "You can choose from the ones left over, Ives. My father has excellent taste."

Gerard barked a laugh and sipped his champagne. "You forget, my lord, we are related through maternal lines only. I am an Ives and you are a mere Malcolm. We Ives proliferate with males. We have an overabundance of heirs to the marquisate. And the pater will probably live until eternity, so there is no rush at all."

"Money, not heirs, drives *us*," Bran announced from the far end of the table. "We'll accept your leftovers, Rainford."

The non-talkative twin intervened. "Rainford's prospects will have no interest in impoverished, untitled sons of diplomats."

Max gestured at the array of guests, many of them his mother's students and teachers. "Look out there, my friends, at some of the finest ladies in the kingdom. If they do not have wealth, they have intelligence and integrity, and that is worth far more than gold."

"And they've been known to drive men mad with their talk of ghosts and auras and spirits and things that go bump in the night," Gerard grumbled.

Lydia whispered in Max's ears. "Tell him he's the next one destined to marry a barmy Malcolm. A barmy Malcolm says so."

Max laughed and kissed her, in front of friends and family. Their guests cheered and lifted their glasses in unspoken toast.

"This is the happiest day of my life," he murmured, touching his crystal glass against hers. "Let us remember this moment forever."

"Look this way and smile," Azmin shouted.

As they turned in her direction, she flashed her blinding camera lights.

When Max could see again, he spied his uncle speaking with Hugh Morgan and Miss Trivedi, the team he hoped would be overseeing their financial future, once he talked to the judge. There was the meteor on his sunlit horizon.

He gulped down the rest of his champagne.

TWENTY-NINE

"I WISH WE'D HAD TIME FOR A HONEYMOON," MAX WHISPERED IN LYDIA'S ear as he removed the pins and lace from her hair later that evening. "I'd take you away from all this, to a place with warm breezes and moonlight and the ocean tide lapping at our feet."

"If I'm with you, it does not matter about tides and breezes," Lydia said, stretching her aching neck as the weight of all the folderol was lifted from her head. Her hair rippled down her chemise—Max had already divested her of her sumptuous gown.

She did not mention that what she really wanted to do was go into the library and test her new gift. Max might be as pragmatic as she, but this was their wedding night. She would never have another—even if they'd already anticipated their vows these past weeks.

"You really don't long for romantic strolls down a sandy beach or a fancy hotel with gilded cherubs?" he asked, kissing her throat. "You are that tied to this castle?"

"Why do you ask?" She was terrified he meant to ask her to leave the castle—or that *he* meant to leave.

"I'll admit," he said reluctantly, "That I am not the world's most romantic person. I was hoping to hear your thoughts on the matter."

Lydia muffled a laugh and worked on his shirt studs. "It is not romance I require. It's you, just as you are, who I admire. But we were discussing honeymoons. Are you saying you do not want a beach but something else?"

"I want you." He nibbled her ear, sending a thrill to her midsection. "Never doubt that. But your performance today as a Latin-speaking lady intrigues me more than any beach or gilded cherub. Will that ever happen again, do you think?"

Filled with joy, Lydia laughed aloud. "I am wondering the same. If it were not our wedding day, I would have buried myself in the stacks in an attempt to raise her again."

"We've had our wedding night already, and as much as I would love to ravish you now, I am just half-rats enough to think ravishment should wait."

"Half-rats?" she asked with curiosity.

He chuckled. "Tipsy, half-drunk, not thinking straight, as is obvious from my next question. If the solicitors really have sent testers, shouldn't we practice this exciting new gift you've displayed?"

"I did not think it was possible for me to love you more, but you keep surprising me." She brought his head down so she could kiss him for his half-rats suggestion.

Max caressed her breasts and responded with alacrity, then reluctantly set her back. "If that means you wish to explore instead of being ravished, you'd better find a safer way of expressing yourself, my love."

It never failed to thrill her to be called *his love*. She knew this man. Those words did not come to him easily, so she cherished them more.

"Would we shock the books if we tried both?" she asked teasingly, pleased that he did not mind her forwardness. "I believe the testers drank themselves into a stupor in the cellar, and Mr. Folkston had them carried to Crowley's carriage, but I fear they will be back tomorrow."

"If they come back, it will be after I've left for the city," he said regretfully. "The barrister has arranged to meet with the judge while my cousins and schoolmates are still here to act as my witnesses. We'll have to leave after breakfast."

She wrapped her arms around his waist and rested her head against his shoulder. "I cannot believe your uncle will continue with this lawsuit. Surely he must admit you are who you are after today."

"Not if he and Crowley have other plans for this property. They'd hoped to have you cast out today, it seems. They wanted to settle the matter before the judge rules. I don't know what they plan next. Since Crowley mines his land, he may have discovered the shale. My uncle may be one of his investors. If they suspect there is oil, they will fight us tooth and nail." He kissed her temple. "I'm sorry if my woes have complicated yours."

"We're in this together," she said firmly. "Tomorrow will be a terrible or glorious day. We can celebrate or commiserate here tomorrow night. Let's use our few spare hours to see what we can do. I really think you're the one who has given me the confidence to be what I must be."

Max kissed her again, then reached for the robes the servants had laid upon the bed. "Wrap yourself up and let us visit our ancestors."

"I am so very fortunate that you are a Malcolm as well as an Ives and understand." She wrapped the robe around her while he lit a lantern.

He draped an arm over her shoulders and led the way back to the small salon and the stairs. "Do not expect me to always be so understanding. Tonight, I am blotto with drink and love and excitement and cannot give you the attention you deserve. Tomorrow may be a different story."

"I like all your stories. Just keep me in them, please." Lydia held her breath as she stepped through the hidden portal to her secret world. The structure might not be so secret, she supposed, but the contents were known only to her.

Max held up the light, illuminating the shadows of dark shelves, and she attuned herself to the whispers.

"I will read you the pertinent passages on the tower's foundation later," she said. "If you need more, we can ask again. Right now, I need to know about *me*."

"Just tell me what to do," he murmured, almost in reverence. "Your Latin lady was quite impressive."

"I think she was more likely Scots," Lydia said. "Just educated. And a bit cynical." She touched her belly but didn't mention her hopes and fears. It was much too soon to mention a child who might bear the same bold spirit. "I need to know how librarians are tested and what makes a good librarian."

She said it with confidence, because she'd *heard* these books. She simply had to open herself to them in ways different from Mr. C's. She was fairly certain no spirit had ever possessed him.

The books responded to her certainty, calling to her through that part of her mind she opened to them. She could hear disapproval and confusion from some. But one spoke louder than the others, with irritation and impatience. She could *hear* the voice! Had Mr. C heard voices?

Smiling, she lifted her robe and hurried down the spiraling stairs to the place where the book pushed out at her. Max followed more slowly, holding up the lantern.

"If you ever wanted to murder me, you could push me down these steps, and no one would ever find me," she said absently, letting the book open to relevant pages.

"Why the devil would you say something like that?" he asked in shock.

Lydia blinked, reviewed what she'd said, then held up the book. "It has happened. Apparently the lady is speaking."

Max stared at the book in horror. "That's what those pages say? Someone was murdered here?"

"It's a very, very old tower and not always a library. Probably lots of someones have died here," she said absently, scanning the pages and flipping rapidly, fascinated. "But it is the murdered librarian who interests me. This is the journal of the woman who had to earn her way into the librarian's position after her predecessor was killed by a jealous stepsister. Apparently, the stepsister thought she could acquire the castle upon her sister's death or disappearance."

"She killed her sister and left her body in the library?" Max asked in revulsion, looking over her shoulder at the pages she read.

"It seems so. The younger stepsister had no gift and no interest in the library, but she was financially supported by her older stepsister, who was only interested in books, not the parties the younger one wanted. Or so it is surmised by the Malcolm lady who wrote this. She was the one who heeded the library's call and traveled many miles to visit the castle."

"Take it upstairs and read it to me, please. This is why they test librarians now?" He took her arm and helped her up the stairs while she clung to the book.

"Yes, it seems so," Lydia said excitedly. "The trust's solicitors were called in. The younger sister claimed the older one had disappeared, so she was taking over the position. But she was not a Malcolm, and ladies who may have been your ancestors warned she wasn't qualified. Then the owner of this journal appeared, knew how to enter the library because the books told her, and they found the body. It's all very horrible and sad."

But it was *knowledge*. The library was speaking to her!

"Well, they can't claim you murdered Mr. Cadwallader, but I can see where there might be concern. Do you need any more of these volumes?" He waited, letting her listen.

Lydia shook her head. "I understand now. Let's go to bed." She kissed his jaw. "I'll read you the pages until you fall asleep. I want you well rested so you can be magnificent tomorrow."

STANDING IN THE ENTRANCE OF A NARROW, DARK COURTROOM, MAX squared his shoulders in his fancy new coat, and remembered Lydia's bedtime tale. It had been as chilling and uplifting as any good novel. He had never considered women to be quite that bloodthirsty.

Their display of swords yesterday should have given him a hint.

He watched as his uncle and his barrister entered from a far door. They didn't even glance in Max's direction.

The spectators were mostly men. A few ladies attended—probably some of Max's nosy relations. None of them seemed abnormally interested in him. He tugged at his cravat and breathed a little easier. Lydia was a miracle worker in more ways than one. He'd feared that not having her by his side would be an invitation to any stray female, but his magnetic ability had apparently fastened on Lydia. He hoped.

If so, he might stay in Scotland! Did he want to? He liked working.

His barrister gestured for Max to take the chair next to him. The men who had traveled all this way to serve as his witnesses began taking seats on the benches. No matter how hungover they might be, his cousins had dressed as gentlemen and sauntered in with the arrogance of the privileged. Except for Dingo, his schoolmates were mostly the ones Max had prevented from being bullied in those long-ago years—not prepossessing sorts but apparently grateful ones. Dingo either wanted another round of fisticuffs or figured he owed Max for not breaking his nose the last time they'd fought.

Once everyone was seated, the judge called both barristers to the stand, where they presented whatever documentation they'd gathered, including witness statements. Max gritted his molars in frustration that he even had to submit to this nonsense. Where was George? After yesterday, his cousin had to know he wasn't an impostor.

What would happen if he were declared dead in front of all his old friends and family? What would happen to Lydia? He was cursing himself for three times a fool for even thinking he'd be better off declared dead—

A bailiff shouted George's name.

Heads turned expectantly, anticipating a dramatic entrance perhaps. Max just sank deeper into his seat. His cousin had to think of his own family first, of course. Refusing to testify wouldn't help anyone but would be typical for the conflict-avoider he remembered. Maybe sitting on his head had taught George a lesson he'd never forgotten.

Grunts of satisfaction emerged from the audience directly behind Max. What had his esteemed, immensely aristocratic reprobates of cousins done now? He refused to express curiosity.

George walked out from the aisle dividing the courtroom benches. Ah, question answered. His cousins must have shoved the coward forward.

He wore one of his flashy suits with the stiff collar and cravat and a vest of black silk with gold embroidery. Max thought he looked like a Western gunfighter, except the black sling on his arm and his hobbling gait ruined any swash and buckle. George had been pretty banged up.

"Mr. Franklin." The judge's voice dripped disapproval. "We are pleased you have chosen to grace us with your attendance, however belated."

"I couldn't very well sit with my father, now, could I? We're no longer on the same side. And Max isn't likely to look on me kindly. But I'm here. Tell me what to do." George cradled his broken arm, as if he might be in pain.

Max almost sympathized, except he was too shocked.

"The court wishes you to attest to this documentation stating the man claiming to be Maxwell Ives is an impostor, that you have personally—"

George shrugged and grimaced. "Can't do that."

The entire courtroom silenced. Max sat up straight and stared. His uncle turned purple. For that matter, so did the judge.

Max had hoped George might simply refuse to commit to one side or another, but he hadn't hoped for a complete reversal. He studied his step-cousin with wary interest.

"What do you mean, *you can't do that*?" the judge asked in tones dripping with ice and sarcasm.

George usually brought out that response in everyone, sooner or later, Max recalled. One would think he'd outgrow the habit of simple declarations without explanation.

"Can't say Maxie is dead." George didn't even glance in Max's direction as he spoke. "Might wish I could. The man is still an obnoxious bully, and he did nothing to deserve his riches except be born. But it's Max, all right. I daresay if you care to look, you'll find he has a scar on his shin where I kicked him with my boot when we weren't old enough for school. He sat on my head afterward. He remembers that. That's how I know it's him."

"He *sat* on your head?" The judge glanced incredulously at Max, as did everyone else. "Would you care to bare your shin, sir?" he asked in a tone dry as toast.

"If I may speak?" Max stood and glanced at his barrister for permission. At his nod, he continued. "You might prefer to examine the burn scar on my hand and wrist." He undid his cufflink to reveal the welt. "I sustained this while attempting to rescue my drawings after the brat flung them in the fire. Had I known scars were admissible evidence, I could bare the one on my derriere from the arrow Dingo shot at me. He's in the audience and can confirm it. I prefer to hope his testimony of the incident is sufficient."

The chuckles in the audience grew closer to guffaws.

The judge looked as if he'd suffered enough. Sourly, he flung down the documents he'd been reading and nodded at the bailiff. "This farce is adjourned. Take the arguing parties to my chambers. In the face of witness testimony and evidence, the plaintiff has no case."

Uncle David stood, enraged. "You can't do that! You haven't even heard my side."

The judge tossed a stack of documents at him in annoyance. "Read these. Your nephew has done just as he promised—produced a marquess, an earl, the head of one of the most esteemed academies in the kingdom. . ."

Percy? Was he talking about the bespectacled bore who had needed Max to prevent him from being regularly beat up?

". . .and a distinguished representative from one of our wealthiest districts to bear witness in his favor."

Dingo? Dingo's parents had royal connections and wealth. Max didn't dare turn and glare at the bully. Proving this case meant Max would be rich again. He also had aristocratic relations worth cultivating. Appearing to support Max would be just the thing a politician would do. Civilization still had its downside.

But Lydia cancelled all negativity.

"You, on the other hand, Mr. Franklin," the judge continued, "bring me numbers and testimony from toadies who wish to continue doing business with you. You may appeal, of course, but I recommend you join us in my chambers to determine how and when the estate's assets are disbursed."

Max didn't dare believe it was done so easily, until Rainford slapped him on the shoulder and Ives shook his hand. The stoic Hugh Morgan stood and waited, prepared to follow the judge and begin counting Max's money.

"It's all over but the shouting," the marquess declared, pounding Max once more for good measure. "If you need investment to mine that shale, let us know. Although I'd advise building an easier access road on the slope so people might actually reach the place."

As everyone crowded out the narrow aisle, Percy came up to congratulate Max. "I talked to your son Bakari yesterday. Quite an interesting lad, more so than you ever were, old chum. When you're ready to send him off to school, I hope you'll consider mine. We pride ourselves on an eclectic body of students with the intelligence and background to lead international diplomacy into the next century."

Dingo joined them, grinning broadly. "I'll sign his references. We'll need diplomats in the future who can navigate Egypt's murky waters."

"He's six years old, drat you," Max cried, pushing them out of the courtroom into the hall. "He can't even ride a horse yet. And just because his skin is brown doesn't mean he isn't as English as. . ."

Dingo grinned and smacked Max on the back. "You don't have to defend yourself anymore, Dwarf. Just accept our goodwill and kiss your lovely bride for us."

Shouts of "He has a gun!" rang out in the high-ceilinged hall.

As one, Max's friends and family pulled weapons from their tailored suits and formed a phalanx to guard Max, as if he were royalty.

They didn't count on gunshots ricocheting off marble pilasters.

THIRTY

"THEY'RE COMING," LADY AGNES SAID PLACIDLY, CLICKING HER KNITTING needles. "Positions, ladies."

Lydia rolled her eyes at this prediction. She could not see outside the hall to the road up the mountain. Still, if she accepted the lady's odd gifts, she had to listen. At the urging of her new cousins-in-law, Lydia took the enormous throne of a chair the ladies designated as hers.

A deputation of Malcolms had remained at the castle to defend Lydia from impostor testers. Lydia had tried to tell them she could handle this, but one did not tell forces of nature like Lady Phoebe and Lady Dare that they weren't needed. They were enjoying themselves too much.

Lydia glanced ruefully at Miss Trivedi, who was handing her more documents to sign. "You realize if I fail this test, that the solicitors will go to court to stop me from transferring the trust to Mr. Morgan?"

"You won't fail," Miss Trivedi said with certainty. "The trust's solicitors chose the wrong side and must pay the price."

Lydia admired the ruby on the bookkeeper's ring finger. "That is new, isn't it?"

The Hindu lady smiled briefly. "Your wedding and too much champagne finally persuaded Mr. Morgan to ask. We are to be wed in autumn.

I have insisted that he must meet my family, so we will leave for India shortly after the nuptials."

That alarmed Lydia more than the impending arrival of the testers. "What about Max's investments? And the trust? How will we know how much we have to spend on the tower?"

"Everything will be prepared and in good hands before we leave. Do not worry. And Mr. Ives is a very astute businessman. He simply prefers that other people manage the paperwork. We will have competent solicitors to assist his endeavors, and there is always the telegraph."

"And Lady Dare's studio? Weren't you helping her look for abused women?" Lydia asked in concern, darting a glance to the photographer, who was busy setting up equipment.

"Now that Azmin understands her gift, anyone can be her assistant. She's employing one of the school's art students, plus a normal photographer. She's more involved with finding abused women and helping them than doing studio portraits." Miss Trivedi placed the signed documents into her folder.

The door knocker pounded the ancient plate, followed by the tolling of the entrance bell as the visitor discovered the rope.

"Anxious, aren't they?" Lydia said, almost amused. "I'm amazed they're still functional after all they imbibed yesterday. And very bad wine it must have been. Mr. C didn't like wine, so it's been moldering down there for decades."

"Better than drinking your whisky barrels dry," Lady Phoebe said, coming to stand by them.

"Oh, Mr. Folkston emptied those for the reception. We need to restock." Lydia nervously watched the wide foyer entrance.

"Your reception was quite grand. You need to have more gatherings in this gorgeous hall," Phoebe advised. "It is good for local business. Drew and several of your guests enjoyed your whisky so well that they have ordered from your supplier."

Lydia knew absolutely nothing of spirits but nodded as if she did. "We're hoping to hire locally for the construction Max anticipates. And we're keeping a tailor and seamstress busy with new uniforms as we add staff. But if this goes all wrong and the trust doesn't come to me. . ."

"We will not allow that to happen," Lady Phoebe said firmly. "We will hire lawyers, if necessary. We are Malcolms, and this is our library, and that's what the trust intended."

While Lydia appreciated the loyalty, she knew Calder Castle would languish if they fought legal battles. She couldn't allow that to happen. She had to carry out Mr. C's prediction and assert her hitherto invisible authority. Somehow, she must save the tower so the library might continue—in front of men who wouldn't believe her.

"Misters Lawrence and Harrison esquires," the footman announced from the doorway, as if the hall truly were a queen's throne room.

The two gray-suited gentleman strolled in as if they'd been invited. Lydia wondered if that attitude of authority was arrogance or terror. They had to be just a little bit intimidated by the towering ancient oak hall adorned in weaponry and even more so by the nearly dozen ladies scattered about the seating area who had locked them up yesterday. Lydia didn't think she knew all the women who had taken residence in her front room. She suspected the gray-haired ones might be friends of Lady Agnes and Lady Gertrude.

The visitors pretended not to notice the swords or the ladies. Lydia suspected their male bravado was derived from wearing guns or knives beneath those baggy, unflattering coats. She'd rather this test did not come to an outright battle.

Without rising to greet the new arrivals, Lydia spoke. "Your business, sirs?"

They had to look past her sea of feminine bodyguards to the far end of the hall, where she sat enthroned before the towering fireplace. The ladies truly did have a sense of the dramatic. She doubted the visitors could see her clearly in the filtered light from the floor-length, gothic-style windows.

The gentleman proceeded further into the hall. Small game tables blocked their path.

"We have come to test Miss. . . Mrs. Ives' suitability as a librarian as required by the trust," the older, taller gentleman said.

Mrs. Ives. Lydia considered the sound of that. She had never thought to be a wife. She'd always wished to be the Malcolm Librarian. She was both now, but in this instance, she was very definitely the librarian.

"I am the Malcolm Librarian," she responded with the soul-deep certainty she hadn't felt the last time she'd said it. Today, she was the authority here, and she rather enjoyed the power. It was as if she'd spent a lifetime preparing for this position. "Do you have credentials?"

The taller gentleman waved a document. Nearly as tall as he, Lady Gertrude snatched it from his hand and perused it. "It's signed by the bounders currently managing the trust," she said grudgingly.

Lydia really hadn't doubted that. She'd met the bounders. "Then, gentlemen, how may I help you?"

"We have here a list of questions the librarian must answer to prove her right to the position." The shorter, younger gentleman skirted an empty table, avoiding Olivia's enormous skirt and the skein of yarn she dropped at their feet. They came to a halt when Azmin set up her camera tripod in front of Lydia.

Lydia wanted to laugh at the silly annoyances. She knew the ladies were simply expressing their disapproval. But after reading the journal last night, she'd decided to maintain the solemn demeanor of a judge.

Lydia didn't accept the papers they brandished. Instead, she held up the early librarian's journal. "According to this, there are no lists of questions. The only test to be administered is finding this book. I found it. Anything else is purely spurious pageantry for the sake of the solicitors. Turn around, address the ladies who own the library and represent its origins. If there are any objections to my status, *they* are the ones who must speak up. The trust's solicitors are merely there to handle necessary business, not pass judgment."

Lydia's chair was on a small rise in front of the fireplace. Combined with her height, she looked down on the gentlemen from a lofty position. She could tell they didn't like that. Both appeared flustered and annoyed.

"There is nothing in the trust agreement about the means of testing," the older, more distinguished of them blustered. "We are perfectly in our rights—"

Lydia pointed at the ladies. "The trust belongs to the Malcolm family. Speak to them. Ladies, would you care to see the journal of Aldith Morrigan, the fifth librarian?"

"I've read it, dear," Lady Agnes said placidly, helping Olivia with her skein of wool.

"I'd love to see it," one of the unfamiliar gray-haired ladies said. "I'm

Faith Merriweather, the Northumberland librarian. I daresay you were originally intended for my position, but your father's unexpected demise sent you off in a different direction. I've heard of Miss Morrigan, of course. There are quite a few references to her in our journals."

Another librarian! Lydia thrilled at the news, but she maintained her composure. "Miss Merriweather, how lovely to meet you. We've corresponded a time or two, I believe." She handed the journal to the slight lady who approached—not the one who had spoken but the second of the unfamiliar gray-haired ladies.

"I'm Lady Abbott, from the new Highlands library. Your resources have been of immense help to us. Mr. Cadwallader has served us well, and you as his assistant have been a pleasure to work with."

Even though she was scarcely half Lydia's size, Lady Abbott turned on the two visitors with ferocity. "You should be ashamed of yourselves, and so should the men who sent you. The library is a repository of Malcolm knowledge. We *know* our librarians, and so do the books. Lydia would not have found this journal if the library hadn't wished her to find it."

She turned back to Lydia. "I may call you Lydia, mayn't I? We've corresponded enough that I feel I know you."

Lydia refrained from hugging the delightful lady out of fear she'd crush frail bones. "Of course. Thank you for coming all this way. Was the journey difficult?"

Leafing through the volume's pages, Lady Abbott described the travails of her journey, completely ignoring the suited gentlemen. The men rustled their papers and attempted to speak, but they were ordinary gentlemen, unable to be rude to ladies, particularly aristocratic ones with the power to jeopardize their positions, if they wished.

Lady Agnes and Miss Merriweather joined Lady Abbott in admiring the ancient tome. Their ancient, billowing crinolines pushed the gentlemen even further from Lydia.

Lady Phoebe snatched the list of questions from the tall gentleman and carried it off to a far corner where the younger ladies gathered around her. Peals of laughter erupted as they read the questions aloud.

With her visitors reduced to embarrassed, annoyed irrelevance, Lydia concentrated on her fellow librarians. She pointed out interesting passages and a few amusing drawings in the journal. Then excusing herself, she sailed past the gaping gentlemen, signaling Zach, the footman, as she did so.

"I believe Misters Lawrence and Harrison have completed their business, if you would escort them out. After you show them the door, I'll have tea in my office." As if she really were owner of all she surveyed, Lydia strolled toward the corridor leading to her safe haven.

The Malcolm ladies accepted her. *The library was hers.* She could feel the triumph in her bones. She could hear the books in her head.

She was really and truly the Librarian.

Which meant she had to deal with whatever that dreadful din coming up the mountain represented.

FEELING SO AT HOME THAT HE ALMOST BURST OUT IN SONG, MAX LED THE wagon train of carts and equipment up the long, winding mountain path. He had enough funds now to buy fancy horse flesh to match anything his cousins owned, but he liked old Matilda. He patted the mare reassuringly. She hadn't been in the least fazed by the noisy oxen and mules.

Nor had she sidestepped Lord Crowley's carriage as it had barreled toward them, bearing the two gray-suited gentlemen Max had locked in the cellar yesterday. Max grinned and waved his hat at the trio. Crowley scowled and maneuvered his high-strung steeds off the road so the wagon train could pass.

Scowling surely meant his Lydia had won the day, and Max hummed happily.

One of the engineers he'd just hired rode up to join him. He studied the enormous fort at the top of the hill with admiration. "You need to build a road up the easier slope so we can haul in rock."

"I think you'll find the slope is riddled with tunnels and possibly mine shafts. We'll be bringing in engineers who know shale oil mining. They'll dictate where it's safe to build a road." Reaching the castle drive, Max pulled his mount to one side and gestured for the train of carts and animals to follow the path to the stable.

The engineer stopped beside Max. "You've traced the tunnels?"

"Not all of them, not yet. But from my explorations, I deduce that the original Roman sewer was disguised by a newer medieval sewer, presumably to prevent invasion." Max had studied the drawings in the journals Lydia had given him, and she'd read relevant pages to him over breakfast. He loved that woman madly. Who else would even think to feed him words with food?

"Invasion?" The engineer tilted his head back to examine the tower. "That's disgusting. Who invades through *sewers*?"

"Clever enemies. Castles have fallen to such tricks. In this fort, if invaders took the obvious opening, they fell into traps. We'll hope there are no bones down there. The Roman drain, on the other hand, allowed waste to fertilize those grounds. It didn't provide an obvious entrance into the tower. I don't want any mining to disturb that hillside. We have farmers who need to till it." Max had listened when his cousins had spoken of their lands. He'd just never thought to apply those lessons until now. "So we need experts who can tell us how to mine without disturbing the fertile soil."

Lydia appeared on the portico. She looked grand in a sweeping silver skirt and a blue bodice to match her gorgeous eyes. Her red-gold hair had been carelessly stacked and now dangled in enticing curls along her nape. Max's heart swelled to twice its size.

"Come meet my lady," he told the engineer. "Just be wary of her friends. They're a conniving lot."

"And your wife isn't?" the engineer asked skeptically.

"My wife will tell you bluntly to your face whatever she wishes you to know. Just don't argue with her. She is a font of wisdom and you'll lose." Max happily steered his mount up the drive.

Bakari and Richard came running from the direction of the garden gate. They studied the caravan of equipment and animals in awe, then finally spotted Max.

He winced as they shouted and raced over to him in concern. Lydia was already rushing down the stairs. Here was the hard part of learning to live in civilization—dealing with family.

"Your arm," Lydia cried as she approached. "What has happened to your arm?"

The engineer wisely rode off as Max awkwardly swung down from the saddle, trying not to wince in the process.

"I'm fine. I'm more than fine. Admire the gifts I have brought." He gestured in satisfaction at an entire camp of men who knew how to build and mine, the kind of men he'd spent the better part of his life with. "They will fix the tower, determine if we'll be rich with oil, and perhaps even build us a better road for your visitors."

Lydia flung herself against him, hugging his waist in a gratifying manner, while avoiding the bandaged arm he'd not inserted into his coat. Max hugged her against him and relaxed. He was finally home. "How did your day go, my dear?"

She huffed and pinched him through his shirt and backed off to study his arm. "I believe I am officially the Malcolm Librarian. Lord Crowley's minions have been cowed and routed. Miss Trivedi will be transferring the trust to more female-friendly solicitors."

"I knew you could do it!" Max crowed, hugging her again. He ruffled Bakari's hair, pointed out a digging machine, and sent the boys off to question strangers. They'd be safe and might even learn a thing or two.

"Did you have to fight your way out of the courthouse?" his beautiful wife asked, studying his face.

He kissed her for good measure.

"Something like that. Should we go inside where I can lie to all the ladies at once? Then you won't know the difference and won't have to pretend. You're not a very good liar." Capturing her waist with his good arm, he headed for the stairs, waiting for Lydia to bite off his ear.

"You can tell them the truth," she foolishly insisted. "But first, you must tell us the outcome of your uncle's lawsuit. I am gathering from the plethora of equipment that you are now enormously wealthy and have money to waste."

"Not wasting. It takes money to make money. I mean to provide an income for your castle for decades to come. Maintenance will eat through your funds otherwise." Max stepped into the towering foyer with satisfaction. If he must settle down, it should be to a place that required his talents.

Lydia tugged him into the great hall, where his mother, aunt, cousins, and who-the-hell-knew else waited. Max wished for the Ives males to balance this sea of femininity, but they'd wisely opted to visit men of commerce in the city to avoid this scene.

Although it seemed now he could enjoy the company of women without fear of consequences. He could learn to appreciate that. He hugged Lydia for all to see.

"I trust there is an explanation?" his mother asked from her comfortable seat in front of the windows, where she was working on her knitting.

"This is Max's home," Lydia reminded her. "He needn't explain anything he doesn't wish."

She spoiled the effect by taking his hand and turning to him anxiously. "But please tell us no one was killed."

Max laughed. He couldn't help it. Bloodthirsty women, he had to remember. He kissed her nose, then helped himself to the whisky decanter. His home. *This was his home.* He gazed at the enormous hall and decided it was quite large and eccentric enough to suit him.

"Uncle David went off his nut a bit before George and I settled him down. A gun accidentally went off, and I was nicked, but no harm done. Hugh Morgan is quite happy to work with a court-appointed attorney to divide up the estate in some equitable manner. All is well, and I have my brilliant mother and lovely wife to thank."

Lydia clutched his good arm and whispered, "That was the lie, right? You had all your cousins with you. There had to have been a brawl that will be recounted for years to come."

"And will grow ever more improbable in the telling," he agreed. "But I really am fine."

The ladies clucked and chattered. Max deftly dodged pointed questions. And as soon as he finished his drink, he steered Lydia toward the door. "I thank you for taking care of Lydia and being our support through all this, but we're newlyweds. You'll forgive us if we have a little private time."

Regretting that his injured arm wouldn't allow him to sweep Lydia off her feet, Max ushered her into the tower and threw the bolt.

THIRTY-ONE

L YDIA CAREFULLY UNFASTENED THE BANDAGE AROUND MAX'S ARM AS HE soaked in their tub. Aware that she wore only a thin robe over her chemise and Max was spending more time gazing at her breasts than washing, she warmed all over. "Now tell me the real story. This is a nasty gash."

"But that's all it is, a gash. It probably hurt worse when George kicked my shin." He sank deeper into the bubbles she'd added.

"Your uncle really lost his mind?" she asked, prying information out of him the same way she pried off the bandage.

"Mad as hops, at least. He brandished a gun. People objected. George tried to take it away, and my uncle started shooting cherubs off the ceiling. I got nicked by flying marble. So did a few others." He shrugged. "It's not a badge of honor. The real surprise was my cousins flocking to save me from being murdered."

Lydia breathed easier, from his tale and from examining the wound. It was nasty and someone had added a few stitches, but it didn't seem red after the strain he must have put on it riding up here. "I must find some way to thank them from keeping you away from a brawl."

"Oh, well, there was a bit of a collie-shangles, if I'm to be totally honest." He checked the wound and scrubbed around it.

"Collie-shangles?" Lydia asked weakly. "A gun sounds like a little more than a quarrel."

"Someone had to stop more lead from ricocheting into the crowd," he replied pragmatically. "Do you know the place on your elbow that almost paralyzes your arm if you bang it wrong?"

Lydia winced and patted his wound dry so she could wrap it fresh. "It hurts awfully."

"Well, the quickest way to make someone drop something is to whack that bone. So I borrowed a walking stick and hit the old. . ." He cut off the word he meant to say and said instead, "Gentleman."

"Oh, dear. And then?"

"He lost his grip on the gun. It hit the floor. The bullet in the chamber went off and nicked someone else, and before long, we had a little contretemps going. Jolly good fun and all that, but the coppers looked poorly on it. Uncle David got hauled off. But I was bleeding all over the place and they thought me a victim, so I escaped. I owe my cousins and some friends a barrel of whisky."

Lydia sighed. "And you didn't tell this to the ladies, why? You were a hero! Your uncle could have hurt someone very badly." She leaned over and kissed him square on the mouth.

He circled her waist and half pulled her into the tub with him. "Better heroes than me out there. I just want to be a good husband and engineer." He kissed her thoroughly.

She pushed away and handed him a towel. "And father," she added. "Do you think you'll ever see your third son?"

Max dried his hair. "He's in Colorado, living in a mansion. I left him funds for when he turns eighteen, if he wants to find me. I'd rather he used them for school." He stood in all his naked glory and watched her worriedly. "Is that wrong of me?"

"Not necessarily, but he needs to know to find you here. What if he has Malcolm traits?" Distracted by his casual toweling off, Lydia wasn't sure where she'd meant to take this conversation.

"Unlikely, but we can write. His mother will tear any letters apart, so I'll write the banker in charge of the trust. Or you'll write him for me." He grinned and stepped out of the tub. "Just think of all the money I'll save by not hiring assistants to keep up with family for me."

"You'll hire your own secretary," she said firmly, not backing away when he advanced on her, still wet. She was already soaked anyway. "I am busy and other people can use the work. With wealth comes responsibility."

"I think I just hired an entire village," he said with a laugh, capturing her waist with his good arm. "We will be poor wastrels if we do not find oil that's easily removed from the ground. We will need to be inventive to keep all those men employed and productive. Shall we build a new stable? Housing for tenants?"

"As long as we have the tower for us," she murmured, reaching to kiss his whiskery jaw. "You can build a new city out there for all I care. A good dressmaker would be convenient."

"I like the way you think!" And then, with just his one good arm, he carried her to the bed.

After that, neither of them engaged in thinking. Lydia was quite certain Max had her seeing the moon and stars above.

Perhaps their child would be clairvoyant. Or better yet, a librarian engineer who would keep the library in good repair into the next century.

CHARACTERS

Lydia Wystan—the Malcolm Librarian's assistant
Maxwell Ives—an engineer
Mr. Cadwallader—the Malcolm Librarian
Lady Agnes—Max's mother, part owner of School of Malcolms
Lady Gertrude—Max's aunt, part owner of School of Malcolms
Bakari Ives Elmahdy —Max's six-year-old son
Richard—Max's sixteen-year-old son
Susan—Richard's mother
Lord Crowley—baron, the librarian's neighbor
Hugh Morgan—investor; Max's business partner
Keya Trivedi—Hugh Morgan's partner
David Franklin—Max's step-uncle
George Franklin—Max's step-cousin
Estes—Max's barrister
Dobbs and Henry—solicitors for the librarian's trust
Sara Brown—Lydia's sister
Mrs. Lovell Wystan—Lydia's mother
Jasper Winchester—Marquess of Rainford; Max's distant cousin
Gerard Ives—Earl of Ives and Wystan; Max's distant cousin
Bran and Brendan Pascoe-Ives—twins; Max's distant cousins

Lord Dare—doctor, professor, viscount
Azmin, Lady Dare—photographer
Lady Phoebe Blair and Andrew Blair—friends of the School of Malcolms
Dingo—diplomat; former schoolmate of Max's
Percy—schoolmaster; former schoolmate of Max's

SERVANTS
    Hamish Lloyd—manservant
    Marta—Librarian's cook
    Beryl—Librarian's housemaid
    Old Tom—Marta's uncle
    Laddie—stable boy
    Zach—footman
    Mary—young kitchen maid
    Sally—scullery maid
    Mr. and Mrs. Folkston—housekeeper and butler
    Belle Malcolm—new steward

ACKNOWLEDGMENTS

The list of people who help me through every book is so extensive that it might make another book. I cannot possibly repeat them all here and will limit myself to major contributors.

Since much of this story was written through a time of isolation from a pandemic, my Muse hid under a bed quite frequently. She might never have been dragged out without the brilliant aid of my fellow brainstormers, Mary Jo Putney and Susan King. They've been with me through tears and tirades for decades and probably ought to just shoot me and put me out of my misery. Instead, they always come through with sparkly ideas that lure my contrary Muse from hiding.

To my dear, dear companions in the Book View Café, my immense gratitude for your patience with my forgetfulness and your expertise in the development of this book. In particular, my thanks to Sherwood Smith and Phyllis Radford, editors extraordinaire, for their attention to detail amid my creative wandering.

Most of all, to my dear readers, whose emails and comments remind me of why I sit at this desk every day and argue with contrary characters. Hugs to each and every one of you!

AUTHOR'S NOTE

Due to the pandemic, I was unable to return to Scotland to continue my explorations outside of Edinburgh. I've had to rely on the books I've brought home on previous trips and the occasionally unreliable internet. Let's blame any errors on my bad memory and the corona virus!

But I did not entirely make up my Calder Castle's architecture and history (which will also continue into the next book). It is well known that the Romans pushed into southern Scotland during the first century AD. Admittedly, hill forts were the main means of construction that far north, but Romans knew how to build. Who can say a few Roman engineers didn't linger?

At the same time, we also have the mystery of the odd brochs in and around that same area. Brochs are well known in the far north, but they've also been located close to the Firth of Tay and along the eastern Borders. Built of drywall stone, the unusual brochs were considered high-status buildings, which suits my Druidic Malcolms and ambitious Ives. For a brief glimpse of broch history, take a look here: https://www.historic-uk.com/HistoryUK/HistoryofScotland/Brochs-the-Tallest-Prehistoric-Buildings-in-Britain/

And then, of course, we all know about the violent history of defending borders that led to the magnificent stone fortresses scattered across the Scotland countryside. What better reason to build a castle than to protect a growing Malcolm library? So, yes, that part is my fantasy—protecting books instead of kings.

I do hope you'll enjoy reading my fantasy as much as I enjoyed writing it!

SCHOOL OF MAGIC SERIES

Lessons in Enchantment
Book 1 of School of Magic

Can a straitlaced engineer, three psychic children, and a lonely witch find love?

The daughter of an earl, Lady Phoebe Malcolm Duncan has the ability to talk to animals. She longs to be a veterinarian, but education requires more coin than she possesses. When the walls of her home come tumbling down, she has to take two steps back—to servitude.

Inventor Andrew Blair keeps his nose to the grindstone, knowing his friends and family depend on his talent for turning machines into money. He is about to embark on his biggest investment yet—rebuilding crumbling tenements in Old Town Edinburgh— until his beleaguered cousin begs him to hide his precocious children from a killer.

When the School of Malcolms sends Lady Phoebe as governess for his wards, Drew's well-ordered beliefs are upended. Ladies don't live in slum housing like the one he's about to tear down, nor do they command ravens or encourage children to talk to dead mothers. It might take a vengeful ghost to show the disparate pair how to join forces, fight their fears and their enemies, and reveal a path to love.

A Bewitching Governess
Book 2 of School of Magic

She's the mistress of illusion; How can he trust her lessons on love?

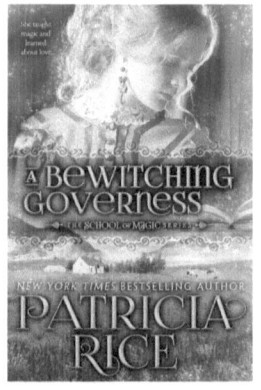

Lady Olivia Malcolm Hargreaves is a viscountess, a widow, a governess, the adopted mother of a disabled toddler—but above all else, she is a survivor. When the father of the young children she's been caring for arrives on Christmas Eve, drunk and ranting, his aura and her own sad experience tell her he's dangerous.

Heart hardened after the murder of his beloved wife, Simon Blair is an industrialist who has no use for another psychic Malcolm. His late wife's weird family is more than enough interference. But his twin daughters are talking to their mother's ghost, his son and heir is floating objects that shouldn't float, and he's beleaguered by aristocrats who refuse to acknowledge his plebeian existence.

When Simon learns that Lady Olivia is in a position to help him obtain the land he needs for his business, and she recognizes that by helping him, she might regain the home she's lost, they must fight their respective prejudices and forge an uneasy alliance. It might take a ghost, an army of children, and a criminal gang to force them to recognize that they want far more than real estate.

An Illusion of Love

Book 3 of School of Magic

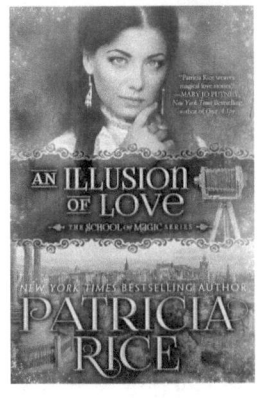

Victorian Edinburgh belongs to staid professors, not the daughter of a Hindu princess.

Apparently lacking the psychic ability of her Malcolm father's gifted British family, Azmin Dougall feels like a pigeon in a family of peacocks. Returning to her ancestral home of India, she finds solace in photography—until her film mysteriously reveals that a woman is being abused by her powerful husband. Helping the wife escape, Azmin flees for the safety of Scotland.

Dr. Zane Dare is done with risk. Because his work introduced disease to his family home, his sister is dead and his niece suffers from the results of the same infection. Louisa has been left in his care, but the bachelor physician has no time to educate an adolescent while he researches a cure. In desperation, he asks the School of Malcolms to provide a governess. The school sends Azmin—the defiant sprite who enchanted him a decade ago.

That long-ago summer crushed both their dreams, leaving them unwilling to open their hearts again. Zane's position at the university is already precarious—introducing a rebellious Hindu princess to his household will only jeopardize his research. Azmin cannot trust a man who scoffs at the psychic abilities she's just discovered, except his frail niece wins her love.

But when Azmin's photography reveals an abusive man may be courting Louisa, Zane and Azmin must set aside their differences to protect the girl who could teach their hearts to love again . . .

∾

The Librarian's Spell
Book 4 of School of Magic

Can a timid librarian and a bold engineer save a castle's toppling tower of books?

The stereotypical reserved librarian, Lydia Wystan has only one true love, the books that whisper to her. But unless she can *understand* the whispers, she cannot become what she wants to be more than anything—the Malcolm Librarian.

Maxwell Ives has a disastrous gift for attracting women, a trait that has resulted in three sons and a desire for solitude. Returning to England to find a school for one of his boys, Max seeks privacy in the isolated Malcolm library. But to Max's dismay, the old librarian dies, leaving Miss Wystan, a *female*, in charge. Before he can run far, far away, he learns the library tower is in danger of toppling, and his cousin is stealing from his mother's School of Malcolms.

To save the library and Max's family funds, Lydia must claim to be what she is not—a real librarian. Fascinated that his magnetism doesn't affect the one woman who can help him, Max must choose between his freedom and his family. In the process of helping others, Max and Lydia just might learn that sometimes, love is the secret that makes magic happen.

ABOUT THE AUTHOR

With several million books in print and *New York Times* and *USA Today's* bestseller lists under her belt, former CPA Patricia Rice is one of romance's hottest authors. Her emotionally-charged contemporary and historical romances have won numerous awards, including the *RT Book Reviews* Reviewers Choice and Career Achievement Awards. Her books have been honored as Romance Writers of America RITA® finalists in the historical, regency and contemporary categories.

A firm believer in happily-ever-after, Patricia Rice is married to her high school sweetheart and has two children. A native of Kentucky and New York, a past resident of North Carolina and Missouri, she currently resides in Southern California, and now does accounting only for herself.

ALSO BY PATRICIA RICE

The World of Magic:

ABOUT BOOK VIEW CAFÉ

Book View Café Publishing Cooperative (BVC) is an author-owned cooperative of over fifty professional writers, publishing in a variety of genres including fantasy, romance, mystery, and science fiction. Since its debut in 2008, BVC has gained a reputation for producing high-quality ebooks. BVC's ebooks are DRM-free and are distributed around the world. The cooperative is now bringing that same quality to its print editions.

BVC authors include New York Times and USA Today bestsellers as well as winners and nominees of many prestigious awards, including:

Agatha Award
Campbell Award
Hugo Award
Lambda Award
Locus Award
Nebula Award
Nicholl Fellowship
PEN/Malamud Award
Philip K. Dick Award
RITA Award

World Fantasy Award
Writers of the Future Award